MEET ME IN THE MIDDLE OF THE AIR

Dark Miracles and Black Comedies

ERIC SCHALLER

UP UNDERTOW PUBLICATIONS

For my mother, my father, and Paulette

"Love Signs," previously unpublished
"Turing Test," previously unpublished
"8) – 5.8," previously unpublished
 "Asleep at the Mortuary," *Dead Lines Magazine* #2, May 1995
"The Assistant to Dr. Jacob," *Nemonymous* #2, May 2002
"Crystal Vision," *Polyphony* #5, Wheatland Press, 2005
"Talking at Sixty Watts," *Postscripts* #11, Summer 2007
"Are You Properly Desensitized?" *Postscripts* #14, Spring 2008
"Going Back for What Got Left Behind" *Nemonymous* #8 (Cone Zero), 2008
"The Sparrow Mumbler," *New Genre* #6, 2009
"Cabinet Number 42," *The Pedestal Magazine* #55, Dec. 2009
"Number One Fan," *Postscripts* #20/21, Fall/Winter 2009
"The Baby in the Forest," *The Dream People* #34, 2010
"Voices Carry," *Shadows & Tall Trees* #2, 2011
"The Bright Air That Breathes No Pain," *Triangulation: Last Contact*, 2011
"The Parasite," *Postscripts* #26/27, Dec. 2011
"Hemoglobin," *Gone Lawn* #11, Summer 2013
"To Assume the Writer's Crown," *Shadows & Tall Trees* #6, 2014
"The Three Familiars," *The Dark* #6, November 2014

First Edition 2016
All Rights Reserved
ISBN: 978-0-9938951-8-0

Table of Contents

AUTHOR'S NOTE

In 1934, a 12-year-old boy named Claude Ely fell sick with tuberculosis. His family gathered around his deathbed to pray but Claude said, "I ain't going to die" and sang a song that had come to him in his sickness. That song was *Ain't No Grave Gonna Hold My Body Down* and it's had a life of its own ever since. The first recording was by Bozie Sturdivant in 1941 for the Library of Congress. Ely recorded his own version and copyrighted the song in 1953. It later appeared on the soundtrack to *Cool Hand Luke* during a grave-digging scene with Paul Newman, and more recently in *The Apostle* as performed by Robert Duvall. Perhaps the best-known cover version of the song is by Johnny Cash, featured appropriately enough as the title track on his posthumous album *American VI: Ain't No Grave.*

The title of my short-story collection as well as the section headings all come from lines in that song. I chose *Meet Me in the Middle of the Air* as the title because, to me, it epitomizes the strange sadomasochistic relationship that exists between writer and reader, especially those partial to dark tales. There's an invitation and, once accepted, entrance into a dimension where the writer holds all the cards, makes all the rules. This isn't just unstable ground, this isn't just having the rug pulled out from under you, this is stepping through a doorway and finding that like Wile E. Coyote there is nothing below you but *nothing.*

The intent of Ely's song, given the nature of its author and the conditions of its creation, suggests reconciliation beyond the grave with Jesus. Nevertheless, I derive something else from it. Divorced of the gospel connotations, it's all too easy to envision the song as celebrating the rise and afterlife of a zombie. As Professor Hubert Farnsworth in the cartoon *Futurama* exclaims, "Sweet zombie Jesus!" Yes, Jesus, raised from the dead on Easter morning was for all intents and purposes a zombie. Even more, Jesus was the original Zombie Master, able to resurrect the dead into some semblance of life (go ask Lazarus when you're feeling six-feet-under). I find it significant that the title to Ely's song isn't, *Ain't no grave gonna hold my soul down*, but is instead the very corporeal, *Ain't no grave gonna hold my **body** down* (emphasis mine).

Strangely enough, it was only after choosing this title and the section headings that I discovered Claude Ely and I share the same birthday.

Meet me in the middle of the air.

I.

THEY'RE COMING AFTER ME

The Assistant to Doctor Jacob

Past a certain age, one lives in memories instead of dreams.

I stand before the kitchen window, Whiskers cradled in my arms, and I feel the soft vibration as she purrs, voicing the unconcern of all her species. She does not care about tomorrow. Or yesterday. Just that her food dish is filled, that she has a warm place to sleep, and that the songs of birds entertain her at suitable intervals. I do not believe she has ever been disappointed.

I am not so lucky as she is. I know that with each new year, the window through which I gaze will add another layer of grime and the wind that rattles the glass will only blow more chill.

Winter and the new year are two curses on my bones.

As if hearing my thoughts, the policeman passing below turns his collar up and pulls his coat tighter across his shoulders.

Still, I remember a more expansive time when the first winter snowfall was a magical act of creation and cold seemed incapable of penetrating even the thinnest fabric. Once again, I am eight years old and running along the sidewalk, puffs of snow evading my footsteps, my breath visible and streaming. I slip rounding the turn to my house, but recover and take the three steps that lead up to the front door in a single bound. I sit at the lunch table, my coat still on, and spoon down tomato soup and chomp half-moons out of my salami sandwich. My cheeks prickle with warmth and returned circulation. Behind me and beside me, my mother is a hovering angel with red hair and freckles; she kisses my forehead, thanks me for coming home at lunchtime without being called, and busies herself with a floral arrangement on the table. "There," she says and steps back to admire her handiwork. "How do you like that?"

This is the scene preserved in the crisp winter light of that long ago afternoon, but there is something wrong here—I no longer trust the memory.

Any memory.

But of this I said nothing to the policeman when we spoke earlier.

❖

The policeman, a plain-clothes man, sat across from me on the edge of a stuffed chair over which I had draped a patterned blanket. In the corner, by the bookcase, Whiskers eyed the man who had usurped her seat.

He held a small notepad and tapped it with a gnawed ballpoint pen.

"Do you remember a Dr. Samuel Jacob?" he asked me. He had a scar or birth defect that twisted the left side of his mouth; it gave him the appearance of constantly smirking.

My face must have revealed my lack of comprehension, for he leaned forward and said again more loudly, "Dr. Samuel Jacob. He lived at 224 Maple Street in Danbury. In the house next to yours." He smelled of mustard and corned beef.

Still I looked at him, not knowing whom he was asking about.

Then I knew.

"Dr. Jacob! But that was fifty years ago. At the very least. I was just a boy."

Once again, in memory, I was that boy.

I did know Dr. Jacob, although I doubt if I ever knew his first name and, if I did at one point, I would never have addressed him by it—he was a well-respected man and those were respectable times. He owned the largest house on the block, a rambling white colonial built over a century before, and although he was a wealthy man he had no family with which to share his good fortune. Perhaps it was for this reason that he noticed me, the neighbor's child. Young and noisy, how could he not notice me. I was only too happy to spend a portion of my afterschool hours and weekends with him. His house was a treasure trove of books and memorabilia. But it was not these, not even the extensive collection of wooden and ivory sailing vessels that lined mantle and bookshelves, or the large black camera on tripod, to which I was most attracted. It was simply this—Dr. Jacob was a gardener. He was not the sort you find grubbing in the backyard dirt. He had his own hothouse, a small crystal palace abutting his home, a secret kingdom sheltered from prying eyes by shrubs and hedgerows. I would spend uncounted hours with him among his orchids, lilies, and roses, as he watered, trimmed, and otherwise coddled those sometimes fragile blooms.

He was a consummate artist in his chosen hobby, and he must have belonged to a variety of garden clubs for an endless parade of vegetation passed through his glass house. I remember a profusion of colour—although Dr. Jacob dressed in somber gray suits, he did not expect his wards to share his wardrobe—colors both garish and sexual, so much so in the orchids that sometimes I would blush and feel my stomach churn, and not know why I could not look at the blooms for long. I remember also how, as Dr. Jacob moved about the pots, as he handled his pruning shears with the deft sobriety of his profession, he named each plant and flower, giving both the common and the Latin phrasing. He would lift a scarlet bloom between his fore and middle fingers, other digits curled into his palm, and say softly, caressing the foreign tongue, "Haemanthus coccineus." He would then glance down to where I hovered at his elbow and say, "To you, the blood lily."

Do I remember the many and varied tongue twisters he pressed upon me?

No.

But I do remember how his eyes sparkled and how sometimes, with a sly look, as if ashamed of pleasure, he would snip off a fragrant bloom and insert it into the buttonhole of his jacket. Then he would seem to bloom himself, turning slowly toward me, chest thrown out to show off that single brilliant splash of colour in the midst of the most neutral of grays.

That was a simple pleasure and one might think that there could be none greater for the amateur horticulturist.

But there were other days when Dr. Jacob brought in new plants, rarities, and on those days from the look on his face you might have thought that he heard the angels singing, for his broad shiny face beamed with an uncontainable joy made manifest.

Of particular beauty were the massive rose bushes that he occasionally set up in the hot house. These came wrapped in burlap around the roots, the body of the plant nothing to speak of at first, with perhaps only a few tender buds revealing the thinnest lips of pink and red. Under his ministrations, the clipping of stray branches, a nip here and there with his sheers and Japanese knife, small chocks of wood to spread certain branches, and wires twisted around others, the plants would take on more perfect form. I would watch in awed fascination as he circled one of his massive rose bushes, then darted in with sharpened tools. He seemed to be always circling, responding to each change in the plant with further changes of his own device. Later, I held my breath as the bushes came into full bloom for, depending on Dr. Jacob's earlier handling, the flowers might open gradually, radiating outward from one initial location such that a wave of colour passed across the bush, while in other cases the flowers might hold themselves back day after day, until it seemed that the buds must burst, and then they would burst, an explosion of colour that transformed the bush from green to burning red in the space of a single night.

I say I watched Dr. Jacob, and I did, through a long humid summer and a chill winter during which the kerosene heaters roared and that hothouse seemed transplanted from a foreign jungle into our snow-carpeted suburbs. I watched for a year, and then Dr. Jacob handed me a pair of pruning sheers. He said, "You have watched enough," and pointed me toward a small rosebush in one corner. "She is yours."

I lived next door to Dr. Jacob for only two years, but those two years remain etched in my mind with all the intensity of youth.

To the policeman I said, still unsure as to the exact nature of his business, "Yes. I knew him. But not too well. I was very young."

"He died recently," said the policeman. "He was ninety-one."

He paused and looked at me the gauge my reaction, working his tongue at a piece of meat stuck in his teeth.

I said nothing and waited for him to continue.

"He still lived at the Danbury residence, from where you would know him. Lived there all his life. He lived alone but had a nurse on call. She was the one who found his body. No known relatives."

I wondered if perhaps I had been named in Dr. Jacob's will.

"Some interesting items turned up in his house when preparing it for auction. Photographs. That's why we were called in." He set his notebook down upon his knee— the upturned page was covered with small crosshatched doodles. He then burrowed into his jacket pocket, pulled out an envelope, and extracted a stack of photographs from the envelope. "These are not the originals, of course."

He laid the photographs on the coffee table and pushed them across toward me. "Have a look. It's not pleasant."

The photographs were of dead people.

They were the close-up photographs of a surgeon's handiwork: sections of the body from which the skin had been cut, then peeled back to reveal the fat and muscle beneath; and deeper explorations, where muscle had been stripped from bone and the interior of the body laid open, the rib cage sawed and bent back to expose the organs.

I saw a hand, naked of skin and lacking its thumb, on which the fingers were spread so wide apart that they described a full half-circle.

I saw the head of a woman, her eyes exhumed from their

sockets and braced upon her cheekbones, her lips removed so that she grinned hideously into the camera.

Dr. Jacob was a doctor after all.

But the images were more disturbing than their graphic nature might indicate for they did not seem consistent with the normal process of surgery. They were more like what one would find in an anatomy text, rendered personal by the intimacy of a photograph. However, even granting this, there seemed an excess of blood. The skin was stained in dark patches, and elsewhere blood coagulated in gelatinous knots and obscured the wounds.

I would have expected the results of an anatomy lesson to be more thoroughly cleaned.

I did not think that corpses bled.

The policeman watched as I thumbed through the photographs and, as I continued, it became apparent that he had established a certain order within the photographs.

The initial photographs had shown details of the surgery, but now I came upon ones that showed the bodies in their entirety. Rather than laid out on a hospital or mortuary table, the bodies were vertical, trussed to and supported by poles, and held in strange animation—legs caught as if in mid-step, arms gesticulating, heads turned as if to speak—these effects maintained by wires or string twisted about and in some cases penetrating the bodies. I could also see the blood. Every wound or laceration, and there were many, had released a dark stream of blood, black in the grainy photographs, that slid down the body and outlined the tortured forms beneath. The patterns of blood were not simply those dictated by gravity, but in places had been smeared by hand, the indecipherable calligraphy of a madman.

My eyes filled with tears.

I shook my head and handed the photographs back to the policeman.

"I didn't know," I said, I meant to say. My mouth moved but no words came out.

"Did you see where the photos were taken?" he asked.

"It was in the greenhouse he had behind his house. That's why you have the better lighting. More windows. See." He pushed a photograph toward me of a bloody woman meshed in chickenwire. The shot was overexposed and the woman's skin, where not darkened by blood, seemed to glow white. Behind her were shelves with pots and foliage. "It would have been too dark indoors in the big house."

I nodded my head numbly.

He pulled the photo out of my hand and added it back to his stack, making sure to place it in the same position from which he had removed it.

"After finding these, we did a search of the grounds. We thought there might be bodies buried on the property. Didn't find a thing. Only the bones of a dog beside the porch."

That would have been Blackie, I thought. But perhaps there had been other dogs later of which I knew nothing.

"He was a doctor, and they have different avenues of disposal. The victims were probably buried in a cemetery or cremated. Just like anyone else. Very hard to trace."

"But of one thing I want you to be sure. One thing we do know." He leaned across the table and glared into my eyes with such intensity that I was afraid to look away. "That man was a murderer. Those people when he started on them were alive."

I thought of the blood, the black blood on the bodies in photographs.

"I don't know how long he kept them alive. But there were gags on some of their mouths in the pictures. Others had their tongues cut out, their throats mutilated. So they couldn't scream."

I swallowed.

"You may be wondering why I'm telling you this. Or even showing you these things."

I nodded my head. My reflection bobbed up and down in his dark eyes.

"There was a photo in there which you may not have looked at closely. One photo that interested us in particular." He settled back a little bit and looked at me expectantly.

"Did you see it?"

He riffled through the photos like a card deck. "This one." He handed the photograph across to me.

Yes, I had seen the photograph. I had seen it the first time I went through the stack, but I had said nothing. I wasn't surprised that he had singled it out, that he was now asking me about it.

That was what I expected.

There were two children in the photograph. The first was a girl, her blond hair flipped out like wings, maybe five or six years old. Her face was butchered past recognition, and one of her arms was bent back, apparently broken, so as to twist behind her head, fingers pointed upward. The second child was a boy. He kneeled beside the girl. He did not look at the camera but, with knife in his right hand, carved within her exposed stomach cavity, engrossed in the removal of her internal organs.

The policeman reached over and tapped the picture with his pen. "It's the boy we're wondering about."

The boy beneath his pen was turned away from the camera.

"Do you know who he is? One of the kids from around your neighborhood? Look closely. I know it's not an easy thing to do."

In addition, although the brutalized body of the girl was clearly in focus, the boy's image was slightly blurred, a result of his movements while the photography was in progress.

I shook my head and mumbled "No."

"What?"

"No," I said.

❖

I press my forehead against the cold window and watch the policeman get into his car. The policeman with his photographs.

That photograph: the boy, the girl, and the blood.

Warm tears gather in my eyes again and spill over, and I

hear the distant sound as they impact the floor.

Whiskers tenses in my arms and I pet her clumsily.

I recognize the girl from memory. I knew her as soon as I saw the photograph, the way she twisted toward the sun, her outstretched limbs seeming to both yearn and shrink from the sky, the way the roses bloomed in patches at face and belly. I knew every blossoming turn of her.

I remember how I trimmed and cajoled her, emulating Dr. Jacob, the patience of his approach, the knowledge that sometimes certain blooms, beautiful in their own right, had to be sacrificed to the overall appearance of the shrub, that by cutting back parts of the plant, one could obtain larger and healthier blooms later. I strove to demonstrate that although I could not match his accomplishment, I could pursue the same vision.

So it is this image that I hold in my memory, that of a rose bush growing toward the sun of a winter's day, and of a young boy emulating his mentor.

There must be something false about the photographs the policeman held. Perhaps the light entering a camera's lens can shift and take on new forms, alien to the original subject. Or perhaps time itself alters the nature of things, adapting them to the dark dreams of the viewer, such that a rose bush can metamorphose into a bloody child.

I cannot accept the alternative.

For I remember holding the shears, the knife, and cutting back the flowers. I remember the thick fragrance and the warmth within the hothouse.

I had come over in the morning, a Saturday with many precious hours to spend, and when next I looked up, I realized that the sun had moved considerably, and I had promised my mother that I would be home for lunch at noon.

Dr. Jacob sat on a wooden stool, bent over his pots of orchids, a small trowel in his hand, chips of wood and spongy moss in tidy piles on the bench beside him. I apologized for disturbing his work and asked the time. He smiled. He wiped his hands on a towel, then pulled a gold watch from his pocket and pressed the fob so that the cover swung back.

"Twelve-o-five," he said. "Time for you to go home, I suppose. Your mother will be waiting for you."

He looked over to where I had been working on the rose bush and I, following his gaze, saw the loose twigs, leaves, and snipped blooms beneath it, which I did not have time to clean up.

"Beautiful," Dr. Jacob said. "You have done well. Very well. Tell your mother that she should be proud of you." He waved a hand in the direction of my handiwork.

I blushed with pride.

"Hurry now. I will clean up here."

Then I was running through the house. I deftly avoided the camera on its tripod, grabbed my coat from the rack by the front door, and ran along the sidewalk, my coat unzipped and billowing behind me. The snow that had fallen the previous night swirled about my footsteps and glinted in perfect crystalline beauty.

I turned up the walkway to my house, still running, and there, inside the house, was warmth, lunch, and my mother.

She looked down at me as I came bursting in the door. She smiled and her crooked teeth shone.

"Here you are, my little general."

Seeing my arm hidden behind my back, she said, "Oh, and what have you brought me?"

She craned her head so that she could peer over my shoulder and I, in response, backed up against the wall to obstruct her view. "Nothing. Nothing at all," I said.

But I could not keep up the charade, nor did I want to. I held out the roses to her, presenting them as a knight might to his queen, the ones from the hothouse, the ones that I had trimmed from my rose bush. There were five of them, each perfect with concentric rings of petals, a deep burgundy red with the velvety texture of skin. A few droplets of water glistened on them from where flakes of snow kicked up in my mad rush home had melted.

All this is as I remember it. My memory.

But what I want to know is what did my mother see

there in my outstretched hands? What was it that she took from me, and arranged upon the dining room table as I sat eating?

What did *she* see?

THE PARASITE

The Midnight Call

Robert Balthus did not think he drank too much but his wife, Amber Wellman, disagreed. His point was that with time one develops resistance to alcohol and that, although his consumption might have increased since their college days, the effects on his system had certainly diminished. Besides, he added, tapping the rim of his wine glass, half-full if anyone was counting, he didn't drink that much anyway. Amber was willing to agree with the overall thrust of his argument, but felt that it was beside the point. And what was the point? It wasn't that he couldn't handle his alcohol, for she in fact found him more amusing after he had consumed a glass or two. It was because the effects of alcohol upon his system had changed over the years. More precisely the effects of alcohol upon his sleep habits and, as a corollary, upon her sleep habits as well. Meaning what? "When you drink, you snore," she said.

"I never snore," was his response.

This argument continued for several weeks, with neither aggrieved party acquiescing to the other. Robert drank and snored. Amber stifled the sound with a pillow, first over her head and then, less charitably, applied to Robert's noisy maw. Neither action was sufficient to the task. Nor was a shove, explosive hand clapping, or a pointed knee directed at Robert's spine. The final resolution came only when Amber discovered an extravagant pair of headphones advertised in a catalog of gifts for those who have everything. The headphones analyzed the sound waves entering at each earpiece and, by producing a contrasting and interfering set of sound waves, bestowed upon their owner a beneficence of absolute silence. Miraculously, they were as good as advertised.

Robert and Amber both worked at the same Boston accounting firm, although not, thank God, they had each said on separate occasions, in the same division. He specialized in small business tax preparation, she in customer relations. Soon after the April 15 tax-filing deadline, the company hosted a celebration to mark the end of the long work weeks. Corporate magnanimity is no incentive for teetotalism, and both Robert and Amber drank freely at the open bar. They returned home on the Blue line and then collapsed into bed, still tipsy, the ceiling swirling above them as if it were made of milk. Within minutes they were sound asleep, he on his back and snoring to beat the band, she with the wondrous headphones engulfing her tiny but sensitive ears.

Although Robert and Amber were, for lack of a better phrase, dead to the world, there are many creatures that call our night their day and, for this reason, go undiscovered except by the most diligent of scientists. Such was the parasite. It had reached the point that it must from necessity, alone and naked, explore the city in search of a host. The parasite was now at its greatest vulnerability, its rudimentary limbs not designed for extensive mobility, its eyes easily confused by the slashing lights of on-coming traffic. It inched along the street curb, picking its way over broken glass and gum wrappers, circumnavigating a plastic soda bottle, not sure where it was headed but searching by instinct for something it could not yet define.

At first that something arrived in only the faintest of tones, a smattering of notes upon the parasite's cursory ears. But these were enough. A shiver of joy rippled the length of the parasite's meager body. It stiffened and turned, true as a compass needle, until aimed directly toward the haunting sound.

No deviations from its path were now allowed. It humped over the curb, shuffled down several blocks of sidewalk, crossing each intersection by clinging with its dozen tiny legs to the humming power lines, and, when it reached the renovated building in which Robert and Amber shared an open-concept apartment, dug the points of its fore-claws into the brickwork and dragged itself, defying gravity, up the five floors required to reach their window. The nylon window screen presented no difficulties. Nor did the bed, its sheets already cast aside to form a sort of ladder that extended from mattress to floor. The smooth sheets, of Egyptian cotton and a high-thread count, provided welcome relief from the many rough surfaces that had come before.

The parasite followed the midnight call to its source and there, perched on Robert's down pillow, began the delicate operation. Two novel limbs, thin, hollow, and sharp as hypodermic needles, extended from their protective skin flap, hovered above the open mouth, and then darted inside to lance the lolling tongue. The anesthesia quickly spread to numb all sensation, an additional narcotic inducing a mildly euphoric dream state, one characterized in Robert's case by several Muppets performing a strip tease to the Bad Company song, "Feel like Making Love." Robert had always wondered what was under those furry costumes. He did not even wince when the parasite, making use of two additional blade-like appendages, severed his tongue at the root and cauterized the wound by application of a metabolic acid. The parasite consumed the pebbly but muscular flesh and then crawled into the vacated cavity. It buried its six hind legs deep within the soft flesh of the host's throat. Its front limbs, their work now finished, dissolved to leave behind nothing but a minty aftertaste. It had been a long and event-filled evening and, if the parasite could be assumed to have anything like our emotional response to the situation, it would have undoubtedly breathed a sigh of relief and said, "Home at last," before drifting off into a well-earned sleep.

Symbiosis

Robert woke the next morning, Saturday, with a headache the size of the U. S. National Debt. Amber slept peacefully beside him, lipstick smeared across her cheek and mascara smudged upon her pillow. She stirred but did not open her eyes when Robert disentangled the headphones from her hair and lifted aside one earpiece. "Where's the coffee?" he said. Or rather tried to say. His tongue had a mind of its own and what came out sounded like, "Why don't I make us both some coffee?"

"Mmmm," Amber said, agreeably.

Robert cursed to himself. Amber's idea of a palatable cup of coffee required beans ground to the micrometer, frothed milk, a pinch of fresh nutmeg, and the use of a finicky metal contraption imported from Italy. Despite his concerns, Robert was finished within fifteen minutes and suffered only one minor burn in the process. He set Amber's favourite mug down on the nightstand by her head, rubbed the painful pink splotch on his knuckle—he hoped it wouldn't blister—and flopped down next to her. "Maybe you can make the toast?" he said. Or, again, tried to say. What came out was quite clearly, "I'll make us some toast and eggs. Over-medium, right?"

"That would be wonderful," Amber said. She opened her eyes and looked at Robert a bit strangely. "Is it my birthday or something?"

"No, I thought you deserved to sleep in this morning. I've seen how hard you work." Robert hadn't even tried to speak, and the words issuing from his mouth surprised him as much as they did Amber. But there was no point in arguing with himself so back he went to the kitchen. But now he was awake enough to be concerned. While waiting for the bread to brown, he slipped off to the bathroom mirror. Are my eyes always that bloodshot, he wondered? Then, turning to the problem at hand, he opened his mouth.

Two bright beady eyes, each balanced on either side of his tongue, stared back at him.

Then just as quickly they snapped shut.

Leaving behind only the pink nubs of his taste buds.

"I see you," Robert said. "You think I don't see you, but I see you." This time the words came out normally. But then his tongue surged forward on its own accord, shoving between his teeth, and waggled in an obscene dance. The clustered legs revealed at its base were pale and fibrous like the roots of a sun-starved dandelion. Then, having made whatever point it was trying to make, Robert's tongue withdrew, leaving a mass of night saliva slathered across his upper lip.

Robert clapped his hand across his mouth.

"I smell something burning," Amber called from the bedroom.

"It's all under control," Robert's tongue said but the words came out muffled by his fingers.

"What?"

Robert removed his hand. "It's all under control." He didn't know this time if it was his tongue speaking or he repeating what his tongue had just tried to say.

The toast was indeed burned. But there was more bread where that came from and Robert managed the eggs without major mishap. Vaguely proud of his culinary triumph, he arranged the food along with a semi-circle of orange slices on a plate and returned to the bedroom, then promptly dropped everything as soon as he walked through the doorway. "What?" he said, unable to take his eyes off Amber even to circumnavigate the wreckage at his feet.

"You were so nice that I thought you deserved a little present yourself." The negligee that Amber now wore had come to them as a wedding gift, with a pink card that read to open the box in private. The last time Robert had seen it had been five years ago on their wedding night, after which it had been retired although not due to any recommendation on his part. He didn't even know that Amber still owned it. Perhaps, Robert thought, forty minutes later after Amber had revealed talents that made him wonder what was in those romance novels she devoured, talents that put their wedding night to shame, perhaps there was something to be said for his new tongue and its way with words after all.

The months that followed were some of the happiest of Robert's life. He always said just the right thing, and in just the right way, whether it was a proposal to bring Amber some flowers or to make her dinner, or just that she looked beautiful in whatever clownish outfit she chose to wear. What had always seemed difficult now seemed so simple.

And the rewards? Well they were beyond anything he could have predicted. The situation had reached a position of balance. The word for it was mutualism or symbiosis, Robert thought, remembering the biology course he had taken as a general education requirement in college. Both he and his new tongue accrued benefits from their relationship. And, he mustn't forget, Amber as well. They all lived together in three-part harmony.

But the parasite's existence was not so static as Robert assumed. Robert ate and, each meal, the parasite siphoned off a portion of the nutrients for itself. It grew, expanding within the narrow confines of its home. Perhaps Robert noticed but, if so, not in any conscious way for he had readily acquiesced to their division of labour. However, on the night that the parasite gave birth, Robert's dreams were not entirely pleasant. The Muppet striptease went on as usual but this time, when Fozzy Bear dropped his costume, he revealed a horde of little Fozzy Bears, and each had a full set of small but very sharp teeth.

A Mother's Advice

Amber woke the next morning from a deep sleep and pleasant dreams to the smell of fried bacon. Eggs as well, scrambled with garlic and rosemary. And coffee, of course, with just a pinch of freshly grated nutmeg. Robert was up and about, moving with muffled steps to bring her day off to a perfect start. His footsteps grew louder then he paused, silhouetted in the bedroom doorway, bathrobe cinched about his waist, her breakfast supported on an enameled tray. He hesitated, almost bashful, as if afraid to enter.

"I'm awake," Amber said, smiling at him.

"You look beautiful." Robert's head was tilted sideways at an awkward angle, perhaps to take in her full measure.

"Thank you." Amber smoothed the nighttime snarls from her hair, sure she looked anything but beautiful, but pleased nevertheless. If she had had any disposition toward divorce, and she had voiced this possibility at times in the past to her girlfriends, marriage not being "all it's cracked up to be" as she put it, the advent of the new considerate Robert had driven such thoughts from her mind.

But Robert seemed different. Nervous. Tentative. He clutched his bathrobe as if embarrassed to be seen naked, wearing it all through breakfast and not disrobing even to slip on his underwear and pants. But it wasn't just his attitude. It was physical as well. Robert had tended toward flabbiness, his waist size having increased from 32 to 36 inches since their marriage, but now his slacks hung loose about his hips.

"Are you all right?" Amber asked, placing a hand on Robert's shoulder. She immediately retracted it. In that brief moment of contact she had felt his flesh crawl beneath his shirt, literally crawl, for it seemed to writhe away from her grip of its own accord. It was as if something or some *things* beneath his skin were evading her grasp. She shook the thought from her mind.

"The window was open last night. I think I caught a chill." Robert rubbed the shoulder she had just touched, adjusting it. "Or maybe it was something I ate." He smiled as if sharing a private joke although really, when you thought about it, there was nothing funny about being sick.

"Maybe you should stay home from work?"

"I'll be fine. Better than ever. A whole new me, in fact." His inappropriate smile, if anything, spread even wider. Maybe he was just putting a brave face on things.

Amber had her doubts, but Robert turned out to be right. Within a few days he gained back the weight he had lost and moved about the apartment with comfortable ease once again. But one difference still remained.

Some years ago, during a margarita-soaked Sunday afternoon, Amber's mom had shared a bawdy ditty that ran: "Long and thin goes too far in, and doesn't please the ladies. Short and thick does the trick, is good for making babies." Now Amber discovered the pleasurable truth behind this rhyme. She attributed this difference in Robert's physique to age and a redistribution of his muscle or body fat. Or maybe he had begun secretly taking those drugs advertised on late-night television. Regardless of the reason, Amber found herself becoming almost predatory in her sexual appetite, lying in wait for Robert and stripping the clothes off his back, then demanding repeat performances until she fell to the mattress spent, her muscles quivering.

But, as her mother had also warned her on that same earlier Sunday afternoon: "Sex makes you stupid." Amber overlooked the other truth of which the ditty spoke.

She was pregnant.

Her pregnancy was a short one. It lasted barely a month and, although she ate more than usual, her weight gain was a measly two pounds. To be precise, Amber never knew she was pregnant. Nor was she aware when she gave birth, an event that occurred on a warm August night following supper with Robert at the local Italian restaurant. Amber consumed two glasses of chardonnay, a plate of seafood linguini, and a chocolate cannoli, and fell asleep early. In her dreams Kermit the Frog rowed her in a dinghy across star-lit waters, the wee frog somehow managing to work the oars and play "Moon River" on his ukulele all at the same time.

Robert did not sleep. He lay fully clothed next to Amber, his mouth open, two beady eyes perched on either side of his tongue watching her every move and never blinking. Robert was there waiting when the newborn parasite crawled free of Amber at a little past midnight. He then rose, kissed Amber lightly on her forehead, and tiptoed from the room, his newborn child cradled in his palms. Together they left the apartment, together they rode the elevator to the first floor, and together they walked out into the night. They had only these few minutes to share, but Robert would savor them for the rest of his life.

Both pedestrian and automobile traffic had slowed in the late hour. Robert set his child down alongside the curb where all it would encounter was the detritus tossed by careless passersby. "Run," he whispered. The young parasite looked up at him, slightly confused, then trundled off, its path erratic, still unsure of its legs and purpose. "Good luck," Robert whispered, watching the diminutive form transit streetlight and shadow, already difficult to pick out although not yet a block removed. But then, just before the young parasite disappeared into the darkness, Robert saw it stiffen and swing true as any compass needle toward an intoxicating melody that only those two, parent and child, could pick out among the myriad night-time sounds of the city.

Somewhere in the distance a sleeper snored.

TURING TEST

"**O**r, if you prefer, you can call me Giant Lunar." Alan's stammering laugh invites a reciprocal reaction from the curator of the Ashmolean Museum. The curator does not even raise an eyebrow in acknowledgement. "That's an anagram," Alan says. Alan loves permutations and crossword puzzles.

"If you say so." The curator is twice Alan's age and shaves so assiduously his jaw shines.

"I'm here to see the automata."

"You know they are not for public display." The curator's tone suggests that this shared knowledge somehow damns Alan.

"My friends are quite enthusiastic about them."

"Your friends." Is that a sneer? "I'm sure they are."

Alan touches his tie, suddenly embarrassed. He discovered a gravy stain on it not minutes before entering the museum. These are his failings: a sloppiness that borders on the compulsive; a love for mathematics that supersedes any personal relationship, including that for his fiancée Joan; and an unspoken desire to be accepted for secrets that he refuses to divulge to even his closest friends.

"All art is useless, except that it is intensely admired," the curator says. He looks disappointed when Alan fails to recognize the quote. He pivots. "Follow me."

They pass through a hall that reeks of preservatives and animal decay, another hall packed with pygmy spears, reed-woven shields, and amulets of teeth and shells, and another hall devoted to Egyptian sarcophagi and curios of the time period. "Treasures of the ancients," the curator says. They pass through yet another hall, this one with cases of somnolent watches and music boxes. The curator gestures. "The automata might be displayed here were they suitable..."

"Where are the automata kept?"

"In storage."

Storage is a room subdivided and banked with oaken shelves. These lean as if about to collapse and entomb Alan beneath a landslide of catalogued, flyspecked detritus. Alan's nose twitches. He sneezes, wipes liquid from his upper lip. "Just a little further," the curator says, smiling.

"Where do the automata come from?" Alan is doing more than just making conversation. He really knows nothing about them or their provenance.

"A *friend* of the director's." That sneer again.

They stop before a carved case. The curator removes a whisk from his jacket pocket and brushes the case almost angrily. He dons gloves before unlocking its front panel. Through the warped glass, Alan has already seen the manikins. He flushes, bites his lip. Now he understands the giggles of his fellow code-breakers, his co-workers at what they euphemistically call the Golf, Cheese and Chess Society, officially demarcated as the Government Code and Cypher School at Bletchley Park. Hugh: *But really you, more than anyone, must see the automata.* Harry: *It will be a learning experience.* Patrick: *It'll be wild.* More giggles, as if they were schoolgirls, not the nation's brightest and best bent on conquering the Nazi menace. His fiancé Joan, to her credit, does not understand the ritualistic hazing perpetrated by men under the guise of camaraderie. She expresses disbelief as to why he must now safeguard his coffee mug by chaining it to the radiator.

The interior of the case is decorated like a florid setting room, wallpapered, the floor spread with a rug of oriental design. There are three automata and all three are instantly recognizable as permutations of that same diseased genius, Oscar Wilde. The curator does not perceive Alan's agony, cannot see his strangled guts. The curator putters about the case, touching it here and there with gloved fingers. He lifts a miniature key from its hook. "The happy prince," he says, directing Alan's attention to the left-most manikin. This Oscar is splayed across a fur-upholstered couch, elbow submerged in a pillow of iridescent silk. The curator tilts the Oscar forward and inserts the key through a slit in the back of its velvet jacket. The internal mechanism, cranked, emits the *tchh, tchh, tchh* of a disapproving schoolmarm.

The manikin is so still, so silent that Alan thinks it defective. Then an eyelid twitches and its fingers tighten into the pillow. It seems bestirred in slumber. When Alan next glances at the manikin's face, he notes that its eyes are now open but heavy-lidded, as if uninterested, bored. The pupils are of a pale blue that borders on gray.

The Oscar rises to its feet then freezes in place, poised, a somnolent statue. It is dressed so finely, so peacock-proud, it seems the antithesis of Alan. Alan once again fingers his dirty tie. A bird is perched on the Oscar's shoulder. Alan thinks this an affectation, much like the lily in its lapel, but then the bird—a swallow—takes wing. It rises, swoops, and twirls. The wire that supports it is thin, the room illumination wan. The bird might as well be flying.

Alan claps his hands, transported with wonder.

Then, horror of horrors, the swallow descends and plucks out one of the Oscar's eyes. The Oscar does not even raise a hand in self-defense. Self-defense would surely be welcome for the swallow has not concluded its business. It glides on the end of its wire then returns to rake the Oscar's face and abscond with the second and terminal eye. The swallow makes three triumphant circles then settles on the Oscar's shoulder, the two eyes clamped like petrified eggs in its beak.

The Oscar looks positively beatific, as if it might be martyred Christ incarnate. Then, although it has no eyes, each socket a desolate hole, the Oscar...winks. For a moment Alan finds this impossible to believe. The smirk that follows is no lie. However truthful, however painful its performance, it is of a kind with the automaton: an artifice. The Oscar bows, one hand on its chest, the other out-flung as if giving the bird its wing.

"I will return his eyes in good time." The curator, until that moment forgotten, wields his words with the care of a surgeon.

The second of the Oscar Wildes enjoys the largess of the fêted, its youthful frame still comfortable with a burgeoning weight. Alan does not begrudge the Oscar its appetites. There is an innocence about the features that invokes trust, as if humbling experience has passed the Oscar by on its winged carriage, each unnoticed to the other. Alan glances at the shiny cheeks of the curator and detects a similarity.

This Oscar is gracious but regal, a true Prince Charming. Alan saw Disney's magnificent *Snow White and the Seven Dwarfs* while at Princeton and was moved to tears. His heart stirs in response to the Oscar's sad, sweet smile, as if it has been awakened from a decade-long slumber. The Oscar rises from a sumptuous chair, brushes an imaginary mote of dust from its hose, fingers lingering. Its many rings catch and ravage the pallid light.

The curator strikes a match. Sulfurous smoke curls upward. He cups the flame in his palm, extends it toward the automaton. The Oscar extends its own tiny hand into the heart of the flame, the smile never leaving its lips. The hand languishes in the flame for some seconds, as if forgotten, and is removed unscathed. Some things are more precious because of their abbreviated lifespans. But the Oscar, like its automata brethren, has not aged, will never age, although centuries may devour its elaborately named and perverse template, may tramp Oscar Fingal O'Flahertie Wills Wilde's children and his children's children into dust. "I represent to you all the sins you never had the courage to commit," says the Oscar. The words emerge from the ever-smiling lips with a tinny whistle.

"That's from *The Picture of Dorian Gray*," says the curator.

"Yes," says Alan. By which he means that he is not

surprised. He remembers Joan pawing at his clothing not long after they had become engaged, a half-empty bottle of wine as courage and excuse. He had removed her hands, carefully, and explained to her again, carefully, that he could not care for her in that manner. He had nevertheless confirmed his intent to marry her.

The third of the Oscars might as well be the portrait of Dorian Gray itself, animated into a shattered semblance of life. Its skin sags like a gluttonous man who no longer has the means to sate his appetites. The suit is shabby, loose at the shoulders, the belly constricted. A gangrenous lily hangs from the lapel. The Oscar totters forward, braces on its cane. "I am Sebastian Melmoth," it says and quotes from *The Ballad of Reading Gaol*:

> "Yet each man kills the thing he loves,
> By each let this be heard,
> Some do it with a bitter look,
> Some with a flattering word.
> The coward does it with a kiss…"

The tinny voice ends abruptly as if choked off, as if the construct could cry. Recovering its composure, the Oscar nods several times, desperate for an applause held most dear in memory.

Alan notes a whiff of alcohol. "Once a month," the curator explains, "I refill an internal receptacle with ethanol, to be vaporized by a friction wheel. Do not begrudge him. Alcohol has always been the truest friend to those abandoned by hope."

Alan is stricken, shakes his head. "Horrible."

"Horrible?"

"To be so trapped, to go through a semblance of life, ever repeating the same thing again and again. That is the most horrible of fates."

"They are toys."

"They are something more, and something less."

The curator's features soften, caught for a moment

between propriety and pity. "Let me tell you a story." He points to the case's latch. "Do you see that lock? I installed it. Do you know why?"

Alan shakes his head.

"Because the Oscar Wildes will not stay put." The curator almost spits out the last words. "The first thing I do every morning, before the museum opens, is to come here and check that each Oscar is accounted for. Most times they are here in their case. But sometimes they go missing, the group of them, like truant schoolboys."

Alan smiles at the analogy.

"I usually find them among the Egyptian artifacts. There's a jade sphinx of which they are particularly fond. But that's not the worst of it."

Alan raises an eyebrow, amused in spite of himself.

The curator whispers—who is there to overhear?—only the Oscars. "Sometimes they are naked. Together." The tone of his voice suggests more than he says. "And it is I...I...who must touch them. I who must dress them." He shudders.

"But now you have the lock."

"It makes no difference. If anything they are more liable to go missing, as if to spite me."

It does not take a genius to locate the holes in the curator's narrative. "Thank you," says Alan. He is weary of artifice, however well intentioned. "If you don't mind, I'm ready to leave."

"One minute. The show is not over. Hold out your hand." The curator takes Alan's wrist, avoiding his skin, and positions his hand before the first of the Oscar Wildes. The automaton is still blinded, fearful hollows in place of its eyes, but—lo and behold—it bows and touches its tiny lips to Alan's hand. Each of the other Oscars does likewise. "There is life in them," says the curator. "Who is to say how much is imparted by my key?"

Alan's hand is branded with the three tiny kisses. He feels their fire as he leaves the Ashmolean, as he sits waiting for his train, and all the rattling way from Oxford to Bletchley Park. The three kisses burn throughout a long tortured night of twisted sheets and brutalized pillows. They burn all through the morning, distracting Alan from his tasteless breakfast and, at work, from the ciphers hidden within an intercepted military transcript. Alan imagines kisses planted on the thighs and haunches of a jade sphinx, of kisses applied time and again, overlapping, of kisses so hot that spittle evaporates into steam, of kisses so numerous that a body might combust. That day, over lunch, even before the waiter fills their glasses with iced water, Alan breaks off his engagement to Joan.

Talking at Sixty Watts

Mike woke to what he thought was the clock-radio spewing gibberish. Then he remembered that he didn't own the clock-radio anymore. It was still in the house with his ex-wife Noreen and their son Jack, and he hadn't lived with them for almost a year.

A glance at the travel alarm that he now used revealed that it was three o'clock in the morning. The travel alarm was on the nightstand near the base of the lamp. The lamp was on. He had come home from the Salt Hill Pub, flipped on his bedside lamp, and slipped into his Sponge-Bob Squarepants boxers. The boxers were a birthday present from Jack and were Mike's preferred sleepwear. Then he had fallen asleep. He had crashed out on his bed without bothering to turn the lamp off.

The lamp was talking to him. Mike knew this because the light flickered in time with the words.

What the lamp was saying went something like this: "Please please please don't turn me off. Please please please. I know why you might want to but I would really prefer that you don't. So please please please don't turn me off. Please?"

Mike pretended that he didn't hear. He pulled the pillow over his head and made loud snoring noises. These were pretty fake sounding, but he had hopes that the lamp wasn't an expert in nighttime linguistics. Better yet, maybe he really would fall asleep again and when he woke up everything would be back to normal.

The lamp just spoke louder. "Will you just listen to me and please please please not turn off my light."

Mike threw the pillow aside and sat up. The beer still hadn't worn off from the bar and that was probably a good thing. Another beer would certainly be a better thing. Mike stumbled out of the bedroom and slowly ricocheted down the hallway to the kitchen. He shoved aside the piles of dirty plates and bowls in the sink, turned on the faucet, and splashed his face with cold water. Then he opened the refrigerator. The refrigerator did not let him down. Inside there were two jars of spaghetti-sauce, a jar of salsa, and, most importantly, a six-pack of Sam Adams. He returned to his bedroom with a bottle of beer, leaving behind a trail of water droplets.

The lamp was still talking.

He knocked back two slugs of beer.

Still talking.

"I didn't know you could talk."

"Bless you. You heard. I was beginning to think that maybe I was mute after all. Just your ordinary table lamp but with delusions of grandeur."

Mike leaned in a bit closer to the lamp and pursed his lips. The lamp had a white ceramic base shaped like a raindrop and an ivory shade. It looked ordinary enough. He tapped its base, three short raps, each a bit harder than the last.

"What do you think I am? A coconut?"

"You're hollow."

"No shit, Sherlock."

"Is that any way to talk?"

"Sorry. From now on I will be a beacon of politeness. Please note the pun. Also please please don't turn me off."

"All right." But in spite of what he said, Mike reached across the distance that separated him from the lamp and punched the switch on its stem. Click. His bedroom dipped into shades of gray. "You talk too much," he said, although there was no one to hear him.

❖

"You said that you wouldn't turn me off."

"That was just to show you who's boss."

"As if I could forget."

"You lipping off to me?" Mike raised his hand, forefinger extended.

"Sorry. You just don't know what it's like to be turned on and off, on and off, again and again. It gives me such a headache."

"A headache? More like a bulb-ache." Mike laughed, dribbling beer onto his belly. He had brought the six-pack over to his bed so that he would be well provisioned for his interrogation.

"Well it is hard on the filament."

"Like I care. New bulbs are a dime a dozen. Anyway, I didn't come here to talk about the cranial problems of the common table lamp. I want to know what you're doing here. Where did you come from?"

"Are you sure you want to hear?"

"Sure. Why not?"

"Well it doesn't reflect that well on you."

"Hold on just a second then." Mike took a healthy slurp from his beer. In his experience there was no pain that could not be eased by the proper application of alcohol. Beer was good for the general day-to-day perils of existence. Should that not be enough, there was a large blue bottle of vodka in his freezer. As his friend Bob liked to say, we're all alcoholics, and anyone who tells you different is just an alcoholic in denial. "Okay. Lay it on me Lamp." Mike had decided that the lamp needed a name and he figured that Lamp was one that he could remember without too much of an effort.

"Do you remember the Monty Python movie, 'The Meaning of Life'?"

"Sure. I've got it on video. Not that I have a VCR anymore, mind you. That's the one with Mr. Creosote." Mike put on the cajoling voice of the waiter: "Just one thin mint?" His imitation wasn't very good, but he was persistent. "Surely you have room for just one thin mint?"

"Give yourself a gold star."

"Sarcasm. I hope what I just heard wasn't sarcasm."

"Do you remember the skit where the woman stands at the sink and gives birth to babies as she washes the dishes? She doesn't stop what she's doing and the babies just keep falling to the floor."

"The Catholics. They have to sell their babies to science because they have so many of them." Mike chuckled.

"Do you remember the song that she and her family sang?"

"Every Sperm is Sacred."

"Give the man a beer."

"Thanks. Don't mind if I do." Mike drained the bottle and returned the empty to the six-pack carton. He then opened a new bottle. "You can continue. I still don't see why you thought I would take offense."

"Well consider your daily routine. And I don't mean eating, sleeping, working, and drinking. I'm talking about pounding your pud until it's sore. Pounding it even when you're too drunk to get it up."

"What are you saying?"

"All that wasted life force had to go somewhere. I'm that somewhere."

Click.

❖

"Okay. Okay. So I made that up. But you've got to admit that you've got an addiction there. You could at least wash your sheets every once in a while. Some days I wish I were blind so that I didn't have to watch."

"That could be arranged. Now tell me what really happened."

"Would you believe aliens?"

"No, but try me anyway."

"They came to your house over a year ago. Almost two years ago now."

"I don't remember any aliens."

"These aliens were really small, so small that you

probably wouldn't notice them. They flew to earth in a tiny flying saucer and parked it on top of your refrigerator. You probably thought that it was just an aluminum pie plate. They stayed at your house for three days."

"Tiny aliens? Where did they come from? The planet of the elves? The planet of the fairies?"

"No. I don't think that they could have been confused with elves or fairies. They looked more like olives. Green olives stuffed with pimentos. Impaled on a toothpick."

"You're making me thirsty."

"Because the aliens were small and easily damaged, they wanted to know how earthlings treated others. They decided to use their advanced technologies to unlock the secrets held in household objects. I was the first object that they animated."

"Not saying that I buy any of your story, but why you? Why a lamp?"

"They didn't say. But I've had plenty of time to think about that. It's sometimes lonely being a lamp, and introspection is my chief solace. I came up with two reasons. First, household objects such as myself are good witnesses. We see everything. It's just that usually we are silent witnesses."

"Well you certainly aren't silent anymore."

"Second, the manner by which people treat what they consider 'common' objects tells a lot about the limits of their behavior. Do you know that there are people who, when angered by a spouse, will actually pick up a lamp, a lamp that never caused anyone any harm, that was not involved in the fight, and throw it at the spouse."

Mike choked on his beer. "What are you saying? Are you accusing me?"

"Well I don't think this person really wanted to hit his spouse. I think this person intentionally missed. Still the lamp smashed against the wall. It was a nice lamp too. Well kind of nice. What made it nice was the sentiment attached to it. This guy had made it for his girlfriend many years before, back when they were first dating. It was from a kit that he bought at a hobby store to make a Tiffany-style stained-glass lampshade. It had all these little pieces of pre-cut glass in different colors and coils of lead wire with which to join them together. But he smashed it. I'm just lucky that it wasn't me."

Click.

❖

"Mike, I've got a favour to ask you."

"You haven't exactly earned my undying gratitude. What makes you think that I'd do you any favors?"

"I just want you to cut my wire."

"Your power cord?"

"No. The one up here." The lampshade jiggled. When Mike leaned over it, he saw a tremor run through the brassy metal loop that arched over the bulb. The lampshade was connected to this loop by an ornate screw that Mike remembered undoing each time he had removed the shade to change the bulb.

"You want me to cut this?" Mike strummed the metal loop with his forefinger.

"Yes. In the middle right where the screw is."

"Why?"

"Must you question everything?"

"No. Just inanimate objects that wake me at three in the morning."

"I catch your drift, as the shovel said to the snow bank. Maybe a demonstration is in order. Why don't you raise both your hands above your head? Better yet, lift the six-pack and hold that above your head. Call it a stick-up. With beer."

Mike didn't lift a finger, not even to open a new Sam Adams, although all of Lamp's talk about beer was giving him a powerful thirst.

"You're not doing it." Lamp sounded petulant.

"Because it's stupid."

"If that's the way you're going to be..."

"That's the way I'm going to be."

"Then just imagine that you're holding that six-pack

above your head. You're a well-built man, and I mean that kindly. But how long do you think you could hold that six-pack up before your arms got tired?"

"How long do you think I could hold that six-pack up before I said to myself: 'Why am I holding this six-pack of beer above my head where it's not doing anybody any good.' And by anybody, I mean myself." With that, Mike popped the cherry of a virgin beer, the last remaining holdout of the original six.

"Well just imagine how tired I must be with my arms raised above my head ever since day one. All in the service of a shade that could hardly be called beautiful."

"You got that right."

"What I wouldn't give for a little relief. A chance to rest my arms like everybody else. Is that too much to ask for?"

"If I get rid of your shade and cut your wire, will you tell me the truth?"

"I'll tell you whatever you want to know."

"Okay. But first I'll have to turn you off."

"Why? Haven't you turned me off enough times already? Haven't I told you how much it hurts me every time you do that?"

"Let me see. I'm about to engage in a delicate operation involving a scatter-brained lamp, metal, and electricity. Maybe I just don't want to take the chance on you electrocuting me."

"Oh. That I can understand."

"I thought you might."

Click.

❖

"That is so much better." Lamp swept its metal arms out and down as if performing the breaststroke in slow motion. The tips of each arm shone where they had been snipped apart and now caught the glow of the bare bulb. "They seem almost weightless. It feels like I could do anything." Lamp curled the end of each arm in turn.

"Now will you tell me who you really are and what you're doing here?"

"Hold on just a second. I'm like a new man." Lamp sent a wave undulating down the length of one arm. "Pretty good, huh?"

"Come on."

"How long have you had me in your home?"

"Let's see. I got you when I was back at Plymouth State, in my junior year. So what would that make it? Ten years and change."

"Close enough. So by your calculations, I've been holding up that shade of yours for more than a decade. I'll give you the benefit of the doubt and say that I was your servant, not your slave. But you still won't grant me just a few more seconds to feel what it's like to be free? For shame."

"Okay. You get another minute. Go crazy. I'm going to dig up a fresh six." Mike stumbled back to the kitchen. He discovered that there was no beer left in the refrigerator, but there was his emergency bottle of vodka in the freezer. There was no orange juice to go with the vodka, but there was a jar of Tang that he had bought out of nostalgia. He stirred the orange powder into the vodka and took a tentative sip. "Breakfast of astronauts, my ass."

Mike licked the powder from his lips and returned to the bedroom. "Okay Lamp. Lay it on me."

"All right. Just don't say that I didn't warn you."

"Warn me about what?"

"The truth. They say it hurts."

"Tell me something I don't know."

"Well how about the story of a man and his son. A baby boy, maybe two, maybe three years old. The apple of his eye as you might say."

"Sounds familiar. I thought you said this was something I didn't know."

"Maybe they're the sort of people that you feel you know, even when you don't."

"Yeah, that's how it seems. Familiar but different."

"Now the father didn't pay too much attention to his

son when he was first born. There was the initial excitement, but then there were sleepless nights and poop-filled diapers. The man was tired and bored. 'What's the point,' the man said, 'if he can't hold a football?'"

"Amen to that."

"But all that changed once the baby learned to say 'Daddy.' Mommy was all about rules and regulations: 'Don't do this' and 'Don't do that.' But Daddy was all about fun, and the game that was the most fun of all was flying."

"Flying?"

"Not real flying, but pretend flying."

"Gotcha. All kids love that. Jack and I used to play until he got too big. But we all get too big eventually." Mike patted his stomach and belched.

"This was back when flying was at its best. The man would throw his son up into the air and catch him, then lower him to the floor if they were indoors, to the grass if they were in the backyard. They played the flying game everywhere. The boy loved the game so much that each time he was put down, he would raise his arms and say 'Fly high.' The boy could never get enough. He would have kept on flying forever if he had his way."

"Just like Jack."

"One evening, mom went shopping, and the man stayed home with his son and they watched Monday night football together. The man pinched the skin on his son's arm and said, 'It feels like pigskin. And if it feels like pigskin, then it probably is pigskin. And if it is pigskin, then it can fly.' The boy didn't understand any of this except the last part. He held up his arms and said, 'Fly high.'"

The lamp paused.

"What happened next?"

"You don't remember? You threw Jack up in the air, but when you tried to catch him, you dropped him. Jack hit his head on the corner of the table by the couch. He bled to death. He died. When he died, his spirit entered into me."

"Bullshit. That's pure and utter bullshit."

Click.

❖

"The thing is that you didn't even have any excuse. You hadn't been drinking or anything. You dropped him because you weren't paying attention. Maybe you were trying to watch the football game. Maybe you were just clumsy. But that's not the worst part."

Click.

❖

"Sorry but I didn't get to finish. The worst part was that even though you hadn't been drinking or anything, you still tried to cover it up so your wife wouldn't know it was your fault. You ran upstairs and then ran back downstairs. You then screamed bloody murder as if you had just discovered the whole thing. Even though there was no one there to hear you. Except for me, of course. Only then did you call nine-one-one. Maybe things could have been different if you hadn't been such a chickenshit and wasted so much time."

Click.

❖

"Now you shut up and let me talk. Do you want to know why it's bullshit? Why I know that it's bullshit, no matter what you say?"

"Go ahead. Tell me. I'm all ears." Lamp twisted his arms so that the tips rested on the sides of his bulb, as if he was trying to cup his ears to better hear.

"Because Jack is still alive. You said he died, but he didn't. I still see him every weekend. Almost every single fucking weekend. So what do you have to say to that?"

"Well maybe he didn't exactly die."

"See. What did I tell you?"

"But he's not all right either. Even you have to admit that he's not all there. He's not all there at all."

Click.

❖

"You heard of Jack the Giant Killer? Well maybe this is a simple case of role-reversal."

Click.

❖

"Or what about Jack be Nimble, Jack be Quick?"

Click.

❖

"Okay. Shut up and listen. Okay?"

Lamp said nothing.

"That's better. You know I could break you? Not just turn you off, but break you."

"Just like you broke that Tiffany knockoff? Just like you broke Jack?"

Mike sucked in his breath. "But I'm not going to break you. I want you to listen to me. Okay?"

Lamp said nothing.

"I want to tell you a story about Jack and me. This is from only about three years ago. I sort of knew that things weren't going to last with Noreen and me, but I still wanted to do right by Jack. I wanted to provide for his future.

"A friend of mine from Wisconsin had told me how he was able to sell his farmland twice. Twice. First, he sold off logging rights to the hardwoods on the land, then he sold the land itself. Do you know that a single black walnut tree can fetch over a thousand dollars? Don't answer that. So I figured that I would plant walnuts for Jack. You can buy a sapling real cheap, but in twenty or thirty years it should be worth a bundle. I bought ten of the suckers and we planted them at the far end of our yard. Jack and me. I had him help me with digging the holes and laying in the trees. They were real tiny things. All skinny and green, and only about a foot or so tall. You could bend them over with your hand. So to give them support, we pounded poles into the dirt beside each sapling, then tied the saplings to the poles with twist-ties, the ones you get with garbage bags.

"After we finished planting, I made Jack sit down with me beside the saplings and I told him that they were his and that he had to help me with them. We then watered them. I should have taken a picture of Jack with that watering can. He was so careful. After watering each plant, he would ask me if he was doing it right. I would say yes, that it was perfect. Then he would go on to the next one.

"But do you know what he did the next day?"

Lamp said nothing.

"He mowed them all down. We had given Jack a push mower because he had this idea that he could mow lawns to make money. But we didn't want him to hurt himself by accident with a power mower, so we gave him the push mower. Anyway, Jack cut a path through the grass all the way to the end of the backyard and mowed all ten of the saplings down. Just them. Nothing else. The mower didn't cut that well unless you got up a good head of steam, so the saplings got caught in the blades and yanked out of the ground. I found them there, chewed up and lying withered in the sun. The mower was there beside them, where Jack had left it.

"Funny, huh?"

Before Lamp had a chance to respond, if he planned to respond, Mike jabbed the switch on the lamp stem.

Click.

❖

"Why did you do that? I didn't say anything." Lamp rubbed the side of his bulb with a circular motion. His light flickered as if he winced in pain.

"Sorry about that. I needed to do some thinking." Mike didn't look at Lamp, but settled back on his bed, head on his pillow, and stared at the ceiling. "You know. It didn't really matter about the walnut trees. I got pretty mad at the time, but it didn't really matter. Who lives in the same house for thirty years? Even if everything had worked out between Noreen and me, by the time the trees were old enough to harvest, what are the chances that we would have still been living there? Or that Jack would have owned the house?"

"It's the thought that counts."

"Thanks. Now, I got a question for you. Why do you keep pretending that being turned on and off hurts you? You fake it pretty well, but no matter what you're just a lamp. Even if I'm talking to you and you're talking to me, you're still just a lamp. You can't feel anything."

"Do you really want to know?"

"Sure."

"Because every time someone turns me off, I don't know if anyone will ever turn me back on."

Mike nodded. "I get it."

"Do you?"

"I think so. It's like every day could be the last day of your life."

"Every night. I never held much truck with daylight."

"Of course." Mike chuckled. "You must really hate the sun. No way you can compete with that. Just knowing that a new day will come means that someone is going to turn you off. After all, what's the use of a lamp during the day?"

"None at all." Lamp's voice was chill. Little wonder, Mike thought, for the darkest hours of the night were now over, and a pale gray halo had begun to form around the window shade.

"Do you dream when you're turned off?" Mike said. "Is it like sleeping?"

"No. You're there and then you're not there. When you're turned back on, the whole world's skipped you by."

"But at least you know that you can be turned back on."

"Do you think that makes it easier?" Lamp's laughter sounded like ice cubes shaken loose from a freezer tray.

"I don't know. I don't really have that choice. Unless there is such a thing as reincarnation. Which would be nice, come to think of it."

"But you wouldn't be yourself then. You'd be something

else."

"That might be preferable."

"What would you choose to be? If you had a choice."

"A dog." A smile spread across Mike's face. "Just a fat and happy dog."

"Really?"

"Or how about a salmon? I've never seen one except to eat, but I always loved those documentaries on TV."

"I used to watch those too." Lamp's voice was warmer again, even nostalgic. "We used to watch those together."

"A salmon. That would be perfect. Can you imagine swimming upstream to the place you were born? You've got to figure that a young salmon doesn't know what its future holds. You're born and you just swim downstream to the sea. How easy is that? Then years later you get seized with this compulsion, like a bolt out of the blue, to return to where you were born, and nothing, no matter how impossible, is going to stand in your way. You've got to swim up waterfalls. You've got to swim past grizzlies. And you're dying the whole time, falling apart even as you swim. But you do it because you've got to. Then after you breed, you die. But you know that you've done something, no matter how hard it was, and that there's going to be another generation of salmon that will be able to do exactly the same thing themselves."

"Salmon have it made."

Mike couldn't tell if Lamp was being sarcastic or not. "Yeah they do," he said, taking Lamp at face value.

"Want to know a secret?"

"What kind of a secret?"

Lamp's voice sank to a whisper. "About what happens after you die."

Mike shifted his head to the right side of his pillow, so that he was closer to Lamp and could hear better. "You know?"

"It's not always a question of what you know. It's what you want to know. Do you really want to know the truth about reincarnation? About heaven and hell?"

"Would you tell me the truth?"

"Of course." Lamp unknotted a golden arm, reached across from the bedside table, and began to stroke Mike's dirty tousled hair.

"Then yes."

"Alright then. But just remember that I offered you the choice." Lamp's bulb flickered as if he intended to say something more, but no words came. He stroked Mike's hair in silence, his bulb pulsing like a heartbeat.

Mike smiled and closed his eyes. "I'll tell you what I wouldn't be."

"If you were reincarnated?"

"Yes."

"What's that?"

"A black walnut tree."

"I can understand that." Lamp raised his arm so that it hovered above Mike's face, shadowing the sunlight that now warmed his eyelids. Lamp seemed about to smooth Mike's hair or even to stroke his cheek. Maybe he was tempted to do one of these things, but in the end he did neither. Instead, Lamp gently tapped the tip of Mike's nose.

Click.

The Baby in the Forest

Three men are rolling stones in the forest. They do not agree on what the forest looks like. The first says that it is a forest of immense gray and black fungi. The second, that it is composed of monoliths carved in the shapes of forgotten gods. The third, that they travel among the withered sticks of an empty bird's nest.

Three men are rolling stones in the forest. The stones are spherical and rough enough to abrade their palms and fingertips to sandpaper tenderness. The men believe that the stones were once rectangular, like oversize bricks, and that years of being rolled have rounded off their edges. The stones are of similar material and size, but the men refuse to believe they are identical. Each is convinced he rolls the heaviest stone. Sometimes they exchange stones in hopes of easing their work but then, seeing the smirk on the other man's face, they realize they have made a mistake and demand back their original stones.

Three men are rolling stones in the forest. They believe that if they reach the far edge of the forest that they will have accomplished a task of significance. Perhaps they will finally be allowed to rest. So it is a matter of some consternation when they come upon a baby in the forest. Or rather, the first man thinks it is a baby, naked and screaming as fungal tendrils crawl over it. The second thinks it is an old man with crippled legs, pinned beneath the rocks. The third that it is a fledgling bird, its skin pimpled and blue from cold.

Three men are rolling stones in the forest. They have to make a decision. Do they save the baby (or the old man, or the bird)? Do they save it, or do they continue rolling their stones on through the forest? Whoever plays the role of savior will have to set aside his stone and will lose valuable time. "It's a trick," hisses one of the men. "I don't know how, but I remember it's a trick. Pass it by." So they do. They ignore the cries and congratulate each other on seeing through the wiles of whatever beast lurked behind the mask of innocence.

Three men are rolling stones in the forest. They hear a cheerless whistling in the distance that draws closer. It is the voice of the wind. The three men are tumbled back along the many miles they have come. They are broken against rocks and trees and discarded in the dirt. But that is not the end. Gradually, over time, their wounds close and their bones knit back together. When they are finally able to stand, slowly, painfully, they see three large stones. Their minds are a tangled mess but they know what they must do. They must start all over again.

Three men are rolling stones in the forest. They are not well. They are in pain and have a long ways to go. Then they see the baby (or the old man, or the bird) crying lonesome in the forest. "It's a trick," says one of the men, his voice a low fearful moan. "I don't know how I remember, but I remember. If we don't help, we will pay."

Three men are rolling stones in the forest. Three men are rolling stones but they stop to help. Barely have their hands left the surface of the stones but they hear the cheerless whistling of the wind drawing closer.

Three men are rolling stones in the forest.

To Assume the Writer's Crown: Notes on the Craft

Introduction

Bookcases proliferate in my home. I could write *house* rather than *home* but, to me—and I think you and I may be alike in this regard—books define my home. One of my bookcases is a magnificent construction of bird's-eye maple. Another is of oak: warm wood with swinging glassed doors. These represent my Platonic ideal of book collecting. Most of my bookcases, sadly enough, are of the *requires-some-assembly* variety and, as soon as one bookcase is filled, I assemble another. There is never enough space. Books pile on their shelves, on my couch, on the floor. My cats knock over the books and piss on them.

I'll let you in on a secret. Although I call myself a writer of fictions—my publications confirm this assessment—much of my library consists of non-fiction. The first book I bought, at the innocuous age of six, was a biography of Cortez. Cortez the Killer, as Mr. Neil Young would have it. One of my most influential books was *Two Little Savages*, which under the guise of a children's tale has much to instruct on wilderness lore. Reading that book, I painted my face with blue clay, deciphered and followed animal tracks, and devised snares to trap pigeons. The following Christmas, my parents gifted me with a wonderful book on knot tying. I still own all three of these books.

But it is not to discuss my facility with knots that I began this essay; rather it is on the craft of writing itself. The secret within the secret I now confess is that my bookshelves contain as many books on writing as they do writings themselves.

I exaggerate, but the truth is that I have always loved the non-fiction that proliferates around fiction as much, if not more, than the fiction itself. In this essay, I will share with you some highlights of what I have learned over the years. Relax. Pour yourself a drink. The next few minutes are ours and ours alone. Writing is not all fun and games, but let's pretend for the moment that it is.

First Things First

In my estimation there are but two classes of writers: those who write and those who don't. "But how can anyone be a writer if they don't write?" you of the first contingent assuredly exclaim. By their own proclamation is my answer. Moreover, I believe this second contingent is in the majority. They are the jealous fools, who upon hearing you have written a story or two, perhaps a dozen, in my case over a hundred, none of which they have read, will declare themselves writers of equal merit, if only... These two words ("If only...") are the key to their thwarted ambition. If only they had not been engaged in more lucrative enterprises. If only they had not raised a family. If only they had found the time to set their words to paper.

If only...

These wasters have assumed the writer's crown without any more exertion than the flapping of their puerile lips. Run, I say, should you meet such a *writer*, run with all alacrity and hide. Above all, do not show them this essay, for they will claim the ideas for their own and, never recognizing the contradiction, scoff that you should sympathize with it.

The Cage of Words

The key to successful fiction, its heart, its soul, is in the character. Some imbeciles will state that a genre, like science fiction, is more about the idea than the character. But an idea without a character is a bodiless brain. Even the most idea-driven science fiction employs characters to carry the reader through the story.

How then to best capture a person in words?

There is the obvious possibility of describing the character's physical features. For instance, a woman—blonde hair, blue eyes, tanned—so close to a cliché that you could be arrested for artistic delinquency. Instead, how about: hair a sun-bleached blonde, eyes the silvery-blue of beach holly, skin a deep natural tan. This description suggests something of the woman's history but at the expense of a truckload of adjectives. All the reader now knows is that the character spends a carcinogenic amount of time in the sun. Let me give you the scientific name for that variety of cancer: *longinquus*. That's Latin for *boring*.

Physical description is wasted unless it is freighted with emotion. David Morrell, in *Lessons from a Lifetime of Writing*, advises writers to emphasize "the *effect* that a character's appearance has on others". To revisit our example: the woman, her blonde hair disheveled, her skin slick with sweat, turned at my approach, her eyes hunted...

Hunted? Haunted, I meant.

The Pathetic Fallacy

This phrase, coined by John Ruskin, was intended as a pejorative against attributing human emotions to nature, of having the universe sentimentally reflect the state of your characters. In my opinion, Ruskin's concern points to the effectiveness of this technique, none having employed it to more success than Edgar Allen Poe ("The Fall of the House of Usher"). Let's give it a shot with our female character. Note how I use this technique to capture her essence:

Mary—for so I shall call my female character—has gone for a run on a blustery October afternoon. She always runs when she's troubled. What has happened? She's thinking about her boyfriend and the gossip that he was seen at the movies with another girl that looked a lot like her. Mary feels a raindrop on her cheek and glancing up sees clouds clotting darkly above the rooftops. How could he cheat on her? How could he touch another girl? The wind gusts, her flesh prickles, and she wishes she'd worn sweats instead of shorts. There's not far to go, just a shortcut through a wooded lot. She gulps air. Smells evergreen. A bird trills, and for the briefest of moments she smiles, a toothy smile at this wonderful inconsequential song in the face of the coming storm. Where is that bird? Why the hell did he do what he did with that girl? Why did he fondle her secret places? There's a slippery movement beneath the pines and then a tug at Mary's shoulder. Mary lashes out. She stumbles. Her hand tears at leaves. Wet fragments stick to her fingers. She's on her knees. Thunder cracks and she's dragged forward. Her cheek smacks metal. Her nose, erupting blood, is engulfed in a carpet that reeks of mildew and cat piss. She screams. Too late. The door of the van slams. Trapped.

The Bare Necessities

Frank O'Connor wrote, "There are three necessary elements in a story—exposition, development, and drama. Exposition we may illustrate as 'John Fortescue was a solicitor in the little town of X'; development as 'One day Mrs. Fortescue told him she was about to leave him for another man'; and drama as 'You will do nothing of the kind,' he said."

This is, in fact, the universal struggle of the author with the written word, with his or her characters. Consider the following:

"The author lived in an oppressively large farmhouse at the end of gravel road.

"One day he decided to write a story.

"'You'll do nothing of the kind,' Mary said."

The Worst Advice

David Morrell describes how he once heard a teacher, intending to simplify the writing process, exhort his students to imagine their stories as movies and to then write what they saw. A fool teaching fools! The limitation of this advice is that it only engages the sense of sight. Writing grants you the supernatural ability to spy inside a character's mind, revealing thoughts and experiences, and engage *all* the senses. Let's return to my character, *our* character, and bring this sensory information into play.

An Exercise

There is just one rule for this exercise: you may not use the sense of sight for your description. Imagine yourself in a darkened room, a basement. I recommend that you try this for real. You descend the stairs, running your hand along the wall to maintain balance. Feel the texture. Describe it. Do the stairs creak? What is the smell of the basement? How is it floored: poured concrete, gravel, barren earth? This is called "Setting the Scene".

Now, to introduce some drama: stepping out onto the basement floor, you turn. What was the sound you heard? A moan. A distinctively feminine moan, in fact. Does this excite you? You come across the body of a woman. Is she naked? You have only your non-visual senses to inform this decision. Her feet, which you encounter first, are certainly bare.

What's this twined around her ankles? Something hard, serpentine: the plastic-coated metal of a bicycle chain. The woman is bound to a chair. What kind of chair? You can determine this through your senses of touch, smell, and yes, even taste.

The woman is cold, as one must expect of a body without the comforting benefit of clothes, but just as assuredly alive. Her skin prickles at your touch. Her calf muscles tighten yet she does not struggle. Her breaths come short and shallow like submerged hiccups. The skin on her legs tastes of salt as if she had been swimming, or running. Her knees are skinned. Her pubic thatch, to your surprise, is shaved, scented, as if in preparation for a boyfriend.

For you?

You avoid her breasts. You don't want her to get that idea. Nevertheless when your hand trails past her shoulder, brushing her neck for the barest instant, she moans again. You can't tell whether from fear or desire. Her cheek shivers. Note the texture of her skin: the fine hair (the cliché of peach fuzz comes to mind), the puffiness, the *fleshiness*, all ending abruptly at the bony lower orbit of her eye. She has, you discover, clenched her eyelids shut. Even though it is dark. Even though she cannot see you. She has not, in fact, ever knowingly observed you.

Mary is not entirely naked as it turns out. She wears a misshapen hat: a bird made of felt fastened to her head with a stretchy band that runs under her chin. The hat was probably once a cat's toy but has been re-purposed. It smells of cat pee, that's for certain.

Write What You Know

One of the most limiting writing recommendations ever set to paper, if interpreted literally. Do you want to produce nothing but thinly disguised autobiographies? Consider a re-interpretation: write from the emotions that you know. Write, as so many books on my shelves implore, from what you care about.

For me, it always returns to a woman, a girl from my high school. Her name was Mary (not her real name) and she had the most gorgeous smile. I think she needed braces, but braces would have ruined that smile. Her smile appeared without preamble in response to the school heaters burping in winter, the rhymes of children jumping rope, the crackle of the PA system. It could light up the room, as they say. Part of me loved her, but I had never pursued a woman before. I sat two seats behind and across the aisle from her on the school bus. Sometimes she wore a red sweater. On those days she rhythmically pressed her thighs together, revealed only by the tension in her legs. I imagined myself as her. I imagined how the cloaked space between her legs felt in response to those rhythms.

Then I dreamed of Mary. Initially she was how I knew her: sweet, innocent, smiling. But she changed. She devolved. Have you ever seen the Bugs Bunny cartoon in which skinny, wisecracking Bugs devolves into a burly Paleolithic version of himself? Something similar happened with Mary. In my dream, she became coarse and broad, hairy and hulking.

Bigger than me. After that, I could never look at Mary the same way again.

In every story since then, I've tried to infuse my female characters with that initial element of desire I felt for Mary, and I've tried to avoid the subsequent revulsion. On the first score I've had some success. On the second, perhaps less.

Dialogue I

Character: Why are you doing this to me?
Author: (no answer)

The Narrator

Who to choose as the narrator for your tale? The girl? She may scream from blind fear until she is hoarse. She doesn't know that she is locked in a basement far from town and the chances she will be heard are slim to none (and slim has already left town). This dawning realization can be communicated from her point of view. But how much more damning if the narrator should be someone else, unnamed, who can describe the same scene from a contrasting viewpoint. Black humour can be effective here, especially when the victim is of limited perception, a girl whose ideas of horror are blinkered by some appallingly bad movies. "Is the key to the lock behind my eye?" she asks. There is of course no answer, and the reader is left wondering if the girl will, in fact, gouge herself blind on the chance that this will illuminate the basis for her captivity.

A remark about Oedipus would be apropos, but would be lost on our character. Hence the silence of the narrator with regards to the victim. But not in regards to you, the reader, who one hopes will understand (relish?) the reference.

One of my favourite stories is by Kipling, the most black-humoured piece I have ever read, and one of the most instructive. The story is called "The Record of Badalia Herodsfoot". It is not frequently reprinted, but it does appear in *The Oxford Book of Short Stories* (1981 edition), as chosen by V. S. Pritchett. "Her husband after two years took to himself another woman, and passed out of Badalia's life, over Badalia's senseless body; for he stifled protest with blows." After that it goes from bad to worse for Badalia, ending in the tragedy of her death. Readers—it's a fact—do not like weak-willed characters that are buffeted by events like tissues in a purse. However, under the guise of humour, any crime may be committed with impunity.

Revision

The sad fact of writing is that nothing will match your initial vision. Our character Mary may seem perfection itself. But try this experiment—I certainly have—leave her alone in the basement for a few days, a week, a month, and then return. Formerly an angel, she will now be dirty, rank as onions, a clawing creature of the pit. With revision, she may once again approach that original ideal. Below, I suggest several strategies for revision.

The Kingectomy: Even Stephen King, one of the most prolific writers of our age, in his book *On Writing*, describes how he excises 10% of a story to achieve final form. Perhaps your character could use a *diet*, her excess ten percent whittled away symmetrically. But don't feel so constrained. How about amputating a leg just below the knee? A one-legged runner has narrative possibilities.

The Straubing: In Peter Straub's short story, "Blue Rose," there is a description of how the narrator inserts a thick needle into the arm of his hypnotized brother. This scene, running for pages, captures the obsession with which an author focuses on a particular scene in need of revision. The author might, for example, flay a fingertip, then deciding this is not sufficient, retract the skin to the second knuckle. Blood dribbles. Something is still not right. The author extracts strands of muscle with a pen point, exposing pink nubs of bone. The author licks and tastes the tainted calcium, then gnaws at it to reveal the divine white bone of memory.

The Flauberation: Gustave Flaubert is quoted as saying, "I spent the morning putting in a comma and the afternoon removing it." Do you remember Mary's silvery blue eyes?

She has only one now, having lost the other in a misguided attempt for freedom. But didn't she function better with binocular vision? Editing is sometimes harder than even Flaubert could imagine.

Dialogue II

Author: I'm doing this for your own good.
Character: (no answer)

The Willing Suspension of Disbelief

First coined by Samuel Coleridge, this is one of the most cumbersome phrases to make its way into common parlance. Yet...

Escapism

I thought I had my character trussed up tighter than a Thanksgiving turkey. I did mention my facility with knots, did I not? I used a good granny knot—not the most elegant choice, but a damn sight better than a square knot.

A knot?

Wasn't it a bicycle chain ("hard and serpentine")? A fumbling inconsistency. So easy to overlook. But, just like that, Mary is

going

going

gone.

Really and truly gone. Not a stray hair remaining. Not a whiff of her sweet salty skin. Only this: that strange felt hat with its stretchy band. A felt bird. Yes, it's true. My character has gone and given me the bird.

On Symbols

In spite of what your English teacher may have told you, there are no hidden meanings in stories. That doesn't mean items in a story can't take on a significance greater than themselves:

an idiosyncratic felt hat, for instance.

The Lonely Voice

How often is an author abandoned by their main character? Far too often, I'm afraid. But on those occasions of true and honest success, when every rope is knotted, every door locked, and your character left no recourse for escape, on those occasions one can spin tresses into gold, guts into glory. Consider Ursula K. Le Guin's finest story, the Hugo-award winning "The Ones Who Walk Away from Omelas". Here we have the earnest depiction of a utopia made real in its last pages by the description of the abused child held captive in the dark basement of the city. It is on the frail shoulders of that child that the whole edifice stands. Yet, for all Le Guin's willingness to exhume that child as a symbol of the horrors that create wonder, I have a feeling that should Le Guin ever read my own small contribution to the literary arts, should she ever meet me in person, she would abhor me. Abhor is not too strong a word for it.

Frank O'Connor titled his influential book on the writing of the short story, *The Lonely Voice*. We are all lonely voices. Remember this. I won't say it again, but it almost owes repeating. Abandoned by our characters, despised by those we love, the author is the lonely ghost haunting the story, refusing to relinquish it.

The Second Person

I'm all out of advice. All out of jokes, too. My main character is gone, lost due to a momentary lapse, a failure in editing, a rupture in your "willing suspension of disbelief". What is left?

Why you, my dear friend, my diligent reader. You who have followed this narrative since its inception, who wonder of wonders is still with me. It was only with your willing participation that I was able to create a character. *Our* character. I wrote the words, but you gave Mary life. You explored her, edited her. You lived with her, breathed the perfume of her flesh, and, dare I say, loved her. This narrative would not exist without you.

What is left? (I repeat myself.)

You and I. Alone, together.

Pablo Neruda, commenting on his great friend Federico Lorca, told of how Lorca would pick up prospective lovers with the line, "Let us be alone, together."

In short stories, any number of texts will warn you against the use of the second person in a narrative. Use of the second person causes a rupture in the uninterrupted dream that is, according to these texts, the ultimate goal for any true short story writer.

However, you and I are not in a short story. We stand outside the story, living our own circumspect lives— different jobs in different cities, maybe different countries, continents—knowing nothing of each other until we meet within the confines of these pages. How did this piece come into your hands? I have no idea, yet here we enter into a collusion. Ours is the faith of long-time friends. Together, we build a grand artifice. Together, we clothe our dreams in flesh. New worlds blossom in the cold, dark reaches of space. Glass cities erupt from the desert sands. A populace dances, loves, fights, and screams in the glittering streets. Together, we create and live the story of their lives.

Who is the writer and who is the reader? Neither? Both? We are all creators. We are all writers. We are alone, you and I, together.

The Gift

I have something for you.

A thank-you gift for having been my accomplice in this enterprise.

It's nothing much, but I want you to have it. A hat. Again, nothing much, but once upon a time it was quite fine: created by a true mad hatter. The hat is of felt. Bird-shaped. Feel how soft it is. Perhaps not so much any more. It was quite fine once but—confession time—the cats got at it. To be frank, it still smells of cat piss on occasion. Only when wet, though. Otherwise it can be quite dandyish. So I've been told. Some might call it a crown.

I trust you'll wear it.

I'm afraid I've nothing more to offer.

II.

MEET ME IN THE MIDDLE OF THE AIR

8) – 5.8

The stone monument that protected Poe's interred remains proved an insurmountable problem, a discovery that precipitated a black funk in Jason. He wandered the streets of Baltimore, ruminating, scheming, and embracing his suffering with an avidity second only to that of Poe's himself. "Like a consumptive lover." Jason said these words aloud and luxuriated in their bitterness. Returning to the tomb on a miserable rainy night, Jason satisfied himself with a remote 3-D recording he made of Poe's brainpan. This was of higher resolution than he had anticipated and might capture Poe's spirit if not his essence.

Poe!

Poe had no children but the descendants of his cousin Neilson, a Baltimore judge, were plentiful. Jason examined their records, their images and vital statistics, and boarded a flight for Chicago. Three days later, in the men's room of the Logan Bar and Grill, Jason bumped into a man five-feet eight-inches in height and with handsome but delicate features. "Excuse me," Jason said. He held his tissue sampler out of sight but at waist level. The sampler released an anesthetic and did not puncture so deeply as to draw blood, at least not so much as might be noticed. "My fault," his quarry said, stepping aside so that Jason could open the door.

Poe!

Of course it was Poe. The immortal Poe. Poe with his luminous forehead and those pale magnetic eyes that captured and held you, lost beyond all decency of sorrow. Poe with his claustrophobic vocabularies. Poe with his lopsided mustache and moon-sallow skin, Poe who alone in the world could understand the loneliness of the outsider, the misunderstood genius that was Jason.

It had to be Poe, and so it was Poe.

And Jason? He was young, of course, fifteen-years-old and flying solo in an efficiency apartment after leaving home. He still reeled from the discovery that the universe cared nothing for him at best. At worst, and Jason took an egotistical delight in the possibility, the universe actively thwarted his ambitions. Jason cut his own hair. He wore an oversize black suit jacket even in summer and hunched his thin shoulders, thinking this bat-like appearance suggested a world-weary rebel. He had friends, lovers, but these inspired mixed emotions. Their obvious flaws—celebrity gossip couched as disdain, flippancy mistaken for irony, guffawing laughter when stoned—reflected poorly on Jason. Yet he was foolish enough to believe the unobtainable friends and lovers he coveted would do otherwise.

Jason was, in other words, more a man of his time than Poe ever presumed to be.

The Petit kit—the name originated from the French but the pronunciation was Anglicized to '*pet*-it'—contained an incubator, packets of nutrients and retroviruses, and a live link to the company site. Jason watched the cell clump grow with increasing anxiety and hope, shifting his attention between the fist-sized plastic globe on his desk to the magnified image on his wall. He zoomed in and out. He cursed the limitations of microscopy: a blob of cells could be any blob of cells. The blob divided asymmetrically over the next two days, elongated, bent like a pink jellybean. It protruded tiny limbs, webbed fingers, developed a bulbous oversized head. The forehead looked familiar but was Jason fooling himself? The miniscule genitalia confirmed its maleness.

Jason maintained his petit in the amniotic substrate for two months, 18 years of relative age for his Poe, the outer limit of the recommended incubation period. Jason had no desire to cater to the whims and tantrums of a child. How Jason grinned when he saw his petit sprout a tiny but unequivocal mustache. He zoomed in on its face. What had seemed a preternatural fineness of detail, a ravishing sensitivity of features, enlarged on the wall screen was monstrous: the hair coarse, the face soft, amorphous, like a melted reflection emerging from a nightmare. The brochure had warned of this, followed by the reminder that, "Significantly, the capacities of a petit are not those of a human, in particular when it comes to its cognitive abilities."

Jason did not repeat that magnification mistake.

He decanted Poe soon thereafter. The little creature rose unsteadily to his knees, retched fluid from his lungs, and drew his first sputtering breath. He swept aside a lank swath of hair and blinked repeatedly, painfully, either from tears or an excess of light. Jason's heart melted. "Edgar," he murmured, heart suffused with the warmth of creation, ersatz childbirth, a continued reference to the surname *Poe* seeming a historical anachronism. Still on his knees, not trusting to his balance, the newly christened Edgar stretched his arms toward the looming mountain of Jason. Jason extended a forefinger. Edgar encircled it—*the sweet sensation of those hands, so small, so perfect*—and, using it as a support, struggled to his feet.

❖

Clothing is naturally foreign to the petit in its initial state. We recommend establishing an ambient temperature of 21 degrees Celsius, but not lower than 16 degrees—the low body mass of the petits renders them susceptible to cold shock—as an incentive to vesture.

❖

Cynthia was a friend of a friend. She had always been on the outskirts of the circles Jason frequented, so outside that he hadn't even remembered her name. But they both had petits and so he acquiesced to a Thursday afternoon at her apartment, calling it tea although he laughingly admitted to a preference for coffee. Jason presented his Edgar dolled up in all his finery. Black on black velvet, with a froth of white about the neck. Edgar's garb was suspiciously similar to that worn by Jason himself although less fitted, loose clothing being recommended for all petits; even the best microfibers were ruffians when it came to chaffing.

Cynthia's Marilyn tottered on her heels but curtsied quite prettily. She was clearly a black-market knockoff of at least three generations removed from the original clone. Her hair was bleached beyond platinum, her cheek decorated with a painted mole, and she wore a push-up bra. That's about as far as the resemblance to Monroe extended.

His Edgar accepted Marilyn's proffered hand, cradling it like a patient dove, then bowed and kissed its back. He twittered excitement and was rewarded with a similar twitter.

"Marilyn Monroe, right?" Jason said. He habitually stated the obvious as a safe conversation starter.

"Yes, isn't she beautiful?" If Cynthia's petit was Marilyn, then Cynthia was her more prosaic alter ego Norma Jean, a brunette who eschewed make-up but lived vicariously through Hollywood artifice. Cynthia was seventeen, the two years difference in their ages rendering her all the more seductive to Jason.

Perhaps sensing the comparable crudeness of her petit, Cynthia soon found an excuse to entice Jason into her bedroom. Marilyn's dollhouse, a palace confectionary frosted in pinks and whites with stiletto towers, uncountable mirrors, and vertiginous stairs, extended from floor to ceiling and encompassed a full quarter of the room. The dollhouse was a world apart from the generic digs Jason had established for Edgar. Every room of the dollhouse was visible, the exteriors being walled with non-reflective glass through which Jason could follow, over Cynthia's naked shoulder, the two petits and their exploration of the interior.

"And so, all the night-tide, I lie down by the side of my darling—my darling—my life and my bride, in her sepulcher there by the sea—in her tomb by the sounding sea." Jason ran his fingers along Cynthia's shoulder, her neck. He hefted her hair.

"Is that what you think of my Marilyn's palace?" Cynthia's hair smelled of shampoo, a springtime fragrance.

"It's a poem I like. By Poe." How could she miss the point so utterly?

"Oh, Poe." She giggled. "That's almost a poem itself. *Oh, Poe.* It rhymes."

"Please," he said, "lie still." Cynthia was one of liveliest lovers he had ever had, in spite of his hint that the emulation of Poe's Annabel Lee was preferable. He kneaded the skin on Cynthia's neck, finding it looser than he expected. Was that what two years wrought?

"Why?"

"Or speak," he added. He placed his lips over hers. She giggled again. Her puffs of breath tickled his mouth, more distracting than words.

A high-pitched scream froze them both momentarily in place. Marilyn's palace! Jason tore aside the sheets, slapped feet to floor, and covered the distance in two strides. He crouched down, a nude but awkward giant, and scanned the transparent walls. Where were they?

Cynthia had followed him. Her thigh slid warm and sweaty against his shoulder. "Marilyn," she cried in the affected voice she used whenever she communicated with her petit. She then swung a glass wall to the side and reached into one of the bedrooms. Marilyn clambered onto her hand. She was crying, a hiccupping twee sound more mouse-like than human. Streaks of blue mascara bisected her cheeks. She was naked, exquisite and vulnerable, and rubbed her forearm compulsively. "He bit her," Cynthia cried. A magnifier confirmed the bruised oval of teeth marks. Cynthia did not comment on the other bruises that discolored Marilyn's skin. Girls were notoriously hard on their petits.

Jason discovered his Edgar huddled by the baseboard of the same bedroom. Edgar was still clothed, arms clutched protectively across his chest. Each fist gripped a bunched lapel of his jacket. Closer inspection revealed that one of the sleeves was ripped, threads popped at its shoulder seam.

Now it was Jason's turn to cry out. "What did she do to him?"

Cynthia gave Jason the strangest look. "Exactly what I was going to do to you. Little Marilyn is quite the randy girl. Just like her owner."

❖

Petits are desirous to please and, after the initial imprinting period, readily adapt to their owner's expectations and actions provided these are clearly and repeatedly communicated. A food reward system is commonly employed due to its effectiveness.

❖

Envy is the most utilitarian of the Deadly Sins and, transformer of potential into kinetic energy, was the spur to Jason's genius. Jason was tempted to emulate the House of Usher, or the castellated abbey of Prince Prospero, or the labyrinthine catacombs of the Montresors. But his fervent desire was not to recreate a character of Poe's but to rather recreate the vivifying character of Poe *himself.* Truly there was only one choice: the Amity Street duplex that served as incubator to Poe's authorial aspirations. Jason made a trip to Baltimore for the sole purpose of acquiring brick scrapings from the original walls, scans of its interior and exterior already being available online. He had the wall plaster synthesized using keratin filaments de-convoluted from genuine horsehair. A friend supplied him with a bonsai elm that, planted outside the Lilliputian property, promptly lost its leaves, its doleful aspect a welcome infliction on the residence.

Jason intended the new house as a surprise and, on the day of its completion, he scooped up Edgar and deposited him inside a jam jar, its lid pocked with holes to allow for air exchange. He then placed Edgar's substandard shoebox-sized home into a metal wastebasket, squirted it with lighter fluid, and dropped a match. Jason thought that Edgar would appreciate the conflagration even if he did not understand its ceremonial nature, that it would hold a Neolithic fascination born deep within our genetic heritage. He was wrong. Edgar pounded his tiny fists against the walls of his glass prison, leapt helplessly, and, even after Jason disposed of the smoldering wastebasket and revealed the pristine Amity-style home to him, refused to uncurl from a fetus-like position made all the more ludicrous due to his somber raiment.

Edgar slept in a corner of Jason's living room floor for two days, an ascetic with a straight pin near at hand for protection. Jason's stomach was queasy with sympathy, even though his actions had been endorsed by the petit instruction manual. He tucked a square of toilet paper around Edgar's shoulders for warmth, Edgar's original blanket having been destroyed in the fire.

On the third day, overcome by hunger, Edgar crawled up the front steps of his new home and consumed the pastry crumbs Jason had placed as bait. Then inside—Jason following Edgar's exploration through camera feeds relayed to his monitor—the parlor and kitchen on the first floor, two bedrooms on the second, and finally, reached by a claustrophobic stairway, a garret bedroom with oppressive ceiling and minimal furnishings, not least of which was a desk appointed with quill and ink. As well as a plate with meat, potato, and beans, and a glass with two thick drops of burgundy wine. Edgar scurried forward, but bumped his head against the ceiling and sat down on the floor with a comedic thump. He bounced upright and, ignoring the chair, leaned over the desk and shoveled the moist food into his mouth.

Jason clapped in triumph. He then clapped again when he saw Edgar's desperation give way to satiation. Jason lowered his eye to the garret window, concurrently watching himself as viewed from the house and displayed on the monitor. Edgar wiped his mouth and lifted his gaze to Jason's immense single eye.

"You're home," Jason whispered. His eye brimmed with a tear that he did not know he possessed and which, following the moment of its creation, dribbled down his cheek to be lost. "Home."

Edgar nodded in assent, an understanding being reached, a realization that all was for the best, the Amity Street house, the food, the wine...yes, the wine...Edgar regarded it for the first time. He lifted the glass, holding it in just the manner that Jason had instructed, swirled the blood-thick vintage, and downed it in one long swallow.

In dark moments Jason had doubted his own genius, finding no suitable vessel by which to display it to optimal effect. No such doubt remained. Each decision he had made, each optimization of his Edgar, had suggested another, each leading to something closer to that unobtainable perfection— Platonic, Poetic—dare he call it that?—a composition that, being rendered in miniature, would display his genius in a manner comprehensible to the limited intellects of his age.

Poe!

❖

As the good bard William Shakespeare wrote, "...the play's the thing wherein I'll catch the conscience of the King."

❖

The waves seethed and crashed, broke across the bow of the ivory ship, the deck awash with silt-roiled water, the air sodden to choking with spray. Edgar hung against the wheel, one wrist lashed to it with a twist-tie, his legs trembling and spread for support. He wore his funereal suit, but this was drenched and clung to his limbs: water raced in rivulets from hair to shoulders to waist, streamed across his thighs, and then cascaded to deck. Edgar's mouth was a perfect O. His voice trilled like a siren. At times, when the ship lifted to the peak of an immaculate wave, he raised his free arm high, his spread fingers projecting like the rays of a symbolic sun.

Jason ran alongside the thrashing stream, actuator in hand. It could not be said that he had abandoned hope, but rather that he had reconsidered his evaluation as to what would provide Edgar the impetus to develop his personality to its fullest potential. There had been more to Poe's life and struggles than the house on Amity Street. For example, the watery voyages that had informed Poe's hallucinogenic sea tales. The ivory ship was a happy accident that had somehow made its way into the plebian ownership of Jason's parents, surreally appropriate, an antique model crafted by the Inuit or a facsimile so accurate that it might as well have been the original. Three-masted, the sails gluttonous before a persistent wind and steadied by ropes of slivered bone, the ship seemed at once phantom-like and uncomfortably heavy. Strangest of all, derived from how such a ship must have appeared to the shore-bound Inuit, the hull was flat at its bottom, the model crafted to reveal only what was obvious above the waterline, as if this was all that existed. Such a ship was not seaworthy and so Jason, in the interest of safety, added a keel synthesized from the waste of dental cosmetics.

"*Moskoe-strom*," Jason said into his actuator.

The water stilled, the mist assumed a coppery sheen and, from just the right angle, took on a rainbow's aspect. The ship, despite the perpetual billow of its ivory sails, appeared becalmed. Three deep breaths, each held behind a bitten lip. The ship perambulated sideways, caught in a grip mightier than the mockery of wind in its sails—it inscribed a curve, like the abbreviated orbit of a planet. Then the ship swung its prow around and into the direction of the new current and there could be no doubt that wind meant nothing to this new path, that this circuit formed the outer circumference of a mighty whirlpool, a maelstrom that at its centre penetrated the stream to its mud-churned bed.

"Oh my oh my oh my!" Jason cried, the spectacle being greater than even his rapturous imaginings. He wondered how it would look replayed on the walls of his apartment, perhaps unannounced while in the company of friends. What should he serve at such a gathering? Nautical fare—limes, hardtack—had little to commend it. Perhaps penguin. Edgar's keening, at first unnoticed, reached a pitch that demanded Jason's attention. The ship had circled halfway down the artificial maelstrom and was now pitched sideways such that water sluiced its decks from above. Edgar had lost his footing and hung in mid-air. Only the twist-tie curtailed his plummet into oblivion. Even as Jason watched, and before he had the presence of mind to still the waters with his actuator, Edgar reached for the twist-tie with his free hand.

At that moment the ship flipped over, keel replacing sails.

Jason remembered the actuator. The ship recovered itself, having inscribed an additional semicircle underwater, the main mast now broken, splintered and trailing behind, the other masts intact but missing sails. And Edgar? The ship rolled over once again to ride the current upside down— Edgar!—doing so before the maelstrom dissipated enough for Jason to wade into the stream and recover the remnants of his family heirloom.

Jason hauled the smashed boneyard of the ivory ship to shore. He settled onto the green sward better suited to a picnicker from *Le déjeuner sur l'herbe*. Then with the desperation of a starved man exploring the chicken carcass that such picnickers might discard, Jason dismantled what remained of the ship. No Edgar. Just a twist of wire linked to the wheel. A calm settled over Jason, an awareness that Edgar had been thrown free of the doomed ship—his Edgar had a pocket watch and chain, and, unlike its nineteenth century model, this watch was waterproof and contained a transmitter—Jason carried its larger cousin in his pocket. He flipped open its case and toggled the homing signal: blips pinged and a green star flashed on its compass screen. Was the watch still with Edgar? More importantly, was Edgar still alive?

Yes, and yes.

Splashing along the shoreline, as if beholden to the technology in his hand, Jason rescued Edgar from beneath a towering forest of grass, pawing at the somnolent duckweed, coughing and spitting up dirty water. Edgar had lost his jacket and his shirt was drenched and torn. His arm was incised with an evil scratch, deep enough to loose a spill of blood. "OhmygodOhmygod!" Jason lifted his beautiful Edgar to his lips and kissed him. Edgar's blood tasted identical to his own, as if they were undisclosed twins, the separation granted by time and dimension as immaterial as spider webs in a rainstorm.

Prior to his adventure, Edgar had spent the requisite two hours a day at his tiny garret desk, recordings of Poe's works playing in the background, while he scrawled on the paper that Jason supplied. There had been something almost comical, girlish, about the looping scribbles that Edgar committed to posterity. After this adventure, Edgar's writings took on a new character, the ink streaked and jagged, the force of his hand sometimes splintering the quill so that the ink splotched, a Rorschach test of projected imaginings. These were the writings Edgar now saved, lining his mattress with them as with the makings of a nest.

The first video that Jason made public on Cloud Kingdom was of Edgar crouched over his desk and fanatically scribbling his beautiful gibberish.

Poe!

❖

We recommend a combination of positive and negative reinforcement for optimal results, each being the more effective when balanced with the other. Please note that, while some have employed electroconvulsive therapy to good effect, the constitution of a petit is such that lower doses are required than might be predicted. Common adverse effects are confusion and memory loss.

❖

On August the fifth, they passed a panhandler: "Can I ask a favour?" The man had a puffy face, his cheeks ruddy and blotched, a short beard, and carried a child's backpack. Jason shook his head. He wanted to be as invisible as Edgar in his shirt pocket.

"Sorry for asking," the panhandler said. It was only then that Jason realized they were standing near a Kevorkian, all sleek plastic and handicap accessible. The stranger entered the booth and disappeared from view, his last solicitation a matter of habit if not necessity.

Jason waited outside the booth for a good five minutes—fifty percent of suicides were aborted—but the man did not reappear. Ever curious, Edgar pulled himself upward to rest his forearm on the lip of Jason's pocket. Jason quoted to him from Poe: "His whole frame at once—within the space of a single minute, or even less, shrunk—crumbled—absolutely rotted beneath my hands. Upon the bed, before that whole company, there lay a nearly liquid mass of loathsome—of detestable putridity."

It was not long thereafter that Jason reacquainted himself with Cynthia. Although she had been a lively and unsatisfactory lover, he had been polite enough to say nothing of this, complimenting her on her technique. He wasn't sure why he called her. Maybe because she had also complimented him on his technique. Maybe because she shared his interests in petits, even if Edgar and Marilyn were oil and water, darkness and light.

❖

A petit will, if the imprinting is successful, be at its happiest within the sight and hearing of its owner. Such imprinting provides the greatest security against loss and, in combination with a personal transmitter, will assure you and your petit a lifetime of mutual satisfaction.

❖

The thing bobbing at the end of the tether was oddly shaped and had a disheveled appearance. Bells tinkled on its underside, their musical throats amplified to the joyous warble of a robin. Hanging below this thing, suspended on blue ribbons but upside down, was an antique hat of genuine beaver fur. "It's a balloon," Jason said proudly, "modeled after one in a Poe story."

"Of course it is," Cynthia said, giving his hand a congratulatory squeeze.

To Jason's surprise, the two months that had followed his re-acquaintance with Cynthia were the most blissful of his life. Bliss arises, not from a paradisiacal continuity, Jason realized—that way lies boredom—but from a sense of continued striving coupled to an unanticipated level of success. Moreover, Cynthia was a willing accomplice in Jason's adventures. Or rather, the adventures he bestowed on Edgar, and to which she now contributed her Marilyn as the eternal companion. The increasing popularity of the videos Jason posted to Cloud Kingdom was due in no small part to the unlikely pairing of their two petits. He had even begun to recoup costs through the advertising revenue.

Jason hauled the balloon down and pinned its securing lines to the turf. It was a glorious day. Only a few clouds, helped along by a breeze gentle and cool, wandered the obscenely blue sky. "It's covered in newspaper," he said of the balloon. "Replicas from an 1835 Dutch newspaper, from Rotterdam." The smudged and curling newsprint rebounded to his touch like the fur of a sated cat.

In response to a hand sign from Jason, Edgar parted the curtains of an Arabic-styled tent and strutted forward. He wore a frock coat and breeches of sky-blue satin, a vest of yellow, as if he sought to emulate the day itself. These were offset by a clownishly large handkerchief of blood-red silk tied about his neck. Nearby was a white mansion with crystalline windows: Cynthia's purse. She unzipped its door and Marilyn skipped forth, sparkling like a newborn star. Marilyn executed a pirouette and curtsied, only a flickering grimace as she took weight on the ankle that Cynthia had injured when dressing her.

Marilyn accepted Edgar's hand with good grace. The two petits appeared to have accomplished a truce, perhaps emulating the camaraderie of their owners, almost certainly yielding to gluttony for, following each shared adventure, Jason rewarded Edgar with treats as compensation for the indignity of Marilyn's company. Curiously, Jason had once caught Edgar sharing his nugget of caramel with Marilyn.

"We'll picnic together, us below and they above," Jason said. He might be addressing Cynthia, their petits, or the anticipated audience for the video he would assemble. "Residents of the earth mirrored in the sky." He exhumed a tiny basket from a larger wicker basket and passed it to Marilyn for safekeeping. In it, to be revealed once the balloon attained height, was a replica of the luncheon he had prepared for Cynthia: a dismembered chicken, Brie and cucumber sandwiches, potato chips, chocolate mousse, and a bottle of rosé wine.

"Up, up, and away." Jason played the tether out slowly. The balloon bobbed and weaved overhead despite his steadying efforts. The two occupants appeared unperturbed, laughing along with each jolt, clinging to each other as if lovers in fact not fiction. They waved colored handkerchiefs from the hat's brim and then dropped from sight, their secrets revealed only to the on-board camera.

"What would you like, my love?" Jason asked Cynthia, unwrapping the parcel of chicken. "Dark meat or white?"

"I'll take a wing," Cynthia said. She rolled her eyes upward, expressing significance. She too had learned to play to an audience.

The balloon inscribed small circles at the end of its tether. Its smudged appearance reminded Jason of the inherent fragility of all manmade creations. *If the future should disrobe before our blinkered eyes, what horrors would be revealed?* Such had always been Jason's credo, although too often he assumed that pain could be mollified by transmutation into art. Too often, he forgot the visceral nature of fear.

Cynthia tore pebbled skin and fibers of flesh from her chicken wing. She held the tender bones in her fingers. Her teeth glowed in the afternoon sun, a white brighter than ivory and acquired only by chemical saturation. She smiled in response to Jason's attention. She was, in her own way, more beautiful than Marilyn. Jason returned her smile, negligent of how the harbingers of horror arrive in guise of those we love.

Cynthia applied greasy fingers to the bottle of rosé and refilled their glasses. "Do you suppose," she said, "that Marilyn and Edgar are toasting each other even now as I toast you?" She clanked her glass against his and slurped a mouthful. She licked her lips.

"Don't you just love the smell of new-mown grass?" Jason said. The smell was alive, even though born of a scythe. He glanced at the monitor:

Blue...

Blue? Sky-blue. Although no clouds were visible within the limited frame.

"The camera's not right," he said.

He turned from the monitor and searched the genuine sky for the balloon. It was smaller than he remembered. The balloon was disappearing into the sky.

Rising into it.

"Hey," he said, dropping his glass. It spilled but did not break.

"What?" Cynthia said.

"The balloon."

The line was slack in his hand. When had he grabbed it? He pulled and there was no resistance. The line was falling. "It's falling," he said. He knew even as he said this that it would confuse Cynthia. He pushed to his feet. "The balloon," he said. "It's broken free." His voice was calm, deadpan, although in his mind he was crying, screaming, the air shivering firestorms in response, his mind back-flashing to his near catastrophic recreation of the maelstrom: *Not again!*

He began to run.

❖

The petit maintains a body temperature similar to that of a full-sized human but to do so, because of its high surface area to volume ratio, the petit functions at a considerably higher metabolism. This may contribute to the petit's relatively short lifespan of one year or, to be exact, 347 days on average for males and 368 days for females.

❖

Jason, Cynthia, and a dozen friends gathered in the park, besieged by a cold rain that bordered on sleet. They wore somber suits and dresses, obsolete by two centuries, and sheltered beneath spidery umbrellas that threatened to invert with every stormy gust. They shivered with a welcome discomfort, the memorial ceremony as dismal as intended.

It was a funeral, after all, although there were no bodies to inter.

Jason placed his foot on the backbone of a spade sharpened to a knife-edge never obtained by whetstone. His shirt cuffs were wet and clung to his wrists. Four perpendicular cuts, the blade sunk each time until his heel met turf. Again, the motions recapitulated for a second interment. Then, kneeling, water blooming across the knees of his pants, he plunged his hands into the crevices and yanked loose rectilinear chunks of turf, grit beneath his fingernails, dirt staining the edge of his cuffs. Soiled. He wiped his hands on his pants and took a perverse joy in the fact they did not come clean, and likewise in the fact that whether he cried or not, his tears became part of the rain. He was, in fact, crying.

He rose and wiped his dirty hands again on his thighs. Everything was wet and cold. "Welcome," he said. He snuffled, a disgusting sound but one that could be forgiven in the here-and-now and later erased from the video. The advertising rights for the funeral were pre-sold. The coffins were properly coffin-shaped, finger-length, and painted a shiny black such that the rain pearled and spilled off them in engaging trickles. He opened Edgar's coffin, the pillowed silk immediately splotched with rain. "These are Edgar," he said, and deposited a miniscule watch and a red handkerchief into the cavernous interior of the coffin. These were the only remnants of Edgar's that had been recovered following his ill-fated adventure, the watch with its transmitter scratched and dented, the torn handkerchief tangled within the twigs of a nearby maple.

Cynthia enlarged on the motif with her own offerings. "These are Marilyn," she said. She proffered the scrap of a white dress, rescued from the same locale, as well as a tiny crown that played no part in this last adventure but was pretty in its own right. Cynthia's face crumpled and Jason attached his arm to her shoulders, lending support. "These are the mementoes by which we remember those we loved," he said. "Those we still love and hold in our hearts." The words, although trite, were surprisingly truthful. "The tiniest of men might be a giant, if judged by his shadow in the dying of the day." On cue, the dark clouds parted and a ruddy finger of sunlight illuminated the sward on which they stood. Their shadows stretched out into the darkness beneath the dripping trees.

❖

Significantly, the capacities of a petit are not those of a human, in particular when it comes to its cognitive abilities. Nevertheless, even while accepting and taking into account the limitations of a petit, avoid the diametrical error of underestimating its intelligence.

❖

"*Crepuscular.* Don't you just love that word?" Jason and Cynthia stood in the park shelter, rain drumming on its roof. Jason hoped she would say something nice about his closing statement at the memorial service. He looked toward the horizon where the clouds had once again drawn together, night rushing in.

"Do you even know what that means?" A gulf had opened between Jason and Cynthia. Without their petits, did anything unite them?

"Can I get you a drink?"

Cynthia paused for longer than Jason thought reasonable. "Champagne," she said. "That was Marilyn Monroe's favourite. And Marilyn's too."

"Your wish..." Jason said, voice trailing off. Most words are meaningless, or implied.

He returned shortly, an effervescent flute in one hand, a snifter of brandy in the other. "Poe's vice," he said, referring to his drink. They twined arms and toasted their departed petits and then each other. One toast led to another, and one drink to another. It seemed they inhabited their own bubble, one in which they shared solitude and perhaps even grief. Cynthia was already more than tipsy, giggling at something Jason had not heard, or had misheard. It was hard to remain commiserate all the time. Circulating friends slowed in their vicinity, available should substitute companionship be required.

"I was thinking of keeping it," Cynthia said. Her head flopped to one side and she tugged at her hair. "It was just a scrap and you have so many. And besides, he left it in Marilyn's house. Maybe he gave it to her. Shouldn't it then be mine?"

"What are you talking about?"

"You should at least see it. No, I want you to *have* it." She set her glass on the floor, stared at it as if surprised that it remained upright. "Maybe you can tell me what it means." Cynthia's purse was a mess but it should not have been difficult to find the item. Indeed, when she extracted the plastic square from an interior pocket, he was sure it was something she had already handled and rejected.

Jason reached for it.

"You won't keep it, will you?" Cynthia's hand retreated.

"It's mine." She looked around distractedly. "Where did I put my drink?"

Jason pointed to its location on the floor.

The angry lines on Cynthia's forehead smoothed and she handed him the plastic square, almost absent-mindedly. She drained the few drops that remained in her glass.

Jason wiped moisture from the clear plastic: a small sheet of paper was encased within, the creases from its original folds still visible. The paper must have originated with the petits, probably from Edgar. "Where did you get this?"

"I found it when looking for Marilyn's crown. It was on her make-up table, in a jewelry box. Do you see the writing?" Most of the sheet was empty but there were squiggles in an upper corner. "Is that Edgar's?" She tapped the plastic with her fingernail.

Jason magnified the image on his handheld monitor until he could make out the writing. The craggy loops and dashes, the mockery of language, were indeed those of his dear sweet Edgar. He remembered fondly the reams of paper that Edgar had covered with his scribbling, so many sheets that Jason had given up tracking them. It wasn't surprising that a few had ended up in Marilyn's possession. Maybe they had been peace offerings of a sort.

But this was different, Jason realized with a shock of recognition. This was not an approximation of the alphabet, but actual numerals and punctuation: 8)-5.8. Jason zoomed in and out with his monitor. There could be no doubt. This was not gibberish but a substitution cipher, one that he had even used himself, most notably while keeping a short-lived diary secret from his parents.

The cipher originated from Poe's story The Gold Bug: 8)-5.8

Six letters, making up one word: *escape*.

This was the message that Edgar had passed on to Marilyn. Tears welled in Jason's eyes. That one word inverted the relationship he had maintained during his own short history with Edgar: not creator, but jailer, and there is world of difference between those poles. He felt nauseous imagining the collusion of their two petits, the facile manner in which they feigned abhorrence. He remembered the way they had clung together in the balloon—perhaps not entirely due to its vagaries of motion—like two halves of one whole. What remnants had been recovered from the crash? Just items that might be cast overboard to distract the searchers.

But still, to think that their petits would dare a world unmonitored, untamed by actuators, that they would flee their creators. It was almost too much to consider. Might they be out there on their own, fighting for survival but still alive? If they had made such an escape was it possible that other petits had done likewise?

"What does it say?"

Jason hesitated, conflicted by the desire to share his pain but not wishing to inflict such suffering on another. Perhaps this potential for pain was all that Cynthia and he now had in common, a parting gift from Edgar and Marilyn. The rain drummed heavily on the shelter's roof, and the wind blew chill around its supports, carrying with it the scent of severed grass and worms. There was dirt beneath Jason's fingernails and within the whorls of his finger pads.

"Nothing," he said. "Everything Edgar ever wrote was gibberish."

CRYSTAL VISION

David stirred a pot on the stove with a wooden spoon that had once belonged to his grandmother. Even without the fancifully carved handle, the origin of the spoon would have been easy to guess. Pretty much everything in the house, as well as the house itself, a century-old saltbox on the outskirts of Rochester, New Hampshire, had been inherited from David's grandmother. From my seat at the kitchen table, I raised my own spoon piled high with soggy cornflakes and made a silent toast to her memory.

David set the wooden spoon down. His long blond hair, normally curly, was lank from where it hung before his eyes in the billowing steam. He raised his arms so that the sleeves of his bathrobe fell back to his elbows. The robe was of red silk faded to pink and missing its belt so that it flopped loosely about his body like a second skin. He spread his fingers, clenched, knuckles crackling, then spread his fingers wide again.

David looked like a sorcerer escaped from some B movie.

He measured out a tablespoon full of yellowish liquid from a Pine-Sol bottle and added it to the pot on the stove.

"Eye of newt," I said.

Two teaspoons from a Mop-and-Glo bottle.

"Wing of bat."

A half-cup of Comet, the pale blue powder leveled with a kitchen knife.

"Dew off a dead man's eyes."

The stuff in the pot was mostly sugar water. I did not

know whether the sugar was an intrinsic part of the recipe or to make it more palatable. I didn't even truly know what were inside the name-brand bottles that David pulled out from their locations in the cabinet beneath the sink.

The proportions varied slightly each time David made up the recipe, like a good cook who follows intuition as much as any book. Except David wrote down the relative proportions each time in a small spiral-bound notepad he kept in his pocket. He used a stubby pencil whittled to a point. He said that in a former life, and by former life he meant five or ten years ago, he had been a chemistry student.

The pot boiled and the mixture became syrupy. Bubbles worked their way loose from below and exploded with a flatulent pop. There was the distinct odor of ammonia. David stirred until the mixture was so thick that it refused to move. The sugar on the bottom began to burn, blackening, the upper levels taking on the dusky appearance of ancient amber.

David gave the mixture a hard whack with the edge of the spoon and crazed lines shot across the surface.

"Crystal," he said.

Saliva filled my mouth. I thought of Pavlov's dog.

David banged the pot upside down on the counter, dislodging the contents, and scraped the inside clean with a knife. He then brushed the wedges and flakes of crystal off the counter into a Tupperware container and put the container into the cupboard. He returned to the counter and, with a moistened finger, picked at the remaining crumbs. He licked his finger clean and dabbed at the counter again.

"You want some?" he asked.

I nodded.

David smiled and held his encrusted finger out to me. I circled his finger with my lips and slid my tongue back and forth along it length, feeling the roughness that adhered to it dislodge and dissolve. The crystal tasted sweet and sour at the same time and bloomed on my tongue like roses in the snow.

"Everything is crystal you know," David said. "Salt.

Proteins. Blood, sweat, and tears. The trick is getting to the crystalline form." He walked back to the stove. "You ever have a crystal garden?"

"No," I said, "What's that?"

"Something I got with a chemistry set when I was a kid. You dropped seeds of different chemicals, small crystals, into a saturated salt solution. They grew day by day, week by week, piling one atop the other, all sorts of different colors depending on what chemicals you used. It was beautiful, like nothing I had ever seen before."

One was David.

Two was me.

Together we were something else.

Of course, back then, I didn't know what that something else was. Or that it would take five of us to get there. Even David may have worked mostly from instinct, any method to his madness revealed only in retrospect, to him as much as to the rest of us. But whatever door he was trying to open, crystal was the key and at some point it became obvious that, even with the key, he couldn't open the door alone.

❖

David kept an ever-expanding menagerie of toys, the kind you find in cereal boxes, in kid's meals at MacDonald's, and in cases at flea markets and next-to-new shops. Plastic cartoon characters, ceramic animals, and metal robots kept watch from nooks and crannies throughout the house. Walking barefoot, you would suddenly recoil in pain and discover a plastic cowboy embedded in your foot, his six-shooters raised as if in victory.

On the day of the party, David collected the characters in his menagerie and arranged them on the pool table in the living room. He made the toys part of a parade that wound around the table and then up a pyramid of books where, on the peak, a white plastic unicorn reared upon her hind legs. Trolls lurked in the pockets of the pool table and gryphons perched on the table's edge, playing the part of spies or outcasts, I wasn't quite sure.

Folks started showing up at the house at around five o'clock. By seven, the party was in full swing. It was bring your own and there was plenty of beer and wine. A couple of former housemates, Casper and Magic Hat, had gathered a group together in the kitchen. They all took turns sucking on Casper's bong, while Magic Hat rummaged through the kitchen drawers. "Let me show you how to make a bong out of a beer can," he said. "I just need something sharp to punch holes in it. You got any nails? It would be really cool if you had an apple. I could make a bong out of an apple too, if you had one."

David wondered from room to room carrying a plate piled high with wedges of crystal. It was a ceramic plate patterned with a Christmas wreath around the circumference, his grandmother's taste in crockery not his own. I slipped a sliver of crystal off the plate and pocketed it in my cheek to let it dissolve. "Any takers?" I asked.

"A few," David said.

There wasn't any food at the party besides some bags of chips, and we ordered out for pizza at around nine o'clock. The fellow who showed up at our door with the pizza wore a red knit cap over black curly hair. He had the placid smile of a stoner, and, from the resinous stench that clung to his sweater, I figured he had been toking in his car on the drive over. "Pretty cool party, man," he said. "Wish I didn't have to work."

"Hold on," I said. "I'll get the cash."

"Hey," the guy said, following along after me, "can I set these boxes down somewhere?" Then, before I could react or say anything, he dumped the stack of pizza boxes down on the pool table. On top of David's parade.

"Shit!" he said after a long pause. One could almost see the gears grinding in his head as he tried to make the connection between his actions and the devastation wrecked upon the parade. "Man, I'm really sorry. I thought it was just a table." He grabbed the boxes back up again and, in so doing, knocked them into the pyramid of books. Plastic characters tumbled in a landslide of dislodged books down to the green felt, some bouncing off the table.

"Shit!" he repeated after another long pause. "Sometimes it just doesn't pay to get up in the morning."

Several other partiers had gathered around us by this time, including David. The pizza fellow came up from beneath the table with a Snow White and a Scooby Doo in his hands. He set them down carefully on their feet in the wreckage of the parade. "Don't worry. I'll fix it all up again," he said.

"Hey, that's okay," David said. "No big deal. It was an accident waiting to happen."

I went off to scavenge money from the folks back in the kitchen. When I returned with the wad of bills, the pizza fellow and David were talking like old friends. "Peace, brother," the pizza fellow said when he left. "Peace to you too, Jacob," David said. "Drop by anytime."

Jacob took him at his word and showed up again the next afternoon.

I opened the door and saw him standing on the front porch, looking slightly awkward in the same clothes from the night before. It was autumn and leaves were rattling overhead in the trees. In our driveway, parked beside a beat-up VW microbus and a rusted tractor, neither of which would ever run again, was a blue station wagon that I did not recognize.

Jacob pulled a joint from the band of his knit cap. "Fair exchange?" he said. I invited him in even though I wasn't really that much into weed anymore. "David," I called, "It's the pizza fellow. But I don't think he's delivering pizza."

David came out of the kitchen naked. That was his customary way of greeting unexpected visitors. He craned his neck sideways. "Jacob," he said, "Good to see you again."

Without missing a beat, Jacob asked "Hey, do you have any more of that crystal, man?"

I didn't even know that Jacob knew about the crystal. Then I realized that David must have given him some the previous night while I was getting the pizza money together.

"Sure," David said. "Step into my laboratory." He swung his arm in a windmilling motion toward the kitchen.

Jacob stayed the night at our house. Within two weeks he called it home.

David's parade stayed up until Casper and Magic Hat came over with a pick-up truck to reclaim their pool table. It was only then, while packing the menagerie into a box, that David noticed the unicorn no longer led the parade. When Jacob had rebuilt the parade the night of the party, he hadn't known there was any particular order to the characters. He just wanted to get them back on their feet and in line. As a result, a troll, naked and plumed with purple hair, had ended up on top of the mountain at the front of the parade.

"That's pretty cool," David said, tossing the troll up and down in his hand, before packing him away in the box. "That's the way it should be."

❖

David found Sally at the Wal-Mart.

The three of us—David, Jacob, and I—had spent the morning driving around, crammed into the station wagon with pieces of David's inheritance, hitting up all the flea markets and antique shops in the area. My favourite shop was one that advertised Antiques and Used Items on its sign outside, just because that last part always made me smile; they bought a metal juicer and two boxes of glasses from the 1939 World's Fair. We also managed to unload four dining room chairs at The Antique Alley, which gave us a little breathing room in the car.

No one was willing to take a chance on the old 78-rpm records, too many scratches they said, so we spent an enjoyable half-hour playing Frisbee with these out by the gravel pit. We couldn't catch the damn things because they were too hard and heavy. Instead we sailed them off the edge of the pit as far as we could send them. Louis Armstrong. Duke Ellington. Benny Goodman. They smashed on the rocks below and sent black fragments flying up like frightened crows.

Then, flush with cash from the earlier sales, we pulled into the Wal-Mart parking lot.

David spent the good part of an hour poking through and reading the labels on the cold medications in the drug aisle. When he was finally ready, he gave us each several packages, and we went to separate check-out lanes. Jacob and I got through, but it turned out that David was held up by a cashier waving a little slip of paper. She pointed at the items on the conveyer belt and explained how only so many items containing pseudoephedrine could be purchased at any one time, that it was a Federal regulation. She shook the slip of paper for emphasis when she said "Federal regulation."

David, of any of us, should not have made that mistake. But maybe he just wanted to test the current limit.

"You'll have to put one of your items back," the cashier said.

"But what about my little friend here, who is terribly congested?" David pulled a PEZ container out of his pocket and held it in front of his face. The PEZ had the head of Garfield the cat.

"You see," David said, talking in a squeaky voice, "I think that Garfield might have an allergy to cat hair. Problem is, as you can see, he is a cat." David made a sneezing noise and pulled back on the Garfield head, so that it expelled one of the PEZ candies. "Pretty disgusting, isn't it?"

The cashier was a blonde, but not a California blonde. An Illinois blonde if such a thing exists: well-fed, but not fat, a couple of zits covered over with makeup, the kind of girl that goes to college but ends up marrying her high-school sweetheart.

"Now Sally," David said, glancing at the tag on her uniform, "Garfield has but two options. One, he could shave off all his hair and go around naked. You ever seen a shaved cat? It's not a pretty sight. And one thing's for damn sure, Garfield would never get any pussy that way."

Sally's face creased with an unexpected smile. I also noticed that instead of a cross around her neck, she wore an ankh. I couldn't imagine a girl with an ankh marrying her high-school sweetheart.

David continued. "So that leaves option two. What is option two? Just a common allergy medication sold throughout this good country of ours. Now the items before us are not for my consumption. Hardly. They are for poor little Garfield." David made Garfield sneeze and pop out another PEZ candy.

Sally said, "Sorry, I don't think so. Rules and regulations you know. I could lose my job."

David's face fell. For a moment he looked like a tired old man, a tramp wearing someone's cast-off clothes.

"But I get off work in two hours," she added. She brushed a strand of hair away from her eyes. "If you like, I can stop by after work and bring your little friend his prescription personally. Make a house-call so to speak."

"You are a saint," David said, brightening. "More than a saint, a goddess."

Or maybe just a number.

❖

Only some of the people who came to the house actually tried crystal, although David was an enthusiastic distributor of that mottled candy—when it came to crystal, it was always Halloween as far as David was concerned—and of those who tried crystal, most did not bother taking a second piece.

A singular taste, or an acquired taste?

It certainly wasn't the revelation most people expected from David's fervent peddling. No orgasmic rush like your first taste of heroin, so powerful that you don't care about the wet stain mushrooming across the crotch of your jeans. No visions of God. No angel brigades. Not even the cold power-trip of that whore cocaine.

But for the four of us, crystal was the only drug that mattered. All our old habits had fallen away like shed skins.

Why? That was a question I am sure David asked himself many times. The closest I came to an answer was after a midnight run to MacDonald's.

It was winter, and so we pulled our coats on along with whatever other clothes we could find. Crazy ugly is how we looked. I wore a plastic raincoat on top of a sweatshirt. David had a pink quilted coat that stretched almost to the ground; he looked like a transvestite pimp. Sally wore a sequined dress with feather boa and a down vest over it. Jacob didn't have a coat, just a stained blue blanket that he wrapped around himself Indian-style. Jacob said it was the same blanket he had used as a kid, that he was never going to throw it away.

At MacDonald's, we pooled our change and bought two super-sized fries and a jumbo Coke to split between us. I set the red cartons of fries upright in the middle of our table and we sat huddled around them, campers clustered for warmth before the yellow flames of a tiny bonfire.

Jacob got some packets of ketchup and came back with his blanket fluttering like a cape. He grabbed the sides of the blanket and swirled it from side to the side—too vigorously, perhaps, as ketchup packets loosened from his hands flew in all directions. Two teenagers seated nearby laughed. Jacob brought both ends of the blanket up to obscure the lower half of his face. "The Batman," he said.

I rose and held my hand out. "Peace," I said. "On this night two heroes meet. I am Superman." I gave my raincoat a theatrical shake.

Jacob slammed the remaining ketchup packets down on the table, where they formed a sweaty pile. "Superman was a pansy."

"Government dupe, I'd say," said David. "Mr. Status Quo. Me, you know who I liked?"

Jacob and I shook our heads. Sally helped herself to a French fry; she swirled it around in the intestines of a ketchup packet.

"Bizarro," David said.

"Bizarro? The freak superman? The guy who talked funny? You got to be kidding," Jacob said.

"He wasn't a freak. He built a whole god-damned planet just so he wouldn't have to deal with the people on earth—

people just like you who thought he was a freak."

I suddenly realized that David was angry. I hadn't seen him angry before. Jacob realized it too. He apologized and we returned to eating our fries, making them last as long as we could.

But it was David's anger that I remembered on our drive back to the house. That, and how we all wanted to be superheroes. Even Sally. I don't think she read comics, but she would have loved to take the whole earth in her arms, hold it and love it as if it were a child.

As a kid I had always thought that secretly I might have super powers. I just had to discover what they were. Or maybe I would develop them as I got older.

Becoming an adult meant giving up that dream.

That's where crystal came in. Crystal made me feel like a kid: everything was new and everything was possible. Crystal made me believe that I could be a superhero. Not that I was a superhero. Just that the possibility existed.

As we drove back to the house, Sally crowded against me for warmth and I drew diamonds in the fogged section of my side window. I extended the diamonds facet upon facet until the whole window was a meshwork of intersecting lines. I decided that if I became a superhero, I would wear the emblem of a diamond on my chest.

❖

From within our darkened house, all that winter, we sat on the second floor, facing the one window that wasn't pasted over with fiberglass insulation and duct tape. It was cold and we sat wrapped in sleeping bags and blankets.

When we were hungry, we ate rice. We passed the pot of rice between us, eating with the same spoon. When we couldn't find a spoon, we dug in with our hands. Just David, Sally, Jacob, and I. No reason for anyone else to come anymore. All we had was crystal and rice.

We sat before the window and didn't move unless we had to. When the crystal ran out, David would get up and make more. "How many days was it that time?" None of us knew.

We fell asleep seated before the window, hardly aware that we had dropped off because in our dreams we were still seated before the window. Then we awoke and found that time had shifted, day become night, or night day.

We watched the sun rise. In our backyard was an old ship's anchor—a huge metal ball that could keep an ocean liner from drifting. It looked like a rusty moon fallen to earth. The sun rose above the anchor and we watched the edge of night retreat from its near side.

Icicles hanging from the gutter overhead began to drip... David smiles as he watches a droplet build on an icicle. He is bearded and his hair tumbles in greasy curls upon his shoulders. He wears the same pink bathrobe that he has worn for weeks. He smiles and he doesn't care if anyone sees the gap in his teeth. One day he just found the tooth loose. After a few days of playing at it with his tongue, the tooth fell out into his hand. Now, he keeps the tooth in the pocket of his robe. Sometimes he takes it out and stares at it as if it were some rare pearl, or a seed that was going to sprout a new person.

Already this day is over, the sun has set, and stars have exploded upon the night.

So we sat, day after day, and watched winter melt into spring. Spring into summer.

❖

David leaned into me and rubbed the top of my head meaningfully. "I need a haircut," he said. "I can't see."

We couldn't find any scissors, but there was a bread knife in a kitchen drawer and razors in the bathroom cabinet.

David took a seat upon a wooden chair and I tied my raincoat around his neck.

"Take it all off," David said. "We have to be smooth like ice, like crystal." He bobbed his head back and forth.

"Hold still," I said.

But he wasn't paying attention. "Do you remember Telemetrics?" he asked.

I did. That was where David and I had first met, although there wasn't much of a story there. Far from it. Just two people working in the same room with a bunch of other people. We sat in gray plastic cubicles and made phone calls all day, following whatever scripts we were handed. When David decided to leave, we all had a little party because he had been there longer than any one of us. He cut the cake, licked the blue frosting from his fingers, and wouldn't say where he was on to next. Then, as he shook my hand goodbye, he pressed a small folded sheet of paper into my palm. "I think you will be wanting this soon," he said. Later, when I unfolded the paper back in my cubicle, I saw it was an address. I crumpled the paper into a tiny ball and tossed it into the wastepaper basket. But I remembered the address.

"Back then I thought that the crystal would be enough," David continued. "The right combination of ingredients, enough people all linked by the same perception, and something would happen."

"I think we're almost out." I had seen Jacob licking the pot that morning. I thought of Winnie the Pooh stumbling around with his head stuck in a jar of honey. "You'll need to make more soon."

"But it's more like a bridge. We can't just stay as we are, we have to move forward. We don't just wait for them. We meet on the bridge. We move toward the crystalline just as they move toward us. Less distance to travel, you see."

"You've got to stop moving. I can't cut if you keep moving your head." I finished sawing with the knife and smeared his stubble with green dishwashing soap. I pulled the razor across his scalp.

"No. You don't see. They're out there and they're waiting. I thought that they would come to us, but we have to go to them."

This was the same pitch that David had used when trying to sell customers on crystal. It still didn't make any sense. I wasn't buying anyway.

"Are you going to make any more crystal? Jacob was licking the pot this morning."

"Sure. Sure."

I shook the razor clean.

"Done," I said.

David raised his hands and ran them backwards across the dome of his head. He brought them down dripping with his own blood. Blood covered his head and was mixed with the droplets of soap and hair that splattered the floor.

"I think that Sally used the razor on her legs," I said. That was meant as a joke, but David said, "No, that was me. I did my legs and pubes this morning."

He laughed and stood up, then walked over to the wall and pressed his hands, fingers spread, against the plaster. He leaned forward and rubbed his head between his two palm prints. "Kilroy was here," he said, admiring the bloody stains on the wall.

❖

There were four of us. Then, one day there were five.

Adelle just appeared, a knock on our door at ten in the morning. We weren't expecting anyone, so David dropped his robe. He wasn't wearing anything else. He had read in a book about some guy who used to answer the door naked as a way to discourage strangers. That made good sense to David, so he hunched over to the door, vertebrae protruding from his back like the plates of a stegosaurus.

Adelle was fifteen years old and had had a habit for five years. Still beautiful, though, her skin pale and luminous, almost transparent so that you could see every vein. A denim tank top, hot pants with hearts for pockets, and hair dyed blond but with a greenish tint that made you think that she might be a mermaid.

She blinked a few times and smiled blissfully.

"She'll do," said David.

After that Adelle stayed at the house.

I only mention Adelle because she was there. She didn't

bring any unwanted child with her. She didn't fall in love with anyone. Nor was she a cold-hearted beauty whose presence inspired heart-sickness and friend turning on friend to win her love. This wasn't a movie.

Maybe Sally took an interest in her when she first arrived. A few times, I saw Sally brushing Adelle's long hair and braiding it. Then I saw Sally crying once in the kitchen, quietly holding her sobs in with her head pressed against Adelle's thin chest. Adelle stared vacantly over Sally's left shoulder at something only a cat could see. After that, things settled down.

David wanted her there, and that was enough.

Before she arrived, he had been getting agitated. Said something had to happen soon. That we couldn't last much longer. Something had to happen or we would all starve to death. David held up his right hand, fingers spread. "Five," he said to me. He curled his hand into a fist, then made a quick karate-like punch at my chest, stopping inches away from contact. "With five we might punch through."

Then Adelle arrived.

First there were four, then there were five.

❖

When the end came, it came fast.

"We've changed," Adelle said. She pointed at our reflections in the window.

It was summer, in the evening, one of those late evenings that seem to last forever. We were naked and content. With the warm weather we had opened some of the windows and a breeze worked its way along our backs and arms. We had to be careful because the mosquitoes were out. The trick was to have only a few windows open and no lights on.

I nodded. I looked from Adelle to Jacob. To David. To Sally. I looked at myself in the glass.

We had changed. That was no secret. But, judging from my reflection, I still looked pretty good.

Adelle continued to stare at the window. Her eyes were

wide. She tried to speak again. Her mouth made tiny spasms and all she got out were some croaking noises.

I thought she was having a seizure and I reached out toward her.

She was ice-cold. Shivering uncontrollably. "It's all right," I said and wrapped my arms around her thin body. I pulled her up against me. "Relax," I said. "It'll be all right."

I held her, but there was hardly anything there to hold. Her skin was like Kleenex stretched over a balsa-wood frame. I remembered a bird that I had to kill after a cat mauled it. I had used a rock and it had been almost too easy, the bird so fragile it was a miracle that it had ever lived.

Then I saw what Adelle saw.

A movement in the window.

I sat up so straight my backbone cracked.

We hadn't changed. Our reflections had.

There were five of them, seated in similar fashion to us and staring back from out of the night. I looked back and forth between us and the reflections. Really they were nothing like us. They were more like how we remembered ourselves, how we pictured ourselves in our minds.

They sparkled like frost on a winter morning.

Adelle had twisted her head so as not to lose sight of the reflections. "They're so beautiful," she said in a mumble that only I could hear. Tears were running down her cheeks. She stretched her open palm out toward the window.

"Beautiful," she said.

In the window, a hand reached toward her, the palm also open.

The hand was like something crafted by Michelangelo, a perfect gesture that reflected moonlight and starlight as it reached forward. Each networked cell on the skin was a tiny facet.

I grabbed Adelle's hand. I pulled it away from the window and held it in my lap.

There was no such answering move by my counterpart in the window. My reflection sat peacefully at ease, legs crossed, a barely perceptible smile on his lips. He reminded me of the sculpted likeness of Buddha. The fasting Buddha.

Adelle's reflection slowly lowered her hand of her own volition and laid it in the naked lap of my counterpart. She looked directly at me and smiled too. A flickering smile like that of a serpent.

In her crystalline eyes, Adelle and I were reflected back—two starving humans twisted in an awkward embrace.

But Adelle and I weren't the only ones who saw what was in the window.

I heard a lurching movement from beside me.

"David," Adelle said.

My sight was temporarily blocked. Then, a shattering roar. The window exploded into shards of glass.

I jumped to my feet.

Adelle screamed.

Sally and Jacob ducked their heads. Then lifted them. "What's going on?" they said almost in unison.

David was gone and the window broken.

❖

David did not get far.

I pulled on my clothes and ran downstairs. I circled around the house, tripped once, legs giving out from the unexpected exertion. Then I stood below the window, now lit.

The window was too far up to do any more than reveal silhouettes of those behind it.

Still, there was a half moon, the reflected light of the invisible sun.

Fragments of glass littered the grass, winking up at me like eyes. I tiptoed barefoot among them until I came to David's body. There was no blood. Nothing really. He was in pieces. Shattered into a thousand pieces. It was hard to tell what was David and what was glass from the window.

But I did find a hand, miraculously intact, amongst the glittering crystal wreckage. Broken off at the wrist. Five fingers slightly curled. The gesture that a man might make to protect his face as he jumped through a window: back of the hand against his eyes, fingers projected outwards. The gesture that a man might make as he reached out to grasp something he had longed for all his life. Now rock-hard. Like ice, but warm as the summer night. Even warmer as if the hand still contained some of the heat that once animated it.

I held the hand up between my eyes and the moon, and light came through. In each facet of the hand, a tiny image of the moon shone. The hand clutched moons like so much loose change.

I ran then. I didn't care where I went. I just wanted to get away from that house. Away from Jacob and Sally and Adelle and the shattered body of David lying on our lawn.

❖

Of course, I couldn't stay away.

I went back the next morning.

I approached from the rear, skulking like a dog. I found a tire iron in the trunk of one of the cars and carried it at the ready. I didn't know for what.

David's body was gone. Beneath the window I found just a few slivers of glass, thin flat fragments of windowpane. Somebody had cleaned up.

I slid in through the side door of the house and climbed the stairs, quietly cursing the creaks that resounded with each step I took.

It didn't matter. When I came to the second floor, there was no one there. I cursed out loud and went back downstairs. My stomach twisted in knots as I ran from one end of the kitchen to the other. I slammed the doors of the sink cabinet open and shut. I tore open the cupboards. I ran upstairs again and looked through the empty closets. I ransacked the attic. Then I repeated every motion I had made once again.

There was nothing there.

Jacob, Sally, and Adelle were gone. More importantly, so was the crystal.

An animal clawed at my stomach. My temples pounded.

I caved forward and fell to my knees in the middle of the kitchen floor.

No hope. And no choice really.

The crystal body I found beneath the window. Was that David? Or his reflection? Did it matter?

All that matters is the hand that I rescued from amongst the broken glass.

I take it out and lay it upon the linoleum in front of me. A perfect hand made of crystal. All that remains to mark David's existence in our world.

The hand doesn't break at my initial attempts, and I have to search out where I dropped the tire iron. That does the trick. Pieces of crystal skitter across the floor. They catch the sunlight and burn like flame.

I swallow a piece and wait for the old magic.

Voices Carry

In this room there is no room for words. This room is a
kitchen, newly remodelled after a stove fire scorched the
ceiling last September. The walls are painted eggshell white.
Cupboards open and close on hidden hinges. There is a new
stove, a dishwasher, and a refrigerator with an ice dispenser.
Copper-bottomed pots hang from hooks above the stove.
Clay pots with rosemary, thyme, parsley, and chives sit on
the window ledges.

Four of us are arranged about this room in a silence that
cannot last.

Karen stands by the west window, looking out at the
night. She scratches a mosquito bite on the back of her
neck.

John sits on a counter top near the sink. He kicks
the cupboard door beneath him with the heel of his right
sneaker, keeping time to a song in his head.

Sheryl and I sit at the kitchen table, neither of us looking
directly at the other.

Overhead is the large globe of a light fixture. It is choked
to overflowing with scorched insects and casts a mottled
light on our faces.

John gets down from the counter and walks toward the
kitchen door. This is usually left open, but fifteen minutes
ago Karen slammed it to make a point. She slammed the
door but did not leave. John puts his hand on the doorknob,
then reconsiders. Instead, he takes a can of Coke from the
refrigerator and returns to his seat on the counter. Reflexively,
the heel of his sneaker begins to beat time again against the

cupboard door beneath him.

He takes a drink from his can of soda and sets it down on the counter.

Karen turns upon hearing the metallic clank.

John opens his mouth as if to say something, then closes it.

Karen speaks very softly. "Are you ever quiet?" she asks. A gray haze rises from her lips and coalesces into the muted forms of moths, small moths that flutter up toward the light and do nothing else.

Across from me, Sheryl breathes a sigh of relief. I do not look at her.

"I live my life," John says. "Sometimes that involves a little incidental noise. No more so than anybody else."

For a moment, I think that nothing has happened. But I am wrong. It is mosquitoes again. Not many and practically invisible, but I hear the shrill whine before I see them, and I have to slap several vagrants. Karen, on the other side of the room, is slaphappy one might say, killing dozens of the little beasts as they attempt to settle on her.

"Except for the noise of somebody else's bed with you in it."

I turn to look at Sheryl, to see if she will respond to Karen.

Sheryl is looking at me. "Oh, don't give me that holier than thou look," she says. Something glittering leaves her mouth and stings my forehead. I slap at it and come away with blood and a horsefly. I do not answer her. I have told myself that I will not say anything. I flick the fly carcass to the floor and look away.

"Hello. Hello. I am talking to you. No one else." Sheryl waves a hand in front of my face. More flies. Turning toward her, I see them forming in her mouth, as if atoms of the air joined and tied themselves into intricate knots. "You always have to be the martyr, don't you?" I shake my head at her, haloed by flies. We don't necessarily choose our roles. Sometimes we are forced into them.

"Why don't you leave him alone. Haven't you done

enough damage already?" Karen says. Her words bite, and I take a certain satisfaction in seeing bumps rise on Sheryl's face. In this argument, Karen and I are unexpected allies, united against our spouses. I briefly consider Karen sexually, wondering if by sleeping with her the situation would become more or less complicated, if symmetry could be a solution.

"You seem to assume that this was a one-time thing. That it's over now and everything will go back to the way it was." Sheryl looks from Karen to me. "Maybe it is all over, but not with us. Maybe it's all over with you." Sheryl makes a sweeping gesture with her hand, taking in both Karen and myself, as the room fills with flying ants.

I am thinking about how in any emotional situation our choice of language becomes hopelessly melodramatic, lines stolen from soap operas.

"What did you say?" Sheryl hisses at me.

"Nothing," I say, surprised, and watch a single large bee cross the table between us.

"I heard you. One of those little mocking comments you like to make. How you are so superior, and we are just too stupid to understand."

"I didn't say anything."

"You heard him, didn't you?" She addresses John and Karen. "And I have to live with that all the time."

After this exchange, the air in the kitchen is clouded with insects. They register on the eye and ear like static, distorting vision and sound. To understand each other we have to keep raising our voices. We are all shouting now.

"I don't care about that," says Karen. "What I care about is some bitch fucking my husband. What I care about is what you are going to do about it. Both you and John. Is it over or isn't it?"

"I already said that I don't know and we'll do what we want," says Sheryl.

"And what about me?" I find that I have thrown my chair back, and that I am standing and yelling at Sheryl.

"You can rot in Hell, sweetheart." She smiles at me. "Or

maybe just roll over and say you're tired like you usually do."
Wasps crawl over her lips. I see that her face is misshapen
from swollen bites and I imagine that mine has a similar
appearance.

"You are so unrepentantly cruel. Nothing else means a
thing to you." I claw at the biting insects that billow about
my head.

She is not even bothering to look at me. "And John,
aren't you going to say anything or do I have to do all the
talking around here? Won't you tell your dear sweet wife that
you really have no further use for her."

But Karen and John do not hear her. They are standing
toe to toe, screaming at each other, their bodies a single
black mass of twitching insects that bridges one to the
other. Their hands move in erratic pantomimes through
the air and across the many lives pumping poison into their
blood. Rising above the millions of tiny voices, I hear Karen
screaming, "Shut up. Shut up. Shut up."

We cannot shut up to save our lives.

THE SPARROW MUMBLER

The man from the fair discovered John Ashbury at The King's Arms working on his third pint although it was not yet noon. John had warmed that stool ever since he lost his job at the tannery and, in his new position, had made it his business to convert hard cash into liquid assets. He sat there, drank his beers and whisky, and, to pass the time, watched the bartender go about his chores. When that didn't provide enough entertainment he examined the mural behind the counter, following the activities of men and women through a progression of seasons where they planted, gathered in the harvest, and then celebrated at a long table weighed down with Christmas food and drink while winter storms raged outside. When he grew bored with that he simply traced the wood grain in the puddles of beer by his mug with a fingertip.

"Well met. Well met." The man clapped John on his shoulder so hard that John was almost knocked off his stool. "Sorry, don't know my own strength." The man's forearms were thick around as twin bread loaves. He was a true patriot as evidenced by the colors of his dress, which, John noted, mimicked those of the flag. The man flipped back the skirts of his coat and slid onto the empty stool next to John.

"No, no, you can't sit there." John shook his head hard enough to whip hair across his eyes, grimaced, and hunched in pain at his twisted neck. "My friends..." He looked at the stool under contention and wrung his hands. He wanted the seats near him for his buddies, for his former co-workers. But like as not, when they got off work now, they didn't sit near him but off in the far corner of the room, laughing, gossiping, splashing beer, scraping their chairs, and not throwing a glance in his direction.

"I don't see anyone else here."

"My friends. I expect my friends very soon."

"Perhaps I can buy you a beer. Ah, you already have one. Then perhaps another. What's your poison?" He gestured to the bartender, pointed to John's mug, and, holding up the requisite number of fingers, said, "Two pots please."

Reminded of the proximity of alcohol, John wrapped a hand around his mug and took a long sip that emptied the mug by a quarter of its contents. He belched and wiped away the foam that had gathered upon his upper lip, the shiny crust that extended from elbow to cuff of his sleeve attesting to the frequency of this operation. "That's very kind of you."

"Let me introduce myself, although some might say that no introductions are necessary." The man's voice shifted to a different register as though he quoted another's assessment of his capabilities. "Perhaps you have heard tell of the exploits of John Bull, the man who boxed for the greater glory of the Empire? The man who triumphed over six champions from the continent, both singly and in concert? The man who raised pugilism to an art form, the performance of which has been commanded by kings?" He thumbed his bushy side-whiskers. "No? Then my reputation does not precede me. Still I am at your service."

"John. John Ashbury," John replied softly. Then, remembering some of his former bravado, he raised his voice and added, "My friends call me John. My enemies don't call me nothing, because they all run off."

"Well John, we are all friends here." John Bull gave him another clap on the shoulder that twisted him three-quarters of the way around the stool. "Even more. We share the same name, so how can you be anything but a brother to me?" He took a sip from the beer that had been set in front of him. "And like a brother, I will take care of you."

They talked a little more, toasting the queen and cursing everyone else, as strangers will do when sharing drink. Pretty soon, however, before he had even finished his pint, John Bull got down to business. "John, if you are willing to listen," he said, "I have a proposition for you."

"A proposition?"

"A job, if you are interested."

"Just so long as it doesn't interfere with my drinking." John had been drunk when they fired him from the tannery. But that was all right, he told anyone that would listen, because now work wouldn't interfere with his drinking. Work wouldn't interfere with his drinking. He loved that joke, was impressed that he had thought it up himself, and was now rewarded once again by an appreciative laugh from John Bull.

"Interfere? I don't think so. In fact, it's almost a prerequisite." John Bull clanked his mug against John's, sending it skidding along the counter. "Drink up. It's on me. And there's plenty more where that came from." John Bull then wrapped an arm around John's shoulder, pulled him in close, and whispered in his ear: "Have you ever mumbled a sparrow?"

Those words conjured forth the memory of various raggedy men that John had seen at fairs and even once at a wedding celebration, strangers whom he had jeered and cheered in the company of his friends. "Does it hurt?" John asked.

"Better to mumble a sparrow than to choke a pear." John Bull punched him in the shoulder, gave him a conspiratorial wink, and laughed.

That was not saying much. The ingenuity of Holland robbers was well recognized, and they would sometimes force a metal contraption into the mouth of a victim from whom they intended to extort money. This contraption was called a choke pear and, by turning a key, the choke pear would thrust forth metal points such that it could not be removed from the mouth. The only way for the victim to be rid of it was for him to use a knife to extend his smile beyond the limits dictated by nature or, should he have an unnatural affection for his God-given features, to advertise a reward for the key. Pleased that he had caught on to the joke, John laughed along with John Bull, a few tentative snorts as if clearing his nose from congestion.

When John Bull heard him join in he laughed all the harder, doubling up on his stool and spraying beer in explosive bursts across the counter. In that moment, it seemed that they were just two old friends sharing a joke over a pot of beer, and, although John had not yet agreed to the offer, it was only a matter of time until he did.

❖

After that first meeting at the pub, John Bull took a proprietary interest in John. A cynic would have concluded that John Bull had been paid extra to find a Mumbler for the fair, but John banished such thoughts from his mind. He only noticed that John Bull left money with the bartender for drinks and that, the following morning, he showed up at the pub to make sure that John got to the fair on time. It was John Bull who mounted the stage at the end of the first performance, when the futility of John's efforts to capture the sparrow was obvious to even the youngest spectator, and called the proceedings to a halt.

John Bull enveloped the bird with one hand and cut the cord that bound the bird's leg to John's shirt with a penknife held in the other. Released, the sparrow sat in John Bull's open palm for a few seconds of befuddled astonishment, then flew off past the tents toward the wheat fields and oak wood beyond, shrieking obscenities the whole while.

"He's earned his freedom," John Bull cried to the crowd. He then steered John off the stage and back behind the tent. In a quieter voice, meant only for John's ears, he added: "They'll find a fresh one for you tomorrow."

"Tomorrow?"

"Of course. We're here until Tuesday." John Bull pulled the loop that loosened John's wrist bindings, wrapped these into a coil, and stuffed the coil into the pocket of his trousers.

"I thought I was done."

"What are you talking about? You wanted a job, right? Something where you could make some money?" He pulled a pouch from his pocket and counted out a shilling's worth of small coins. "Here. Take these."

"Thank you."

John Bull's voice softened. "I said you are like a brother to me and you are. So I will give you some advice. Don't go all the way back into town. Go over to the ale tent, tell them that you work here. Mention my name and they will give you drinks for free. That way you can hang onto the money that you earned."

"Really?"

"Just tell them that John Bull is watching out for you, that Mr. Bull is taking care of the tab."

"Thank you." John clanked the coins against each other in his hand.

"All I ask you to remember are two things." John Bull held a finger up that he centered right between John's eyes and about an inch in front of his nose. "The first time is always the hardest. After that it's like pissing on your shoes. So easy you could do it blindfolded." He raised another finger. "Second—listen good here—your wages are double tomorrow. And you can still drink for free."

John nodded.

"Now go on." John Bull shoved him in the direction of the ale tent but then, as he reached his arm's full extension, grabbed a fistful of material from the back of John's coat and pulled him up short. John flailed at the air. "Sorry. One more thing. Clean yourself off before you go over there. You look a mess."

❖

The next morning, John awoke curled against the outside of a tent, the sun up but barely visible through the morning fog and low-hanging gray clouds. Someone had given him a blanket, and he carried in his pickled brain the dim recollection of small angular woman wrapped in a red shawl pressing it upon him as he stumbled from the ale tent. "Take this," she said, "It will keep you warm." But who she was or why she cared had been lost in the dregs of his glass. The blanket had become wadded between his knees during the night and he had dragged the tent canvas, rank with beer, across his back and shoulders.

From elsewhere came the smells of animal dung, urine-soaked straw, and frying bacon. His cheeks hurt when he flexed his jaw from side to side, and his lips, he found when he moistened them with his tongue, were swollen and tasted of his blood. The damned bird had fought harder than he had thought possible, harder than he would have undoubtedly done if placed in similar circumstances. Nevertheless, seeing where he was, still at the fair and only a short wobbly walk to the stage, there was no longer any question of catching a ride back into Birmingham.

It turned out that being paid double meant that he was doing two shows in one day. But still, he thought, fingering the coins in his pocket, money was money.

Even so he might have quit after the day's first show, if his romantic nature, which is the Achilles heal of all confirmed drinkers, had not overcome the little common sense he was born with and still retained after a lifetime of trying to beat it into submission.

The newly discovered object of his affection stood directly in front of the stage. She had brown hair pulled up into a bonnet that had been decorated with pink roses made from bunched cloth. She had freckles, and her eyebrows were broad and almost as thick as those on a man. Her clothing, although well cared for, was ready-made slop work, perhaps something she had sewn herself.

She was not rich.

Nor was she beautiful.

But there was something angelic about her, and he could more easily imagine her at prayer than drinking in a pub. Even so she had lost the calm normally attendant upon the contemplation of God and the saints, and it was the look on her face—the bloodless cheeks, the lower lip gnawed in concern, the hollowness about her eyes as if she could barely hold back her tears—that snared him.

She reminded John of the kind-hearted girl in a story he had overheard as a kid, although he didn't remember if the story was supposed to be true or not. John's mother and some of the other biddies used to gather together on Saturday nights, while their husbands were at the pub, and knit, gossip, and drink their glasses of gin as good old Mrs. Jenkins read from the latest serials. In the story John remembered, a boy passed out from the sun while raking hay in a farmer's field. The boy was rescued by the farmer's daughter and woke on white sheets in a white room to her tears splashing on his face. The girl's father would not let them marry, and so the boy resolved to better his station in life so that he might be worthy of the girl. After many years and many adventures, he returned to the farm as a handsome gentleman in a carriage drawn by two prancing white stallions only to find the girl on her deathbed. She died in his arms and this time it was his tears that fell upon her upturned face but, unlike him, she did not wake up.

What was the girl's name in that story? Juniper? Jennifer? Jenny? Yes.

"Little Jenny," John said aloud, and in doing so released the grip his teeth held on the sparrow's wing.

The sparrow immediately took flight then bounced back and forth at the end of its tether, John's shirt tugged outward from where the string was attached to his buttonhole. To the crowd's enormous merriment, accompanied by their hoots and hollers, John ran around the stage in a vain attempt to gain enough slack in the string so that he could seize it in his mouth and by this means pull the bird back down. The show, such as it was, ended when he collided with the barker and the two of them fell in a tangle upon the plank flooring, the barker cursing John's clumsiness, the sparrow still beating its wings and to all appearances attempting to draw John to his feet so that the fun could begin anew.

By the time John was sufficiently clear to scan the crowd

again, the young lady had disappeared.

❖

There was a break before the evening show, and John Bull explained that John could not wander at will about the fair: "You're the Mumbler now and that's what you got to play." But John could earn extra pay and food if he continued his role inside the tent. Because he was a wild creature, and because the only difference between man and beast is on which side of the cage bars each stands, John Bull insisted upon confining him, shoving him into a cage previously occupied by a tiger as judged by the musky smell and the turds John found moldering in the straw. The door was bolted but, in deference to the capabilities John had inherited from his primate ancestors, not locked, so that he could reach between the bars and slide the bolt to free himself.

John's cage was in a booth near the front of the tent, an area that customers could visit any time of the day, even when there was no performance on the centre stage. The other occupants of the booth were a skeletally thin man and a fat lady, Jack and Mrs. Sprat as they were named on the sign that depicted the two of them in contrasting dimensions even more extravagant than those they naturally possessed.

Mrs. Sprat consumed the food put before her like a greedy fire while, from across the small table, Jack Sprat perched on his chair like a Daddy Long Legs, all jutting knees and elbows, and hungrily licked his thin lips. Periodically, an emaciated hand would dart forth to pluck a crumb or fragment of food fallen from her mouth onto the table. And not always onto the table: food splattered Mrs. Sprat's bosom like the proverbial manna from Heaven—a dollop of potato, a dribble of gravy, a piece of gristle—and this too was fair game. Jack Sprat's hand moved almost faster than the eye could follow, the chief evidence of his actions being the treasures that he held briefly aloft between thumb and forefinger prior to their consumption.

John was luckier than Jack Sprat for, early on, the fat

lady, smiling at him as if he were a favored dog, tossed him a chicken carcass. This was John's first real food in too many hours to count. He sat in the dirty straw, back braced against the rear bars of his cage, and chewed the smaller bones until they were mushy enough to swallow. He gnawed the thicker bones then broke them open to suck out the insides. With each crack of a bone, he would alternate between saying, "Jenny's coming back this evening" and "Jenny's not coming back." In a deeper part of his mind, one to which he refused to give voice, he knew that by these phrases he meant "She loves me" and "She loves me not."

Finally there was only the wishbone left. John had a short debate with himself as to what each half of the wishbone represented, but then realized the portion in his right hand had to represent his own satisfaction, the portion in his left hand that of the Devil.

He was more scared than he wanted to admit and held the wishbone poised with his eyes closed. He remembered his father's favourite saying: "Shite in one hand and a Wish in the other. Squeeze, and see what comes through." He pulled his hands slightly apart and felt the tension in the bone. Then, although he concentrated all his energies, he discovered that he could not will his hands to move any further apart.

He giggled.

"Do it. Do it you stupid arse," he told himself. "Do it you damned fool. It don't mean nothing, so do it."

There was a soft pop, his hands hung in the air, and he realized that he had indeed done it.

Once he worked up the courage to open his eyes, he let out a yelp of glee: his left hand held a jagged stump of bone, his right almost a full arch.

"So the Devil goes hungry today?"

The voice was strangely familiar, a woman's voice but not that of Mrs. Sprat. John saw, his eyes traveling upward, sandals on feet gray with dust, a black skirt, an embroidered blouse fastened with small white buttons, and a knotted red shawl. The woman's face was the colour of tea, her eyes so dark that he could not distinguish pupil from iris. She smiled, but the smile of a woman can mean anything. She was the one who had loaned John the blanket outside the ale tent the previous night.

"Irene," said Jack Sprat in greeting.

"How are you?" asked Mrs. Sprat, forming her words around a bolus of bread.

"Just fine," the fortuneteller said. "I brought something for the Mumbler." Irene standing was only slightly taller than John seated. She smiled at him, exposing teeth of almost the same colour as her skin. "You remind me of my son. You have the same eyes. What's your name?"

"John."

"My son's name was Nicholas." She repeated John's name a few times as if tasting it. "But John...John is a good name also." She thrust a glass between the cage bars. The ends of her fingers were tipped with golden claws. "Here. Medicine if you will."

The lacerations on John's face throbbed. He snatched the glass and took a sip. It was gin, warm gin diluted with water and sweetened with a lump of sugar. He gulped the remainder and felt the warmth spread throughout his body. "Thank you," he said, then returned the glass, his fingers contacting the cold metal of Irene's.

"You're welcome." Irene stood there a moment longer, one tapping finger calling forth a musical note from the empty glass, then turned and left without another word.

As soon as she was out of earshot, Jack Sprat called over to John in an elevated whisper: "I wouldn't have done that."

Mrs. Sprat nodded her assent.

"What?"

"Touched anything, much less drunk anything, that woman offered."

"It was just gin."

"If it was gin you wanted you should have asked," said Jack Sprat. "We would have found you a glass. Did you taste anything strange? Was it bitter? What did it smell like?"

"There was a design on the glass," said Mrs. Sprat. "At

first I thought it was one thing but then I thought it another. It twisted like a snake. With Irene there are no gifts, only exchanges." She tossed Jack half a roll, as if to emphasize her own sainted nature. "You can be sure that she will now demand something from you and, like as not, it will be something that you hate to part with..." Mrs. Sprat seemed about to continue, but she instead turned back to her plate and stuffed a sausage into her mouth.

Irene had returned.

Irene did not look at Jack or Mrs. Sprat. "Show me your hand," she said to John.

He held both hands out, palms up, between the bars of the cage. Irene pushed his right hand away, but took his left hand in her own. She spit into his palm, then wiped away the dirt against her own. "To better see the lines," she said. She began to trace a line with her forefinger. "This is your lifeline. It begins here between your thumb and forefinger, curves toward your wrist, but then stops." She tapped the centre of his palm. "But here," she said, touching a spot further down his palm, "it begins again and then continues unbroken."

"What does that mean?"

"It was the same with Nicholas. I said there was something about you that reminded me of him."

❖

Although the wishbone had promised the return of Little Jenny to the evening show, John like many a Christian who relies more upon superstition than the providence of God, suffered a lapse in faith as the hour approached. A great pit opened in his stomach and began to swallow him from the inside. He hugged his legs and rocked back and forth "She'll be there," he said to himself, even though he was no longer convinced of the truth in his words.

But she was there, standing right at the front of the crowd. He saw her as soon as he came out on stage. It was clear that she was interested in him, not the barker on anyone else, for she never took her eyes off him and the bird.

He never once saw her blink.

One might have thought that John would take satisfaction in a wish come true. But it was like his father always said, his mouth twisted into a grin as if the only joy he had was in taking responsibility for all the failures in the world: "Wishes all turn to shite in the end." John tried to catch the sparrow, but it was a mocking demon that danced jigs about his head, periodically darting in to spear his upturned face with its beak. At one point he thought he had it. He latched onto the sparrow's leg, and, when the sparrow twisted around to free itself, John opened his mouth and lurched forward. But it was all a clever ploy. The sparrow jabbed downward and took a chunk of flesh from John's tongue.

At that, John started blubbering like a baby. The bird was free but he didn't care. There was only the pain and the blood in his mouth. He closed his eyes and stood there like a statue. He didn't want to see anything. He didn't want to see the bird circling his head and calling out its victory song. He didn't want to see Little Jenny. He knew she watched him but, as long as his eyes were closed, he could pretend that she had already left, that she hadn't seen his moment of failure, that she wasn't watching him at that very moment.

As he stood there with his eyes closed, he made a solemn promise to himself that if Little Jenny returned the next day he would, should all the demons of hell stand in his way, mumble that sparrow.

❖

There was just the one show the next evening and John wanted to ask if he still got paid double, but restrained himself out of fear that John Bull would take it as an affront on their friendship. "Did you see the girl?" he asked instead.

"What girl?" John Bull ran a piece of burnt cork over John's face, shadowing his cheekbones and accentuating the lines of his mouth and forehead.

"There was a girl, a young lady, who came to both shows

yesterday. She was standing right in the front. Below the stage."

"Close your eyes." John Bull said. He smudged soot all around the hollows of John's eyes with his thumbs, then, when he reached the eyelids, pressed down so hard that stars popped forth into John's vision.

"Ow."

"You can open them now."

"Here, have a drink." Jack Sprat, who hovered just behind John Bull, offering his own suggestions on how best to make up the Mumbler, held out a bottle of whisky. "A girl, you say. I think I know what you mean." He tapped the side of his nose and grinned, his lips peeling back to reveal rotted teeth.

"She was there at both shows." John took a mouthful of whisky and swished it around his mouth before swallowing. "Thanks. That's enough to give a blind man second sight."

"There are many kinds of girls who come to the shows," said Jack Sprat. "Our own John Bull is quite popular with the ladies. If he wins, they congratulate him. If he loses, they comfort him. But me, I can't detect the slightest difference between their manner of congratulating and their manner of comforting."

"Ladies all." John Bull snagged the whisky bottle, took a slug, and passed it back to Jack Sprat. "Although I've yet to meet a lady so lacking in love for her country that she won't share it with good John Bull."

Jack Sprat chuckled, then leaned in closer to John, speaking in a hoarse whisper. "But there's all kinds of ladies. Some want our John Bull and who's to blame them. But others want something different. Maybe they want a midget. Maybe they want a slippery man who wriggles like an eel. Maybe they want a man they heard about in a nursery tale, so thin they can wrap their arms around him in a double knot. And their legs. If you gather my meaning." He poked John in the ribs with a pointed elbow.

"Bend your head over here," said John Bull.

"That being the case, who's to say there's not a girl that wants a Mumbler."

John Bull took a raw egg from his pocket and crushed it upon John's head. He scrambled the yolk, gelatinous white, and fragments of shell through John's hair. He then scraped together a handful of dirt, twigs, and leaf bits from around his feet and added that to the gluey mess.

"Do you think she'll be back?" John asked, straightening his back. He raised a hand to touch his ruffled hair, which called to mind nothing so much as a bird's nest.

"I wish you could see yourself." John Bull wiped his hands clean on John's jacket. "I don't see how any girl could resist you."

❖

John was royally drunk by the time the evening show began. The sparrow twisted and jerked, jabbing at John's face with its beak and scratching with its claws, but John did not respond. He stood to the left of the barker on the low outdoor stage, beneath a painted backdrop that illustrated some of the freaks inside the tent, and scanned the crowd, his eyes squinted as protection against the sparrow's attack.

He searched the faces of the crowd for the one belonging to Little Jenny but, to his disappointment, could not find her. All he discovered was the diminutive Irene, who had vacated her gaudy fortuneteller's tent with its painted images of cards, spread palms, and all-seeing eyes, and stationed herself near the outskirts of the crowd, her elongated fingers snared within her red shawl.

"Some of you have no doubt been wondering about the young fellow here beside me." The barker was well into his spiel, having already lauded the bare-knuckles championship to be held between Master Mite and General Flea, the skills of Robert the Armless Carpenter, and the three Fat Ladies whose weight could only be measured in units of elephants. "Well don't come too close because he's not used to the company of Man. We found him in the Hebrides, a child of Nature, with no mother or father, a wild thing raised without the benefits of family or civilization. He was naked and lived in a cave, a hole in the rocks by the sea. All he had to eat were grubs and insects. And eggs. And birds. In fact, we still can't convince him to eat anything else. He doesn't speak of word of English, knows less language than your dog. May I introduce to you a creature that, lacking a Christian name, we simply refer to as the Sparrow Mumbler."

Someone called from the crowd: "From the Hebrides, you say? Looks to me like your Mumbler is a local boy."

Another voice, almost a growl and not as loud as the first, but still audible above the stirrings of the crowd: "He does look familiar."

The barker tugged at his neck cloth and raised a calming hand. "I can assure you good Gentlemen that this creature is about as far removed from your humble city as Paris."

"John! It's young John Ashbury. Son of Big John and Sarah. What used to live out past Ripley's Pond."

"John the Sparrow Mumbler?"

"More like John Chirping Merry."

"John Fuddle Cup."

"Creature John. He had one too many pots of the creature and became one."

The barker held up two hands, fingers spread. "Appearances can be deceiving. Perhaps I should explain why I brought the Sparrow Mumbler on stage with me. I mentioned his gustatory predilections earlier and, as you can see, it's feeding time. But a wild beast, for such I can assure you the Sparrow Mumbler is in all aspects but form, pitted against one small bird? The contest seems hardly fair. We have therefore tied the Mumbler's hands behind his back. He has a grip on one wing of the bird with his teeth. With this hold, and without any assistance but the movement of his teeth and lips, he is to get the head of the sparrow into his mouth."

The barker paused for a silent count of three. "Should he accomplish this feat, his reward is obvious: he gets his dinner. But there's more and, for you, this is the important part. Should he accomplish this feat, you will all gain admission to the show inside at half-price. Only three thin pennies."

An appreciative murmur from the crowd.

"So let's have a big cheer for the Sparrow Mumbler."

A few half-hearted yelps.

The barker cupped a hand behind one ear, miming deafness.

More people joined in, some clapping hands and stomping feet.

Then John saw Little Jenny. She had not joined in with the general applause, but had shoved her way forward through the crowd. She was dressed in the same clothes she had worn the previous day, but her face now shone with perspiration and the ties of her bonnet had come loose so her hair flopped about her shoulders. She elbowed her way between two gentlemen and took position in front of the stage. She tightened her lips into a thin line, and locked her green eyes upon the Mumbler and the fretting sparrow.

"Ah, that's what I like to hear," said the barker. "Now who'll take odds on the sparrow?"

❖

John had failed so often in his quest to mumble the sparrow, that he did not immediately recognize success when it came. His first indication was when he bit down and felt resistance. Bones splintered and his teeth clacked together. He then became aware that the bird no longer fluttered and jabbed at his face, an annoyance that had persisted for so long that he had forgotten what a relief it would be to have it gone. Then he sensed the weight that swung like a pendulum from his shirt. Finally, almost by a process of deduction, he realized that there was something in his mouth that crowded against his palate and his numb, swollen tongue.

He had won.

He had mumbled the sparrow.

He spit the head from his mouth and looked to see if Little Jenny had seen his moment of triumph, if she was applauding. But she was no longer in front of the stage. He stared at the position she had occupied, puzzled.

"Everybody's a winner," the barker said. "Three cheers for the Sparrow Mumbler."

The crowd cheered and John nodded his head to them. He blushed, embarrassed at their warm response to his success, then bowed and almost fell over, the stage quaking like water beneath his feet.

Then he saw Little Jenny. She had made her way up the steps to the stage, circled behind the barker, and was running toward him, tears running down her face.

"Jenny," he cried, astounded that she had come to him.

"Oh you poor thing." She bent down and picked up the sodden bird's head. "You dirty evil man. You bastard." She spit in John's face and grabbed at the string from which the dead bird swung. Then, confused by her emotions, maybe repulsed, she loosed the string, and began to beat upon John's chest and face with her fists. "I hope you go to Hell. I hope you go to bloody Hell."

"Come now. That's enough of that." John Bull took the girl by the shoulders and lifted her a foot off the boards, swiveled, and dropped her off the stage. She sprawled in the dust then clambered to her feet. She stood below them, not bothering to brush the dirt from her dress, and trembled in anger.

"You want the bird?" John Bull reached over to John, grabbed hold of the sparrow, and yanked it loose. The string by which the sparrow's leg was tied to John's buttonhole held, so that the bird's leg ripped from its body. John Bull threw the bloody mess at the girl. The last image John had of Little Jenny was of her frantically brushing bird entrails, both real and imagined, from her dress as she stumbled backward into the arms of a laughing gentleman.

"Come on," John Bull said to John. "Your work here is finished. It's time to go."

❖

Not quite time as it turned out. John Bull had unfinished business that was best administered in privacy and, arm resting heavily across John's shoulders, he steered John around behind the tent in the same way he might a dumb beast.

There was still the sensation of feathers in John's mouth, plastered against his tongue and the inside of his cheeks. He coughed and spit a bloody loogie into the matted grass. "Please," he said. He gestured backward with his head, seeking to indicate his wrists that were still bound. "Can you untie me?"

Then his stomach churned and, leaning over one of the tent's supporting ropes, he vomited out the beer and whisky he drank earlier along with a solitary turnip he had eaten for lunch.

John Bull jerked him upright and laughed. "Brother, have you got a padlock on your arse, that you shite through your teeth?"

John tried to wipe his mouth clean against the shoulder of his jacket. "Please untie me."

But instead of complying, John Bull offered a lesson in economics. "How much are you willing to pay?"

"What?"

"Do you think that we're running a charity?"

John frowned. "No. Why do you say that?"

John Bull undid the buttons on his red jacket, slipped the jacket off, folded it, and set it on a water barrel. The right corner of John Bull's mouth twisted upward in a half-smile. "Let's think for a moment, shall we? What would you say is the point, the mission of any good business? How does it differ from a charity?"

John thought for a moment. "Money?" Seeing John Bull nod, he repeated with more conviction, "A business makes money."

"Very good. But not just money, a profit to be more exact." John Bull removed his cufflinks and slipped these into his pants pocket. He then folded his right cuff back and, with exaggerated care, began to roll up the sleeve. "Now I want you to consider a business situation. Let's say that the owner of a business offers a discount to his customers that depends upon the actions of an employee."

"I don't understand. I only asked you to untie my hands."

"I'm sorry. Perhaps I'm not making myself clear. Perhaps I need to rephrase my question." John Bull rolled up his left sleeve, then detecting some imperfection in the result, unrolled it and began again. "When a customer gains half-price admission if, and only if, the Mumbler bites the head off the sparrow, what should the Mumbler do?"

John stared at John Bull, knowing that he had made a mistake, but also knowing that nothing he said would undo it. He closed his eyes and waited for cause and effect to take its logical course.

"The Mumbler does not bite the head off the fucking sparrow."

❖

"Isn't that enough?"

John, curled on the ground into the fetal ball that had protected the more delicate parts of his body, if not his head, back, and ribs, recognized the voice. "Irene."

It was the fortuneteller.

Irene had positioned herself in front of John Bull, between him and his victim. John Bull was a head taller than Irene and easily twice her weight, but he stepped back when she reached out a hand as if to rest it upon his shoulder, a gesture that but for the glittering claws might have seemed friendly. "I need him," she said. "You should know that."

John Bull spit upon the ground, making sure to avoid Irene's shoes. "Then take him. There's not enough left to put up a decent fight anyway." He then stepped to the side as if to leave but, detecting some spot of cleanliness on the otherwise unblemished coat of filth that John now wore, scuffed his boot along the ground to spatter John about the shoulders with dirt. "I'm sorry I can't stay here to continue our conversation, but I have an appointment in the boxing tent."

"Haven't you forgotten something?"

"Yes?" He arched an eyebrow.

"Your knife."

"Oh, that." John Bull hauled John to his feet by his bound wrists. "Stand up. The little Queen's here on a rescue mission. You may wish, come tomorrow, that you'd never been rescued."

"Why?'

"Those she rescues make a habit of disappearing." John Bull sawed through the cords that bound his wrists. "Or maybe they just know enough to stay out of my way. I don't have to tell you what will happen if I see you again?"

John did not bother answering.

"Come with me," Irene said. When John failed to respond, she took him by the elbow and steered him like she might a blind man.

Her trailer was a short walk from the exhibition tents, part of a ragtag village of carts, wagons, tents, and other trailers, where a dog barked at their approach and where, when John stumbled across a fire pit and knocked the cooking spit into the ashes, the pigeons caged nearby broke into hysterics.

"You've got to watch where you're going, love. I think maybe they recognize you." Irene tittered at her joke. "It's this one. Over here. Now brace yourself for just a moment. Mama's got to unlock the door."

The front boards of Irene's trailer were painted red and yellow, and the canvas stretched across the frame, once white, was now a yellowish gray. Inside, the trailer was so packed with her belongings that even Irene, small as she was, must have found it difficult to maneuver. For John, in the dim light, it was almost impossible. Irene tugged and John ducked beneath hanging bunches of dried thyme, rosemary, and roses, his shoulders gathering fragrant powder from where he brushed against them. He kicked something that rattled across the floor, then something soft, a pillow.

"You can lie down here."

He settled himself onto a blanket, its scratchy wool

calling to mind the one he had discovered when he woke after his first night at the fair. John had expected Irene to open the shutters so as to let in some light, but instead she lit two candles posted on either end of a vanity. Once lit, the candle flames were multiplied in tiny mirrors, each no bigger than his finger nail, that were stitched into the embroidered draperies cloaking the interior. Seeing the spots of light leaping forth from the darkness, he thought of stars, of eyes in the night forest, and felt exposed, the lights giving him a sense of having been discovered at a time when he would have preferred to remain hidden.

Then something else caught his attention.

"What's that?" He pointed at the vanity where, behind a jumble of jars and vials, and occupying the space normally reserved for a mirror, stood a box about three feet tall. The box was gray, made either of dried clay or of wood so old that it looked like clay. The top half of the box was rounded and on it was painted a stylized face: two wavering lines for the lips, two spots for the nose, and two large weeping eyes.

"That came from Egypt." His questioning look inspired her to elaborate. "One of the African states. From a time before Christ." She raised her claw-tipped hand and turned it back and forth in the flickering light. "These also came from Egypt. From a mighty Empress who commanded armies of slaves."

"What happened to her?"

"The same thing that happens to all of us. She died. But in Egypt, death is not the same as it is here. Her body was preserved and laid in a secret chamber within a stone temple, where it remained for centuries. But, given time, even the best-kept secrets will be found out. The Egyptians rob the temples of their own dead. They found her body, carved it up, and sold her flesh on the streets so that in consuming it one might gain some of her powers."

"You ate her?"

"That is the story."

"Is it true."

"I traded my father's gold teeth for a dram of dust scraped

from the bones of an ancient queen. That's what they say. I drank it down with urine from a toad, in a cup made from a child's skull. That's also part of the story. Maybe it's true. Maybe not. People believe it. You saw how John Bull would not strike me. He turned tail and ran like a frightened dog."

She reached down a pitcher, filled a glass, and handed it to John. "Drink," she said.

Thinking of what she had just said, and remembering the warnings of Jack and Mrs. Sprat, John held the glass and stared at the trembling liquid inside, but did not raise it to his lips.

"It's water."

He drank because he was afraid to say no and was then relieved to find that, as far as he could tell, Irene had told the truth.

❖

That night Irene tried to educate John on the geography of a land even more foreign than that of Egypt. John said that he was too tired, that all he was good for was sleep, but Irene kissed his drifting eyelids, nibbled at his bruised lips, and he felt his cock stir against his trousers. But even though Irene brought him to full attention, and in spite of his proddings which argued that a moment's pleasure might be more than recompense for years of servitude to the fruit of that pleasure, Irene would not share all her secrets. To be fair, she allowed John to rub himself between her legs and, because she kept her thighs pressed tightly together, he would have been hard pressed to distinguish the true article from the false.

"That's my baby," Irene said. "That's my boy." She raked her long metal fingernails down his spine, raising goose bumps, then looped upward in twin wavering lines that met at the base of his neck, then down and around again, and again, each time repeating the same serpentine patterns on his skin and each time digging deeper. The scratches welled with blood, but John did not care. He hung on to Irene all the harder, pulling her to him, as she pulled him to her, so that it seemed she would swallow him up.

He clenched his eyes shut and imagined that he lay in the arms of Little Jenny. An unexpected and encompassing sadness rose up inside him, deep and cold as the water in the tannery pond. He gulped for breath and even the air seemed like water. But this sensation was soon replaced by anger. How could she have cared more about the stupid bird than about him? He would have given her anything she wanted. The bird was worth nothing, less than nothing now that it was dead. Stupid girl. He drove downwards and shattered the body beneath his again and again.

When he came, Irene released him with her legs so that his semen spilled across her belly. "That's it. That's my baby." She slid sideways to free herself from where he fell across her and, in spite of her small size, handled him with one arm as easily as she might a child.

John lay braced against the wall of the trailer, shivering slightly. There then occurred an event so singular in John's experience that the pleasant veil of drunkenness through which he liked to view the world slipped, granting him a disturbing clarity of vision. He saw Irene, still on her back, extend an arm, her fingers scurrying like a gigantic spider across the sheets, to drop over the edge of the mattress and pull open a drawer built into the underside of the bed. She fumbled inside the drawer, the contents clinking, and came up with a glass vial. She then used the vial to gather up John's semen from where it had pooled on her belly. "Hush now," she said at one point in response to a faint noise that John made in his throat. His lungs had lost all their power so that his words seemed to evaporate even as he tried to speak.

Irene then rose from the bed and went to the vanity, where she corked the vial and sealed it with dribbles of beeswax from a candle, aromatic smoke twisting upward from the guttering flame. She set the vial down in front of the Egyptian casket, where John immediately lost track of it among the other vials and jars, each of which was sealed with an identical gob of wax, and inside of which he could see dribs and drabs of liquid, sometimes shining as though with trapped moonlight, but mostly clotted yellow, brown, and black with fungal contamination.

Standing naked before the altar she had devised, every mirror now a glittering demon's eye, Irene looked strangely fragile. She had felt strong and alive in John's arms, warm as summer fruit, but now that he saw her in the candlelight she seemed withered, her skin like parchment that had shrunk to mark the outlines of her bones. She stood motionless, her muscles strung like wires, the perspiration that beaded her back beginning to trickle down her spine. She gasped, stretched her right hand out toward the painted casket. Then paused. A shiver ran through her body.

"Did you see that?" She whirled around to look at John. "Did you see that?"

"See what?" His voice was barely audible.

"He moved. Did you see him move?"

"Who moved?"

But she did not answer. She turned back to her altar and reached out again to the casket, this time touching the tip of a trembling finger to its surface just above the painted eyes. She exhaled. "Yes. He moves. He is coming back. Oh, he is coming back." She leaned forward, seized the casket in both arms, and dragged it toward the front of the vanity, scattering the vials and jars. She laid the casket on its back in the cleared space. She then wrestled the lid off and reached inside the casket to pull out a stiff bundle of clothing that she clutched to her chest.

"Nicholas," John said.

Irene's son was dressed in a fashionable black suit with silver buttons, which although designed for a child, hung on the boy like the clothing of a scarecrow. Even the top hat had slipped halfway down his face, its progress halted by boney protuberance situated where one might expect to find a nose. His lips and gums had pulled back to expose a toothy grin. The flesh itself seemed molded from wax to assume the expected features but, over time, had become mottled in colour and flowed to take on novel forms that only approximated their model. Although Irene had insisted that she saw Nicholas' casket move, John saw no movement emanate from the misshapen body.

Irene gently rocked the body in her arms, murmuring to it in a singsong voice. Eventually she returned the body to its casket and replaced the lid. She blinked several times while looking at the painted features on the lid, but her voice was composed when she spoke to John. "I will bring him back," she said.

"How was he taken?"

"A fever."

John nodded, although he did not know if he believed her. For all he knew, if the story was true, it had been Nicholas' skull that formed the cup from which Irene drank her witch's potion. "I lost a brother the same way." The brother was two and John ten at the time, and the only person visibly upset was his mother. "He's the lucky one," his father had whispered to John, his smirk betraying satisfaction in a truth well told.

"Nicholas was four. Curly black hair and the eyes of a lamb. You never saw a boy more beautiful."

John tried to count the jars and vials, thinking in this way to gain some idea as to how many men Irene had slept with, gathering their seed in hopes that it could bring back the life of her son. But the vials seemed to multiply before his eyes and he became dizzy, sensing that he was the small part of a plan that extended back to a time before he was born.

He pushed himself into a seated position, legs over the side of the bed, then slid forward to stand up. He kept one hand on the bed to steady himself. "I have to go now," he said, then thinking himself presumptuous, rephrased the question: "Can I go now?" His words were so faint that he barely heard them himself.

"Where?"

"Anywhere. Away. Back to The King's Arms." He felt a strange buoyancy at saying those words, even if he was the only one who heard them. He waited for her anger, but instead she reached over and stroked his shoulder, touching it as lightly as she might a feather. Her hand felt warm and comforting, the only spot of heat in the trailer. Until that moment he hadn't realized how cold he had become. Her touch released something inside him, and he felt a hiccup rise from within his chest. Then another. Before he knew it, he was crying in shallow sobs that emptied his lungs, only to be followed by desperate attempts to replenish the air he had lost. He didn't have the strength to breathe and although he cried no tears came.

"Oh my dear sweet boy." Irene grasped his forearm. "Don't you know that you're already gone?" She squeezed and her fingers passed through his flesh as if it were made of spider's silk, dusty cobwebs that retained the shape of their original design, that appeared solid, but which could be brushed aside without effort.

John stared at the space where his forearm used to be, at his hand now suspended in midair. He watched it drift downward as if it weighed no more than smoke.

"What have you done? What am I?" His mind scrambled. "A ghost?"

"Not even that. Just a breath, a whisper in the night who came to me but who must now depart. You gave everything up for Nicholas. It was almost enough, but not quite. Someday he will come back and perhaps, if it is God's desire, so will you." She waved her hands and John's body parted before her, swirling dust that retained a momentary memory of his form before disappearing in the eddying air. "Good bye."

Epilogue

Time is conciliatory and, although sometimes misinterpreted as irony, this explains why sinners are elevated to sainthood, outlaws mythologized as heroes, and madmen judged geniuses by later generations. Indeed, although Irene swept the corporeal remains of John Ashbury from her trailer that night, years later those ashes fertilized the roses that won the blue ribbon in floral arrangement, as established and voted on by the Ladies Temperance League at the 1865 Birmingham Competition in Home Beautification.

A small consolation for the Sparrow Mumbler, but a consolation nevertheless.

But there was more, for another portion of John still persisted. The weight of that portion would not have swayed a doctor's scales. Neither would its presence have disturbed the perambulations of a goat's hair rubbed with silk and balanced on a drop of oil. Nevertheless, and in spite of turbulence and magnetic forces that periodically rent its fundament, it persisted, haunting a small Birmingham pub. As hauntings go, it was relatively benign—regulars to the King's Arms described a chill settling across their shoulders like the ghostly arm of an overly familiar acquaintance and, even more difficult to explain, sometimes discovered themselves ordering an extra pint and leaving it untouched at the bar—but that wasn't enough to prevent their returning. Beer is beer, and a bargain's a bargain, and a pub that promises both will never want for customers.

Time passed, the gas lights of the pub giving way to incandescent, and these then to fluorescent and neon, but that tenuous portion of the Sparrow Mumbler still clung to the site, and eventually coalesced and established itself within a vessel of suitable contours, in this case a down-and-out rock singer. The singer, on temporary leave from the music industry as he liked to explain it after being fired from his band, noticed nothing out of the ordinary during the moment of possession, and attributed the electrical current ripping along his nerves to the cocaine he shared in the bathroom with two fans. "Good stuff," he said. He rubbed his nose and shifted the silver straw to another line on the hand-held mirror.

After that it was just beer for breakfast for the next six months.

Which is to say, business as usual.

It was not until the singer walked into the conference room of CBS Records in Los Angeles, ostensibly to negotiate for a solo contract, but nursing a hang-over and wishing like hell that he had a drink right then and there, that he discovered that he had screwed up once again. He flopped down in the one available chair. "What the fuck," he said, thinking to get an immediate laugh. A dozen men in suits looked at him but did not crack a smile. A man with thinning hair turned to his neighbor and began to talk about how much his daughter liked the music of Adam Ant, a pointed reference to the fact that the singer sitting there in his long black coat, sweat-stained shirt, and oversize crucifix could in no way be confused with Adam Ant.

The singer frowned.

The pockets of his long suit coat bulged and he reached into a pocket to discover what he was carrying. He encountered the soft feathery form of a dove. There were two doves, one in each pocket, so calm that they had to be either drugged or sleeping. Too late, he remembered the vodka-fueled plan he had concocted the previous night to impress the suits. He was supposed to make a grand entrance. He was supposed to throw the doves out and then, when they took wing, to stride through the white swirling clouds of feathers, a demon from hell, dressed in black, crucifixes and pagan emblems swinging from the chains around his neck. He had pulled his way up through purgatory and was now prepared to pillage heaven. Spectacle. That was what these people understand. They were willing to pay for that.

But he'd fucked all that up.

The dove he had handled shifted in his pocket, cooed softly, a cozy sleepy sound.

For a moment he thought that no one else had heard, but then the man with thinning hair paused in his conversation, squinted, and looked up as if for the first time really aware of his presence. "What's that?" he said.

The singer grinned. Decades later, after a dozen or so albums, a reality television series, and a constant cycle of drinking, rehab, and drinking, he would still remember that moment and how the answer to his problems had come to him in a flash, fully formed, so obvious that it was more like a memory than an idea. He knew what he had to do without even thinking. He cupped the warm bird in his hand and, through the feathers, felt the pulse of its beating heart.

"What's that?" the man asked again.

"Lunch," the singer said, pulling the dove from his pocket.

Cabinet Number 42

The door opens to reveal a tableau of four dusky figures: dolls arranged in a pattern approximating a circle. Then the music starts, a tinny waltz, and small lights come on in recessed alcoves to spotlight the figures. The figures begin to move—automata!—and their movements serve to shrug the mouse-colored dust from their heads and shoulders. There is a gentleman in a tuxedo, his wife in a blue ball gown decorated with ribbons and pearls, and a golden-haired girl wearing the miniature version of her mother's dress. And a chimpanzee dressed in the garish approximation of a servant's finery.

The spectator watching the Lilliputian scene recognizes the faces of the three human automata. He has seen them before in the memorabilia left in other cabinets of the house.

The automata dance to the waltz, arms linked, but it soon becomes clear that they cannot keep up with the music. They shuffle and miss steps. Occasionally, they stop all together as if confused, then start again but demonstrate no improvement in their control. Soon the mother is dragging her daughter along because she no longer makes any effort to move her feet.

Then all four stop. They have given up.

The woman reaches into the front of her dress and pulls out four white sticks. She holds these straws out in a bundle, only the top ends exposed above her fist. The gentleman, the girl, and the ape reach out in turn to each withdraw one straw from her hand. The drawing completed, they hold up their straws for comparison to each other

The ape gets the short straw.

The head of the ape droops in recognition and acceptance. He pulls open his green jacket and unbuttons his red vest to reveal the gears and wires in his chest. The three human automata each reach into his chest cavity and take a gear. They then tilt their heads back and open their mouths—their mouths are much wider than their painted lips—to swallow the gears. There is a metallic rattling as their mouths chomp up and down.

The three human automata now return to the dance. Renewed, invigorated, they spin with feverish abandon, their feet even leaving the floor of the cabinet on occasion. It seems that they will never stop, but stop they do eventually, although apparently out of pride rather than necessity. They stand side by side, facing the spectator, and bow repeatedly until the spectator shuts the door to the cabinet.

Having shut the door, the spectator realizes that he does not know what happened to the ape, only that it was not part of the final waltz. To resolve this mystery, he opens the cabinet again. He will watch the mechanism run its course, but this time he will watch what happens to the ape after its gears are removed, rather than following the movements of the dancers.

The music starts.

The lights come on.

But this time there are only three figures and the ape is not amongst them. The spectator quickly closes the door but he still hears the muffled sound of the waltz continuing behind it.

The Bright Air That Breathes No Pain

"**D**ig," the girl said. Her dress was the brilliant white of sun-smacked snow, her hair pale as straw and she ran a pink comb through it as she talked. She used Pert shampoo, a fact she had revealed to Todd during recess, even inviting him to smell the botanical aroma. Smell but not touch. She pulled away when he pressed too close to her curls.

Was that why he had followed her into the woods?

"I'm tired." Todd's palms were tender and dirty and he could feel the beginnings of a blister. Probably more than one. He thought he might cry but resisted the tightness in his chest, the pressure behind his eyes. Girls always carried tales.

"The only work worth doing is hard work," the girl said with evangelical conviction. She shook her hair and it glittered in the dappled light.

"I'll just rest a moment." Todd leaned against the shovel and wiped the back of his hand across his forehead, imitating a workman he'd seen laying asphalt along the road to school. The sky seemed to pulse with his breathing. He remembered how once while waiting for the school bus, he had found a dusty bumblebee by the road. Dead he had thought, and stored it in his pants pocket for later inspection. But in the middle of Math class, seated at the tiny desk gouged with graffiti, fire washed across his thigh. The bumblebee, only stunned by a car's windshield, had awakened.

"You mustn't give in to weakness," the girl said. "Or else you'll never finish what you started."

Todd stared at his shallow, pitiful excavation. Like the

kind of grave you might dig to bury a pet, he thought. He slammed the point of the shovel blade against the lowest depression, but the ground was as hard as concrete and he came up with nothing. He stomped on the blade's upper rim, hoping that his extra weight might do the trick. Still nothing. He glared. Why had the girl insisted on this fool's project? He tapped the bottom of the hole with the shovel to emphasize the impossibility of the task. A tap? It was barely that but, in response, the ground shuddered and quaked. It rang like a bell. Todd's legs wobbled. His heart lurched into his throat. "What's that?" he said.

"You're almost there," said the girl, voice buzzing.

Todd no longer wanted to be there at all. He yanked at the shovel but it was stuck. He couldn't see the lower half of the blade. He could have sworn that it hadn't penetrated. But now it was buried to the lip. A wave of deathly cold traveled the shovel's length, and the handle turned to ice in his grip. His fingers froze to the metal. Then his hands went numb, his wrists, his forearms.

"Just a little longer," said the girl. She was quite excited. "Don't give in to weakness."

He tried to speak, but couldn't.

"Todd!" Like a Godsend, he heard his name called from the playground. "We're going to play kickball. We're choosing up sides." It was his best friend Jimmy Sager.

That voice broke the spell. He was fully back in his body, sweaty, dirty, and sore. Suddenly he felt very alone and exposed, even in the girl's company, perhaps *because* he was in the girl's company. She egged him on, but he would have none of that. He dropped the shovel and was running before it hit the ground. He didn't even offer an apology, afraid he would be trapped if she caught his eye.

"I'm here!" he cried, batting aside branches that clutched at him with many-fingered, insistent hands. "I'm here!" he cried, plowing through waist-high grass and milkweed and waving his arms in case he might be missed. He ran until he reached the playing field. There, his legs gave out from under him. He fell sprawling at Jimmy's feet.

"Safe at home," said Jimmy, spreading his arms wide in the time-honored umpire's sign.

❖

Todd flicked from one photograph to the next on his laptop. He studied the faces and checked the names listed below. It had been more than twenty years, but the strange memory from his childhood still troubled him. Who was that girl dressed in white? Would he recognize her? He had been scared at the time. Rightfully so, he reminded himself. But he wondered what would have happened if he had continued digging, if he had held on to the shovel just a little longer.

"What are you doing?" Eileen wore a pile jacket over her nightgown to keep out the winter chill, sleeves bunched at the elbow. Her tone expressed annoyance that Todd was playing at his laptop while she washed dishes.

"I'm on Facebook," he said.

"I thought you hated that stuff." Eileen was behind him now, one hand on his shoulder, breath tickling his neck. She peered into the screen. "Who are those people?"

Todd's impulse was to block her view. "I signed up after my brother had his baby. So I could look at the photos they posted."

"Those aren't baby pictures."

Todd hurried to justify himself. "My high-school class had their twenty-year reunion on Thanksgiving weekend. They searched out everybody who had a Facebook page. That's how they found me." His voice trailed off. "I couldn't go because we always have Thanksgiving up here."

"Who are they?" Eileen pointed at photograph number 26 out of 138. A man and a woman toasted the unknown photographer with glasses of red wine. Two other women seemed unaware, one wearing a fringed leather jacket and the other a blue evening dress, heads pressed together in a private conversation.

"I knew them," Todd said, "but not as close friends."

"They're fat." Eileen made the observation without

apparent judgment. "I'm not like that, am I?"

"No." Todd was being more than politic. Stuck in the bedroom mirror was a childhood photo of Eileen with her sister and parents at the beach in Cape Cod. Todd could still see that lithe girl scampering across the sand in the woman Eileen had become. He wondered if she would say the same about him.

"I'm looking for Jimmy Sager," he said. "He was my best friend." In the moment he said this it became true, although for those first 26 photos all he had thought about was the girl who made him dig the hole in the woods: the smell of her hair, the way the dappled light reflected off her bleached white dress.

"What happened to him?"

"Jimmy? He went to Rensselaer. That's the last I heard."

He clicked through reunion photos, pointing out the more familiar names to Eileen. Her clipped questions suggested boredom, but also jealousy, as if she resented him for having a past that excluded her.

The further Todd skimmed through photos of people eating, dancing, and exploring the old school corridors and grounds, the more uncomfortable he became. He couldn't find Jimmy. The name James Sager wasn't even listed in the labels beneath the photos.

It wasn't until almost the end of the show that he saw the collage. Someone had Xeroxed and pasted everyone's yearbook photo onto a standing display. Whoever assembled the collage grouped students based on friendships and cliques that had existed during high school.

"That's me," Todd said, recognizing the flash of braces in his smile and the ludicrous hairstyle he had affected in those days. But there was no Jimmy next to Todd's photo or anywhere else in the collage.

Todd advanced to the next slide in the series. Number 128, another collage with larger photographs, fewer in number, six to be exact. Todd picked out Jimmy's yearbook photo immediately.

"That's Jimmy," he said, smiling up at Eileen. Then he

read the block letters that ran slantwise across the display: *GONE BUT NOT FORGOTTEN*. He read the words again and their meaning sank home.

He blinked back tears.

"Oh darling," Eileen said and hugged him.

❖

Four in the morning and Todd sat alone in a corner booth at Denny's nibbling at a French fry and sipping burnt coffee. He had become a regular since the insomnia set in. His was a good life, he told himself. He was married to a good woman. But somehow that didn't seem enough. "Just go if you're not going to sleep," Eileen had said. She probably only meant out of earshot, but Todd was too agitated to stay home alone. Having other folks near him, even strangers, suggested a certain normalcy to his life.

Todd counted the typical assortment of night owls as his companions at Denny's. There were a half-dozen hospital interns, some ragged kids hunched over a platter of pancakes, and in the most distant window booth, another solitary pilgrim nursing his own cup of coffee. Todd felt a kinship with the single man although physically they were nothing alike. The man was shorter—maybe five-feet-six in his shoes—and muscular. His hair was cut above his ears, but he moved his head as if accustomed to a ponytail. Todd was wondering if he practiced Tai Chi when a movement from outside the window caught his attention.

There was a full moon out, a wolf moon the Eye-On-the-Sky weather forecast had called it, and the parking lot shone blue-white in its brilliance. A woman was walking past. No, walking away with her back toward Todd. There was a familiarity about her. The way her hair bounced on her shoulders, the confidence in her stride. One of Eileen's friends? Someone he knew from City Hall?

She fumbled in her purse, pulled out a ring of glittering keys, and bent toward a silver sedan. Her hair reflected white in the moonlight and she turned, exposing her profile to

Todd. In that instant, he recognized her as the girl who years before had forced him to dig the hole in the woods. How strange.

"Wait!" Todd leaped from his seat, calling aloud even though she could not hear him. His thigh banged the table's edge. He winced. Heads turned.

"Wait!" He limped for the exit. No coat. No gloves. He shoved open the inner door of the vestibule, then the outer one, and stumbled into the parking lot.

The red taillights of the woman's Toyota turned slowly, carefully, out into the empty street. She accelerated away. Todd waved to gain her attention. "I'm here. I'm ready," he said. Too late. Much too late. Realizing he looked the fool, like one of those inflatable snowmen gesticulating with a candy cane to no one in particular, he let his arm fall back to his hip. He watched the lights until they disappeared around a bend in the road and then continued to watch for several more minutes, awaiting their return.

He trudged back to Denny's, rubbing the winter chill from his arms and puzzling over the vision he had been granted. In the vestibule between the inner and outer doors, he almost bumped into the short man. Todd flinched. "Excuse me," he said.

"My fault," the man said. "You wouldn't happen to have a cigarette?"

"Sorry but I don't smoke."

❖

"Did you hear about Amy?" Eileen asked.

"Amy?" Todd lowered his novel. One of the best ways to combat insomnia, Eileen had learned, was to follow a schedule. So now, at her insistence, Todd ate regular meals and, instead of watching television, read every night in bed before turning out the light at exactly ten o'clock.

"Our dental hygienist. I had a teeth cleaning today. Remember?"

Todd nodded although he had no memory of being told

this.

"She'd done something different with her hair. I complimented her and you should have seen her face. It was like I had slapped her. It wasn't her hair. It was a wig. She has a brain tumor."

"Is she going to be okay?"

"The prognosis is not good. The tumor is the size of a plum." Eileen paused. "Why do they always compare tumors to fruit anyway? Plums. Lemons. Grapefruit. What next, watermelons?"

Todd raised his book, scanning the page for where he had left off. But Eileen wasn't finished.

"I sometimes feel like our bed is a little island," she said. "I used to think we were safe here. It was warm and we had each other. We were in it together. Maybe there were sharks circling around the island but they couldn't come ashore and get us. Now I'm not so sure."

"Why's that?"

"First there was your friend. What was his name?"

"Jimmy. Jimmy Sager." Todd felt uncomfortable saying the name aloud, as if he were calling God's or the devil's attention down on them.

"And now Amy," Ellen said. "That's two. But everything comes in threes."

❖

"Excuse me," Todd said, circling an old man who pushed a squeaky cart down the bread aisle at Price Chopper. The old man muttered, but he had been muttering before Todd spoke. Todd grabbed a box of donuts and dropped it into his hand-basket.

"Raw your teeth," the old man said. His smile gapped where front teeth should have glistened. Todd shivered and hurried on. Some of the folks who shopped in the wee hours reminded him of the walking dead.

Eileen had been moody of late, fluctuating between surly indifference and demonstrative affection. It was probably nothing but, in case it was his fault, Todd had decided to surprise her with breakfast in bed. He picked up a carton of orange juice, no pulp the way she liked it, and a dozen Grade-A eggs, shifting each egg in its cardboard cradle to confirm its integrity. He flipped over a package of bacon and opened the cardboard window to reveal the red and white, meat and fat, of a representative slice. Then another package. And another.

"Try North Country Smokehouse. You won't regret it." It was the short man that Todd sometimes saw at Denny's. Todd wasn't sure if the man also recognized him or was naturally gregarious.

"Really?"

"It's made just down the road in Claremont. Trust me, you'll love it." The man had only microwave popcorn in his hand-basket. "I like this one the best," he said, shoving a block of meat at Todd. "Cob-smoked. And it's cured with real maple syrup."

Todd took the package, barely glancing at the representative slice. "Thanks," he said.

"Trust me, you won't regret it."

Checkout was excruciating. There was just the one cashier and he talked overlong with the customer in front of Todd and then initiated a desperate search for a chit of paper that she absolutely had to sign.

"Do you know who that was?" the cashier asked Todd after she left. "Betsy Bolan. She was on *Survivor*. She's a celebrity but she's so regular. Just like you or me."

In the parking lot, a silver Toyota floated along the plate-glass window. Pearly light shimmered off its hood, then penetrated the windshield. A solitary blonde sat behind the wheel.

It wasn't Betsy Bolan.

It was the woman again.

Mistaking Todd's stare for interest, the cashier said, "Season 19. Samoa. She got voted off early but says she's looking for a new show. Maybe *The Amazing Race*."

Todd was already running, groceries abandoned on the

belt, headed for the sliding door. He felt a horrible sense of *déjà vu* even as he did so, a feeling only accentuated when the door slid open and he saw the car swing out of the parking lot. The car rapidly picked up speed; the red lozenges of its taillights diminished down the street.

Gone again.

Damn. It hurt as if she had punched him in the gut. It hurt as if she had abandoned him.

He went back inside for his groceries. I will write her a poem, he promised himself, feeling both rapture and guilt at the unexpected, but romantic impulse.

❖

Todd woke as if an alarm had gone off in his head. He checked the clock on the nightstand. It was three o'clock on the nose and he was wide-awake. He lay beside Eileen for five minutes, listening to classical music playing faintly on the radio. Eileen loved classical music, but its insistent melody set him on edge. He pealed back the bed covers and slid his feet to the floor.

"Where do you go when you leave me?" Eileen's head was buried beneath her pillow, but her words were clear enough.

"Downstairs. To watch TV." Todd couldn't remember the last time he had any interest in the infomercials and repeats that filled the late night hours.

"Is that all?

He couldn't tell Eileen that he prowled the neighborhood in the middle of the night. "Sometimes I read."

"A book?"

"Yes, a book." He reached beneath the bed and felt for the novel that served as his current bedtime reading. What was its title? Tucking the book under his arm, he exited the bedroom. As he descended creak by creaking step down the stairs, he thought he heard Eileen say, "I wish I was enough for you." But it might have been his imagination. He closed the living room door behind him as a precautionary measure and waited in the kitchen for fifteen minutes before quietly opening the porch door and tiptoeing out into darkness.

❖

Remembering the promise he had made to himself at Price Chopper, Todd wrote a poem to his muse on the back of a paper placemat. He described how his muse guarded a secret door and those knights who sought entrance must be pure of heart and conquer various terrors. In the concluding lines he promised that, should she give him another chance, he would win through to victory. He wrote the poem with a purple crayon because that was all Denny's had, and it took four placemats to get it right. Even then he wasn't sure it was really right—he hadn't written any poetry since college—but it wasn't going to get any better.

He folded the placemat and zippered it into the breast pocket of his winter coat. Then, leaving the coat behind to reserve his seat, he crumpled up his rejects and headed for the garbage can by the entrance.

The woman was there. Outside. Approaching. Perhaps all it had taken was the will to commit the idea of her to paper.

The world contracted into a tunnel with the two of them at either end. The woman was a flame flickering behind layers of glass, separated from him by two doors and then one door, and then the inner door opened and a wintery blast blew in and she was inside. Her coat was the colour of mustard and her knee-length dress bright as a field of daffodils. She tried to edge past, frowning as if, perhaps, she recognized him.

Todd stuffed the wad of rejected poems into the trash and straightened. The swinging lid scraped his wrist. He laughed nervously.

"It's me, Todd," he said. "Todd Bailey. Do you remember?"

The woman opened her mouth, then pressed her lips together and said nothing.

Todd extended his hand. "From grade school. Todd

Bailey. Remember me?"

She backed away, eyes widening.

Todd lurched forward. "Todd Bailey. We were in the woods together. Remember? I wasn't strong enough then. I gave into weakness. But I'm strong enough now."

The woman's mouth hung open, wordless. She raised a hand. Todd caught it. Her skin was cold, the muscles tense like bundled twigs. She tried to yank from his grasp.

"I've got a poem for you," he said. "It's not here. It's back at my seat. In my coat." He tried to pull her along.

"Take your hands off me," she said, voice quavering, but gaining in volume. "Take your hands off me or I swear to God I'm going to scream."

Realization dawned on Todd. Her cold hand was still caught in his fist and she was trying to pull it free. She was pulling away from him. Tears, purpled by mascara, trickled down her cheeks.

He was so stupid. He threw her hand away and then, unsure what to do with his own lost fingers, covered his mouth and stared, almost in tears himself.

She pulled the door open. "Don't you follow me. Don't you dare to follow me. I've got a cell phone." She fumbled through the pockets of her coat as she spoke.

But there was no reason for Todd to follow. Her voice was nothing like the girl in his memory.

❖

A rapping at his office door, the scent of a familiar perfume. Todd raised sandpapery eyes from the spreadsheet on his computer screen and refocused. It was Celia, one of the clerks who worked the front desk.

"There's a man out here," she said, "says he wants to talk to you."

Todd looked past Celia and saw, standing at the head of the line for vehicle registrations, the short man from Denny's. What was he doing here? He smiled and raised his forefinger. Just a minute of your time, he seemed to indicate.

"Send him over," Todd said.

Seconds later, having negotiated the maze of desks with the calm assurance of a shark in familiar waters, the short man stood at the entrance to Todd's office.

"Mind if I close the door?" He flashed his teeth. "For privacy."

"Go ahead."

The door latched with a confirmatory click. Todd extended his hand.

"Todd Bailey," he said. "Can I help you?" The man's handshake was firm, but not uncomfortably so.

"Good to see you again," he said. They each took a seat. "How did you like that bacon? Pretty fine stuff, eh?"

"Sure." Eileen had been truly touched when Todd brought her breakfast in bed, but her moodiness had soon returned and Todd hadn't repeated the gesture. "But you're not here to talk about bacon, are you?"

"Got me dead to rights. Just trying to make pleasant conversation." The man's smile faded.

"How did you know I worked here?"

"That's what I do."

"Do?"

"Look, I like you." The man leaned toward Todd. He reached out a hand, but did not make physical contact. "I feel like I've come to know you. But I've got a job to do, all right?"

"What do you do?" Todd's scalp prickled. He was sure he did not want to know the answer.

"I'm a private investigator."

"What's that got to do with me?"

"Look, I tell you I'm sorry. I didn't have to come here, but I felt you deserved some sort of an explanation. By the time they hire me it's already over. It doesn't matter what I find."

Todd puzzled over the words. He felt like a dope. Like a Neanderthal trying to communicate across a million-year gap in evolution. What was the short man trying to say?

Then it hit him.

"Oh my God." He fumbled in his desk drawer for his car keys. "I've got to go home. I've got to explain."

"Do what you have to do. But it's like I said, once they hire me it's already over."

❖

"Eileen!"

On the kitchen island was a manila envelope with his wife's name. No mailing address. No return address. And no stamps. Just the name EILEEN BAILEY written in ballpoint pen. The envelope was ripped open and its contents disgorged.

"Eileen!"

Photographs.

Of Todd.

In some he was framed front and centre, in others consigned to a tiny fraction of the space. But he was there in all of them. All you had to do was to look. There were photographs of his late-night wanderings, ones of him in his winter jacket trudging along dirty sidewalks, or standing in an empty parking lot, or shadowed by skeletal trees. There were photographs from his visit to Price Chopper, including one of him signaling to a ghostly sedan, arms silhouetted against the sky. But most of the photographs were from Denny's. Most showed him alone in his corner booth, cradling his cup of coffee, a look of intense loneliness in his eyes.

Those photographs meant nothing. Todd could have explained them away without half trying.

"Eileen!"

But there were others. And these meant everything.

Todd found them scattered across the floor at some distance from the kitchen island. Scattered, as if they had been hurled in anger. In one, Todd held a woman's hand pressed against his chest. The portion of the woman's face not obscured by hair was tortured with emotion. In another, a close-up, their two faces almost touched and the woman's eyes dribbled mascara. In some photographs Todd reached for the woman, in others she appeared to reach for him. But there was no escaping the radiance in Todd's eyes, the rapture on his face. Or the utter desolation when he watched her go.

"Eileen."

That wasn't the end of it. There were also the poems. Todd found these in the sink. The rejected versions he had written on placemats. The paper had since been smoothed— a spider-web of wrinkles still visible across his idiot scrawl— and then ripped to pieces. Paper flecks littered the sink like material for an abandoned bird's nest.

"..."

❖

Todd batted at a nylon cord hanging limp from a tetherball pole. It twisted into the air, violent and precise in the same instant. He slogged uphill through the snow, past a playing field and a small pond. The pond was iced over and blanketed in white. This was where he used to capture pollywogs for his science class in fourth grade.

Night had fallen while he was driving, but even in the darkness and after all these years, he experienced a sense of security as he navigated the once familiar terrain. Part of Todd, a larger portion than he would have guessed, was still that little boy, and knew its way around the school grounds.

Some things had changed though. The squat school buildings were smaller than he remembered, the woods closer than he expected. A chain-link fence now marked the school's boundary. But boys will be boys and Todd soon found where the wires had been cut and the metal mesh bent aside.

His coat snagged as he wriggled underneath. He leaned forward against the pull. He yanked at the fabric. Nylon gave. He fell onto his knees, hands plunged past his wrists into icy powder.

He struggled to his feet. White insulating material protruded from a V-shaped rip in his coat. Blood beaded from a cut across his hand. He felt no pain, his flesh still numb from the snow.

He rescued the shovel from where he had dropped it. Had he brought it from the car? He couldn't remember. He pushed into the woods. Overhead, behind the lacework of branches, a purple sky seemed to pulse with his breathing.

The girl was there where he had left her, where she had to be. She wore her white dress with its buttons of bone. She ran the pink comb through pale hair that danced like starlight on her shoulders. She did not seem happy or sad that Todd had returned. Merely expectant.

"Dig," she said.

Todd dug.

The snow gave way easily. Beneath that was a layer of frozen bracken, rotted leaves and twigs that came up in icy chunks. Lower still, the earth was as solid as concrete. The shovel rang and glanced off, twisting Todd's wrists. He banged the shovel down again. Again it bounced back.

He looked up at the girl. "I don't know if I can do this."

"The only work worth doing is hard work."

The shovel was heavy. Todd let it have its way, holding it loosely so it did not jar so much when it struck. A chunk of frozen ground flew. Then another. And another. He was sweating even though it was winter.

He stripped off his coat. "I'll just rest a moment."

"You mustn't give in to weakness."

"But I'm so tired."

"Don't you want to finish what you started?"

The little boy in Todd listened for a voice. This time, however, there was no call from the schoolyard, no Jimmy Sager to rescue him.

"How deep do I have to go?"

"You'll know when you get there."

Todd tried again. Piece by tiny piece he excavated the ground.

"Do you love me?" he asked the girl. His wrists, his back, his throat ached. The rip in his hand dripped blood on the snow.

"Of course."

Beneath his feet, the frozen ground began to shake. The air vibrated to the chime of a great bell.

"Now and forever?" Ice crept up the shovel's handle, bound his fingers in an icy grip, advanced painfully, along his forearms, past his elbows.

"Always."

The tears on his cheeks froze. His vision glazed. He raised the shovel one last time and let it fall.

The earth cracked open like a shell.

Light burst forth. White light. Whiter than the girl's white dress, whiter than the white snow, whiter than his white blood streaking the white snow, and whiter than the white frozen dirt, the white trees, the white star-filled sky. Whiter than everything.

White light poured out of the earth. Todd stepped down to greet it.

HEMOGLOBIN

Ibara

The old woman sharpens her knife, its blade longer than her forearm, on a block of gray stone. She is naked except for her skirt. Her dugs swing loose in the cool air, her nipples gray and hard as pebbles. Back and forth, back and forth, she runs the knife across the bowed whetstone, listens to the faint screech of the blade, the song her knife sings in this lonely house. Particles of metal float into the darkness, flickering orange in the firelight, the ruddy stars in her constellation of hate. Your loss will be your gain, she murmurs to the blade, knowing the knife to be her one true friend, her trusted accomplice in crime. She strokes the cutting edge with her little finger. She feels nothing and, for a moment, it is as if nothing has happened. Then a slit parts among the whorls of her finger pad and a drop of blood springs forth, a bruised pearl grown from her own body that, overburdening, falls to the floor to join the other blood that stains the boards, puddling to the palest of pinks in the drizzle that penetrates the thatch.

Ibara's Blood

Ibara's blood is not a true red. It always contains a touch of blue because her hemoglobin is defective, the result of a mutation such that she can never obtain enough oxygen. Her blood is weak as tears. But she refuses to cry even though she is tired. Her muscles ache, twitching at the slightest exertion. But sometimes...sometimes...she throws her gray hair back, exultant, thinking about those times when her blood is made suddenly fresh and she feels like a newborn child brought forth to conquer the world.

Kura

The young woman enticed back to the Ibara's lonely house has not left yet, although she arrived over three hours ago. She drank the herbal tea and a honeyed warmth spread through her body, washing away her nausea and belly pain. She set the china cup down on the pink floorboards, a little unsteadily, and leaned forward on the straw mat, an arm outstretched to brace herself, a blissful smile dimpling her cheeks. But her arm refused support and she crumpled to the floor, still smiling. When she woke, hours later, she was gagged and suspended upside down. The knotted rope, wrapped twice around her ankles and stretched vertically to a ceiling beam, continues at a diagonal across her vision, its far end secured to a stake buried in the sodden turf outside the house. Her flesh, where the rope gouges her ankles, is mottled purple like the interior of a rotted plum. She feels no pain, not even a prickle of diminished circulation in her feet, just a ghostly absence, a dream of strolling around the lily pond in her master's walled garden, the koi trailing her shadow like forlorn lovers in their hope for a fistful of rice.

Kura's Blood

Kura's blood is that of a normal adult: the four polypeptides of her hemoglobin twist into a lover's knot that blushes the prettiest red when it has bound oxygen. Right now her cheeks are flushed past embarrassment. Burst vessels spider across her skin. Blood bubbles from her nose and trickles across her inverted forehead to coagulate in her hair. But the drug still lingers in her system and, in spite of the sting of blood in her eyes, in spite of the clammy fear she feels watching the old witch sharpen the blade below her, Kura cannot stop smiling.

The Unnamed

There are three women in the lonely house on Adachi Moor, but the third member of this trinity is more possibility than actuality. Kura's belly is distended with pregnancy, sweeping past her hanging breasts, so that together mother and unborn daughter twist and swing from the ceiling like a distorted pendulum. The fetus, still in the womb, floats with the serenity of one who never has and contemplates never leaving the oceanic safety of her mother.

Fetal Blood

The blood of the fetus contains a secret, a hemoglobin of its own, one contained only in the womb and to be lost at birth. This fetal hemoglobin draws oxygen to it like a magnet draws iron filings so that, with each desperate breath of the mother, the fetus draws some of that oxygen to itself, sharing her mother's breath, sharing her life.

Stolen Gold

There are others in this lonely house as well, but none may be counted among living. Behind the bedroom door is a carnal pile of tangled corpses, previous visitors to Ibara's apothecary. The bodies of these women, plumped and rank with death, are each bisected by a vertical slit from vagina to sternum. Their bellies, an immensity once born as proudly as any treasure chest, are evacuated, hollowed, delivered of their gold. But the umbilicals have not been severed. Each fetus is still connected to its mother although she has no maternal bounty left to give. Mummified lips purse for teats never tasted. Dead hands clutch for the excavated womb. On the wrist of each fetus is a small slit bordered with dried blood. Brown blood. The colour of hemoglobin after its proteinacious knot has unraveled, after it has given up the ghost.

Ibara's Question

How many ghosts haunt the lonely house? Ibara, dog-like in her attentiveness to the supernatural, raises her head to sniff the air. She smells greasy soot from her bone-fed fire, the friction-heated steel of her blade, and the flowers on the gourd vine entwining her house, their scent like a bee's comb dripping honey within the ribcage of a dead horse. Ibara knows this last scent for fact, a girlhood memory from when she traveled with her family along the northern road from Edo to Kurozuka. Even then she was weak and could barely raise her head from the cushion. But she heard the gentle drone of the bees, and, twisting sideways, saw the piebald carcass rotting in the summer sun, smelled the distillation of life from death. She was fascinated and now, with the benefit of years, the memory carries with it the whiff of a prophecy long since fulfilled.

A Sound Faint as Memory

Ibara cocks her head, one eye squinted, mouth sagging. Does the sound come from behind the bedroom door? A subtle repositioning of tangled limbs? The scrape of bone on bone, of gristle flexed at joint, of withered tendons as mother fumbles for lost child? How many ghosts haunt the lonely house?

Who Demands Attention?

Truly, someone is calling. Not the young woman who twists overhead, her breath like the trills of a trapped bird. Not the fetus, announcing its intended birth with a barrage of blows against the womb. Do the dead call for Ibara? And, if so, does the language of ghosts sound like rain-dampened reeds whispering their secrets? Does it sound like wind shouldering aside the leaves and blossoms of a heavy vine, like wooden shutters ripped from a window frame, like an ax splintering the sodden door? No. The dead are dead. It is only the living that demand attention.

Rescue

The living? Yes. The townspeople have come at last! It does not matter if the townspeople are led by Kura's penniless lover, the one who serenaded her behind the garden wall eight months ago. It does not matter if they are led by Kura's master who raped her the following night and cannot shake the sound of her stifled moans from his mind. Which of these two fathered her unborn child? It does not matter. None of these things matter at this moment, at this time, because the townspeople have come at last. Stirred to action, almost believing a princess is held captive by that old demon-witch Ibara, they have crossed dread Adachi Moor. They arrive in twisted loincloths, in pajamas, in threadbare blankets worn as armor, in prized kimonos handed down for thirteen generations. They arrive waving rakes and cudgels, axes and knives, wooden clogs and sandals, heirloom swords still tied in their sheaths. They arrive with shouts, curses, whispers, and song. They arrive like a storm beating across the shivering grasses of Adachi Moor.

The Taste

They ask Ibara before they kill her, hauling her from her briny house as if a fish fresh-caught from the sea, they ask her before they bury her under a deluge of boulders, crushing her bones, her tender skull, they ask her, "Why did you do it?" The old witch smiles. She knows she will die, but she smiles, glad of a question that distracts, one that allows her to follow the thin golden thread of nostalgia back to a happier time, a sweeter time, the time when she sliced open a mother's stomach to reveal the treasure within. She holds this memory tenderly, carefully, as if it were the child itself, still attached by its umbilical to the dying mother. Just a prick of the knife, the wrist of the mewling fetus nicked. Careful now. Mustn't spill. Then her lips pressed to the blossoming slit, sucking in the sweet nourishment, the strength returning to her limbs, so that she might be young again. Young and beautiful. A courtesan. A princess. It's true, this is what she was once and will be again. She smiles, lids drifting across her ancient eyes, memory as real as yesterday, today, now. She smiles and, lisping across her broken teeth and torn tongue, the burbling of her own wan blood, she says, "Because it tastes like life."

Based on Yoshitoshi's woodblock print, "The Lonely House on Adachi Moor."

III.

AIN'T NO GRAVE GONNA HOLD MY BODY DOWN

Asleep at the Mortuary

"Horror? You want horror?"

I'm talking to my wife. "At my wife," is probably how she would put it. This is a woman who once said that the only reason I got married was so I would have a captive audience. I can't get mad at her for saying that. First, it was meant as a joke and, second, she might be right.

"Well, imagine this, that no one is really dead. I'm not talking about some zombie or a creature from the late show. I mean that what we call death is not really death.

"Let's say you go through what we call life. Your body is gradually wearing out. Oxidants build up. Individual cells die or are destroyed, like when you cut yourself and lose a piece of flesh. Other cells divide and replace the dead cells. But this is a lot of work, and you can't fix everything perfectly. You get scars, small pains that won't go away. Mistakes happen. And if too many happen then you die.

"Or maybe you don't even get to live a long life. Your body gets caught in a major accident, a car crash or something.

"Anyway, you're dead. They take you to the mortuary, where they pump your body full of chemicals and shove you in a box. Family and friends come by. There's a service. And then they stick you in the ground. Of course, some people don't even get buried, they get cremated, rendered down to a pile of greasy ashes with a few chips of bone thrown in for good measure. Different cultures have different burial customs. Like air burials in the east, where they leave your body on a mountain for vultures to feast on. And if you die out in the woods, who knows what kind of scavengers will pick apart your body.

"The point I want to make here is that after death the body is always destroyed. But what would happen if the body were not destroyed? Maybe death really is a time of resting and healing, a rejuvenating stage for the body. Maybe if you waited long enough the body would repair itself. It would just have to be taken care of properly.

"This really isn't as far-fetched as you might think. Scientifically, we know very little about death. Plenty of chemical reactions are going on, but it's hard to separate those being done by the body from bacteria and stuff inside the body. And it's not like I'm saying you would be able to watch a body knit itself back together, like a film running backward. These things take time, maybe years or who knows how long. We don't know because we've never really looked.

"And, if this is true, just think about how we have been treating our dead. That's the horror part. Every nightmare, every movie, about premature burial come true.

"I know there are a few holes in the idea, but don't you think it's at least possible? That they should at least do some studies?"

I try another tack. "You know the short story by Borges--I can't remember the exact title, but it was a series of four imaginary words. Well, the main point of the story is that we define what is real by our beliefs. The natural world is not independent of us, and we mold it and change it according to what we believe. Even history can change. If we think something happened, then it did. There've also been some other books, not fiction. One about monkeys learning without being in contact with each other. The idea of a critical mental mass allowing something to take place. So if enough people believe something then it will come true. Or if fewer people believe, but very strongly.

"So if we are calling the dead, dead, then it is us who have made it so. The potential for life is there. It just depends on what you believe.

"And really, when you get down to it, it does all come down to belief. I am not so stupid as to think that I have all the answers. But I do know my limitations, and these limitations apply to pretty much everybody. I mean that none of us really knows too much. We are in a universe that dwarfs our powers for comprehension. Yesterday's fictions become today's facts, and today's facts become tomorrow's fictions. So what you are left with inevitably becomes simply a system of beliefs."

I'm talking to my wife. I hold her head cradled in my lap and, as I talk, I comb her hair. This is something she has always loved. Occasionally, I brush the flies away from her face with my free hand. I stick to my beliefs.

Going Back for What Got Left Behind

Don't talk to strangers.

That's good advice as far as it goes.

But I had an armful of groceries and there was only one free seat on the evening train. Even so I was tempted to stand because the guy in the neighboring seat looked like a bum. His hair was greasy, his scraggily beard full of crumbs, and a gray film of hopelessness clung to his skin and clothes. But he didn't look dangerous, more like pathetic, so I flopped down next to him, breathing through my mouth so I wouldn't smell his funk.

I didn't plan on talking. I'd just stare out the opposite window and mind my own business. That's the first rule of train travel. Keep your thoughts to yourself and try not to make eye contact.

Fat lot of good it did me.

The bum was jabbering away a mile a minute as soon as I sat down. More like mumbling a mile a minute because the words tumbled out of him like an avalanche of mushy boulders. I hoped it was a monologue. Then I could treat him like ambient noise. Seriously. The suburban version of relaxation music is a crazy bum talking to himself. Make a recording and you got yourself a gold record.

But he paused.

And he waited.

He wanted a response to whatever he had just been saying. Even though I hadn't the foggiest notion of what that was.

So I kept looking out the train over the bent heads

of two Chinese girls. A stuttering sequence of apartment windows whizzed by, then empty sky, then another sequence of windows.

That's when he said it. "Conezero." He pronounced the name as if it were an Italian wine.

Still there must have been some flicker of recognition on my face. A twitch of the lip. A flicker of an eyelid. It couldn't have been anything more, but that was enough. He knew I was listening and, for some people, desperate people who want to make sense out of a senseless world, a captive audience is all the audience they need.

After that there was no stopping him.

❖

The bum's name was Greg Delaney and he had decided to get off the train at Conezero on the spur of the moment. That had been two weeks ago. Maybe three. Or four. He wasn't sure because he had stopped keeping track of the time and had done nothing but ride the rails ever since.

Greg had been on his way home from work. A Thursday evening, he said. His home was still eight stops away and he leaned his head against the window, using his folded jacket as a cushion. He had just drifted off when the train lurched to a stop. He slammed into the seat in front of him. "No!" he cried, throwing up his arms as he relived a car crash from the previous July. Then, coming fully awake and finding himself still whole, he looked around. Passengers were watching him, but he met their eyes and they turned away. Then he looked out the window to see where the train had stopped.

They were alongside an old platform of crumbling brickwork. Trees leaned down from the steep embankment, their foliage overhanging and crawling across the walkway. The sign on the platform read CONE ZERO. CONEZERO, he decided after inspection. There appeared to be two words because the teeth of the E had flaked off or been scratched away.

Although Greg had passed by that way at least twice a

day, five days a week, for the last two years, he couldn't recall having seen that sign before. It wasn't one of the scheduled stops. "Con-ez-e-ro," he said, sounding the name out under his breath. "Co-ne-za-ro." Probably Greek or Italian. The North End's cafes came to mind. Tiny cups of espresso so strong and sweet they made your teeth tingle. Kaleidoscopes of cannoli displayed on Formica counters.

In that instant he knew he would disembark. He was standing before he knew it, then running before he could think twice. He leapt through the open doors, stumbled when he hit the platform, but caught himself before he fell. He needn't have hurried. The doors to the train were still open when he regained his balance.

Down at the far end of the platform were a man and a woman. They glanced back over their shoulders. They looked familiar but, by the time Greg waved, they had already turned away and begun climbing the gray steps leading up the embankment. By the time Greg reached the top of the gray steps himself, they had disappeared.

Whatever hopes Greg had for a good cup of coffee soon evaporated. Conezero was about as nondescript a neighborhood as you could imagine. He walked past a Pizza Hut, a McDonald's, and a Revco drugstore. He pressed his face up against a bar window and saw nothing on tap but Budweiser and Coors. He passed a Christian bookshop, two kids sharing out wedges from a chocolate bar, and a thin black man talking on his cell phone. Details registered here and there, but by the end of two blocks he had already forgotten everything.

At the end of those two blocks, he decided to turn back. He had made a valiant attempt to do something new, to put himself out there again, but nothing had come of it. So he walked back the way he had come, not even crossing the street.

He walked two blocks and then looked for the sign with the rail symbol. He had taken special note of the sign when he had first turned up this way so he would know how to get back to the platform. But it wasn't where he thought it should be. He walked another block. And another. The street followed a gentle downhill slope now. Had he started out walking uphill? He wasn't sure, but continuing downhill was easier than retracing his steps. If worst came to worst, he could always take a cab.

He continued on this way, stopping at each cross street to look north and south, east and west. He didn't recognize any of the street names or shops.

Then suddenly he did.

He saw a church steeple several blocks in the distance that looked like the steeple on the Congregational Church near where he lived. He had seen that steeple for the last two years of his life.

That was the first sight that he recognized but, as he drew closer, everything became increasingly familiar. There was his neighborhood Pizza Hut, distinguished by a ghostly palm-sized A for Anarchy on its brickwork. Some punks had spray-painted this just over a year ago and sandblasting had not removed it. There was the convenience store where he bought bags of corn chips and jars of salsa, along with six-packs of Seven-Up on good days, Heineken on bad days. He hadn't eaten well since the car crash but that little corner store had been a lifesaver.

There was Chestnut Hill, Shattuck, and his own home street of Linden.

Greg felt a sense of pride as he walked along Linden. He had taken a chance in getting off at Conezero, but had successfully navigated his way home, and had done so before night fell and without having to take a taxi. He walked by the apartment buildings and condos on Linden, mentally checking off the occupants of each as he did so.

The Jacobsmeyers.

The Halloways.

The McCourts.

Then his own apartment on the second floor of an eight-unit brick building. Once he would have thought of it as the Delaneys. He would have taken pride in calling it the Delaneys, knowing that it referred to him and his wife Carol.

But that was before the car crash. Now it was just Delaney.

He circled around back to take the rear stairway up from the parking lot. As usual someone had parked in front of his Camry. There were only eight official parking spaces behind the building but seldom that few cars. This car was unfamiliar, a Lincoln belonging to someone's father or grandfather, and he walked over to check it out more closely.

The Lincoln Continental parked in front of his Camry.

The same Camry that had been destroyed in an accident six months ago.

❖

"Have you ever had a nightmare in which your wife died?" Greg must have noticed the gold band on my ring finger. "You fall asleep. You dream and at first it seems just like a normal dream. As normal as dreams ever seem. Then it changes. It becomes more real. And it becomes bad. Maybe a thief has broken into your apartment. You've just gotten home from work and you find the broken lock on your door. You know what's happened and, even though you run into the house waving your briefcase as a weapon, ready to chase the thief away when you find him, you know that you will be too late. You know what you will find when you reach the bedroom."

Greg looked at me but I refused to answer.

"Or maybe it's something as simple as an icicle. It's a Sunday morning, and you and your wife are talking about how brilliant the winter sun is shining off the snow. Then she says that she'll be just a moment and runs downstairs in her slippers to get the Sunday newspaper. You watch her from the window and see her open the rear door. The door sticks a bit and you feel the vibration snake up the two stories from ground level to the roof and you see the icicle shiver on the gutter overhead. It's just out of your reach even if you were to get the window open in time. You see the icicle sever and fall. Two stories up and accelerating at 32 feet per second per second. You know what's going to happen and there's nothing you can do to stop it."

Greg slouched down in his seat, and pulled his dirty suit jacket about his shoulders as if chilled. "Or maybe," he said, his voice a fevered whisper, "Maybe it's a car crash. Maybe it's a car crash and even though your friends say it wasn't your fault, you know that it was. You had been too happy, talking and laughing with your wife as you drove along. It was a cold but sunny day, and the inside of the car was toasty hot. You were as comfortable as two cats basking in a sunbeam.

"Then bam!" Greg clapped his hands together and I jumped back in my seat. "Next moment you're rolling end over end down the street. The miracle is that the car ends up on its wheels. The windows are all broken, your lap full of jagged crumbs of glass, and the sides smashed in but the car is right side up. But that's the only miracle you're going to get. You know that even as you scream out your wife's name."

Greg took a couple of deep breaths, the air catching in his throat as if it were to narrow for the job at hand. His eyes were closed and I thought he might, in spite of himself, fall asleep. Adrenalin can only stave off exhaustion for so long. But no such luck. He started speaking again without opening his eyes. "Nightmares" he said. "Nightmares of your wife dying. When you wake up from one of those, it's as if you were granted a new life yourself. There is no thief in the house. The icicle never fell. There's just you and the woman you love, and a second chance for happiness."

He raised his head, eyes now open. "You have to understand that I had been living and reliving that car crash for six months. The world spinning end over end through a shattered car window. Carol's bruised and puffy face made up with the mortician's cosmetics. The shiny black coffin being lowered into the wet brown earth. The friends bringing over casseroles to store in my freezer even though I refused to eat. The long slow crawl to work each morning. Then the slow crawl back to the same empty apartment at night. Again and again and again. That was my life. That was my world.

"But when I saw my Camry back in its usual parking spot that evening, looking the same as it had before the accident..." Greg bowed his head.

"I thought that maybe the accident was part of a nightmare that had lasted six months. I thought that maybe I had just woken up."

❖

Greg fumbled his key into the lock of the rear door and pounded up the gray stairs to his apartment. He didn't unlock his own apartment door. He stood in front of it. He then raised his hand and, feeling a little foolish, knocked.

"Coming."

The door was unlocked from the inside.

"Baby." Carol stood there. His Carol. She wore one of his old dress shirts, the tails hanging over a pair of blue sweatpants. She leaned forward and gave him a peck on the lips, her hair brushing against his nose and cheek. Nothing special. Just a little kiss like nothing had ever happened. "I was doing some cleaning before you came home." She held a dust-cloth in her left hand and smelled of Lemon Pledge.

Greg didn't budge. He was afraid that any movement on his part would break the spell and the woman standing in the doorway would disappear.

"Baby you look tired. Hard day at work? I'll make you a cup of coffee." Carol turned and walked back into the apartment. She disappeared behind the wall and Greg's heart beat faster. But he could hear her footsteps on the floorboards. He could hear her voice merging with the voices on the radio into buzzing gibberish.

He found her in the kitchen.

"Carol," he said. He held his breath while he waited for her to answer.

"Yes."

"Coffee sounds good."

Greg pulled out a chair, sat by the breakfast table, and watched Carol move about the kitchen. Carol was not a coffee connoisseur. She popped the plastic lid on a can of Folgers crystals and shoveled two heaping spoonfuls into a mug they had bought at a craft fair. She filled a kettle at the sink and set it on the stove. She turned the surface burner knob to HI. The coil beneath the kettle changed from black to red.

While waiting for the water to boil, Carol turned her attention to the dirty dishes in the sink. She sloshed soapy water about the steel basin. She circled the face of each plate with a sponge. She rinsed the dish and set it in the drainer.

Greg watched, hypnotized.

The kettle whistled.

Carol dried her hands on a cotton towel decorated with songbirds. She poured the hot water onto the Folgers crystals and added one heaping spoonful of sugar. The spoon clattered against the interior of the mug.

He was in Heaven when she set the coffee before him.

"This is the best cup of coffee I've ever had."

"You haven't even tasted it."

"I can tell by the smell." He wrapped the warm mug in his hands but did not raise it.

"You're crazy." She blew him a kiss as she walked back to the sink. She sank her hands into the sudsy dishwater. Once again the water sloshed back and forth. She pulled out a handful of silverware, separated out a fork, sponged it off, rinsed it, and placed it in the drainer. Then another fork. And another. Then a spoon.

Greg couldn't stay seated any longer. He leaped to his feet then walked across the linoleum floor as if he were walking on knives. He came up behind Carol and circled his arms around her waist, crossing them so that his hands settled upon her hips. She leaned her head back against his chest, and his nostrils filled with the scent of her shampoo. Orchids. Mango. Coconut. "Mmmm," he said, breathing in the familiar smell.

"Baby," she said, "That feels good." There was a nasal tone to her words, as if she were fighting a cold.

"I missed you."

"I missed you too." She released the silverware and turned around in his arms. One of his hands slid across her lower back, the other across her warm belly. Her hands were still dripping with soapy water and she held them to the side.

"Hold me," he said.

"My hands are still wet." Her head was beneath his chin, her cheek against his chest, and he could feel her jaw move as she spoke. The words came out distorted, muffled.

"Just hold me."

She settled her wet hands upon his back, fingers pressing against his shoulder blades. Water worked its way through his jacket and shirt, spread out and cooled against his skin.

He pulled her closer. "Carol," he said.

"Yes?" she mumbled. She bent her head back to look up into his eyes.

"I love you." He bent down and touched his lips to her forehead. He then kissed each of her eyes in turn, feeling the flutter of eyelashes beneath his lips. He kissed her nose.

"I love you too."

He pressed his mouth against hers before she finished speaking, and his lips vibrated with her words. He closed his eyes and held her tightly, a puff of her breath entering his mouth. Her lips were soft, her mouth open. But the inside of her mouth was not as he expected. Her mouth was dry. Dry and tangled. Rough fibrous strands choked the inside of her mouth, filling the interior like roots in an earthen cave. Then something inside her mouth dislodged itself. It skittered forward and clawed at Greg's tongue with a jointed leg.

That was it.

That was all it took.

Greg was out of there in an instant. He raced the length of the apartment, swung himself down the stairway, and then ran blindly out into the street. He didn't care where he ran, just as long as he put distance between him and that thing in his apartment. He ran like a crazy sprinter with no sense of direction. He ran until his legs gave out from under him and he fell against a brick wall for support.

There was a stitch in his side sharp as a knife wound.

Sweat from his forehead rained upon the brick walkway.

But even though he didn't know where he was going,

his legs did. When he lifted his eyes, he saw the train waiting for him at the far end of the platform. Its doors were open and light poured out onto the crumbled brickwork. He stumbled inside and the doors closed. He felt a momentary elation as he watched the lights of Conezero diminish into the darkness behind him. But even before Conezero was out of sight, as the train carried him back toward the empty life he had lived for the last six months, he started to wonder if he had made a mistake.

❖

Don't talk to strangers.

Good advice when you can follow it.

Greg and I were both fools. Greg was a fool for thinking that he could ever truly leave Conezero. I was twice the fool for listening to him. His story brought back memories I preferred to leave behind. He had lost his wife to a car crash. I had lost mine to cervical cancer. He found his way to Conezero by train, I by bus.

The details varied but our stories were almost the same.

Like him I returned home expecting to find an empty apartment. Instead I saw lights on in my second-story window and a backlit shadow moving behind the curtains. I was suddenly so angry that I screamed. I screamed curses up at the sky. I screamed at one more indecency inflicted on me by a sadistic God.

I pounded up the stairs, fists clenched, and opened the door.

I thought I was ready for anything.

But that didn't include Cindy. Not Cindy with pink cheeks and a smile seven oceans wide. Not Cindy looking as if she had never felt the touch of cancer or undergone two fruitless rounds of chemotherapy.

One moment I was ready to take on whoever had broken into my apartment and pound them into hamburger meat. The next moment I was in Cindy's arms, weeping into her hair and thanking the same God I had just got done cursing.

Let me have that moment. That brief ecstatic moment when I too thought I had just awakened from a nightmare. I found out soon enough that Cindy wasn't quite as she appeared. Only with Cindy it wasn't her mouth. It was her head. The back of her head.

I had crawled into bed with her that first night of our reunion. She wore a T-shirt I had brought back from a marketing convention. I wore gray gym shorts with the Red Sox emblem. We crawled into bed together and I spooned up against her. But soon enough I was running my hands up her legs and thighs, sliding them up underneath her T-shirt. Cindy rolled over and pressed her body against mine. I took her face in my hands and kissed her.

Then I began to run my hands through her hair. I loved its weight and the way it slid through my fingers. She loved the tension against her scalp. But as I worked my fingers through her hair, raking the tips against her skull, suddenly my hand felt no resistance. The back of Cindy's head was soft and my hand sank to its wrist. My hand is caught in her hair, I thought, refusing to believe that anything worse could happen. But her hair shouldn't feel like fibrous roots, and her hair shouldn't coil and twine about my fingers. Then a rustling horde of many-legged things poured across my hand. I never saw them. I only felt them. Hundreds of segmented bodies pressing one upon the other, thousands of legs and feelers exploring the hand that had invaded their home.

I ran then. Like Greg, I ran. I jumped out of bed and bolted for the door.

But there the story changes.

Cindy called me.

She called me and I heard her.

I don't know if Greg's wife tried to call him back. I can't imagine not. But maybe he didn't hear her. Or maybe he didn't care enough to respond.

But I heard Cindy call my name. I heard the same ache and the same fear in her voice that I remembered from when she first got the news of her cancer. I heard the same absolute sense of betrayal.

That was enough to make me stop. My hand was on the doorknob but I didn't turn it. Even though I could barely form words without screaming, I talked to her as if nothing had happened. I told her that I had to go to the bathroom and then I would be right back.

In the bathroom I looked at my hand. Pink welts had already risen on my skin. Tiny punctures trailed across my flesh. My hand itched but I held it under hot water until it stopped itching.

Then I went back to her. I went back and I held her and loved her all through the night.

Just like I did every night after that night.

Just like I will do again tonight.

Number One Fan

In its day the Winter Gardens must have seemed palatial, but now that Victorian monstrosity had all the charm of the novelty condom Paul Slate kicked aside from its entrance. Travel had never agreed with Slate, and he stumbled into the lobby with a pounding headache, a runny nose, and eyes that felt like they were lined with sandpaper. Nevertheless, his spirits rose when he saw a poster advertising an upcoming concert by David Cassidy. Perhaps, Slate thought, he too might find his long-sundered audience waiting for him inside.

But first he had to find the room where he was reading.

Easier said than done.

Room 6, although listed on the CosmiCon program schedule, was *terra incognita* as far as anyone he encountered was concerned. Slate rushed about the maze of hallways and amphitheatres growing increasingly desperate with each passing minute. His heels slipped on the slick marble floors. Sweat soaked through the armpits of his dress shirt. He discovered a pub modeled after a pirate galleon, a meeting room with sunny Spanish frescoes, and, when he stopped at a restroom to plug his dripping nose with toilet paper, two men in a stall designed for one. But it was only after quizzing a janitor so aged that his existence might have predated construction of the Winter Gardens that he found his way to the shadowy lower level and, behind a trembling stack of folded tables, discovered the unmarked door. Beside it was a placard that listed the day's readings. The name PAUL SLAIGHT headed the list.

For an instant, peering into the room of empty chairs, Slate thought his worst fears had been realized. Then, taking another step, he discovered his mistake. There was one fan in attendance. The fan wore a shapeless black cap, an organizer vest, and cargo pants, and was so large that he sprawled across two of the spindly chairs. His shucked coat took up a third chair. His daypack, shingled with so many slogan-bearing buttons that they could serve as armor, dominated a fourth. But no matter how many chairs are occupied, an audience of one is still just an audience of one.

Slate hurriedly revised his estimate of a worst fear. One fan was worse than no fans at all.

Slate snuffled, phlegm rattling down his throat, to call attention to himself.

The fan turned and checked Slate's nametag. His eyes widened, feathery brows disappearing behind low-hanging bangs, and a smile composed of teeth the size and colour of diseased fingernails split his face. "Jeeze, it really is you. I was getting worried." He pulled a red licorice stick from a bulging vest pocket, stuffed it into his mouth, and chewed with the intensity of a rabid dog worrying a dried pig's ear. Slate wondered if a few premature fans might have been consumed as snacks.

"No one else here?" Slate stated the obvious as a question, hoping that a more progressive math might exist on this side of the Atlantic.

The fan twisted his head from side to side, butt cheeks following his nose's lead so the chairs beneath him squealed. "Not that I've seen." He patted his chest. "I was here first. I'm your number one fan."

First, last, and everything in-between. "I wondered if maybe we should call the reading off." Slate snuffled again. He hoped the fan might honour Slate's suggestion out of respect for his health.

The fan's face turned ashen. "Oh no. I'll admit that I had considered leaving. I thought I might have the wrong room. But then you showed up." His smile returned. "You're here. I'm here. You've just got to read."

"You sure? There's some very good programming upstairs this morning."

"There's no place I'd rather be than here with you. Why it must be more than a decade since your last reading."

Slate did not waste time considering the implications of this last remark. He was intent on convincing his fan that any activity, not excluding trepanning and self-immolation, was preferable to a reading by Paul Slate. "I'm afraid I've a bit of a cold. I'm sure my words are barely intelligible." Slate spoke in a gargled whisper to corroborate the point.

"Not much gets past these ears." The fan, displaying a freakish ability better suited to Coney Island, waggled each ear in turn, repositioning them as if for optimal reception.

"There is also the danger of contagion." Slate coughed without covering his mouth.

The fan didn't wince. "I've had my shots."

Slate could not win. He walked to the front of the room and set his valise upon the greasy table, next to a pewter pitcher and an empty water glass. He then settled into a plastic chair the colour of congealed oatmeal, removed a sheaf of typescript from his valise, and squared the pages against the tabletop.

He checked his wristwatch. It was five minutes after the hour.

"Well let's begin, shall we?" Slate had prepared a short introduction on his flight over from New York, rehearsing this so many times that he could not deviate from the script. "It's so good to see you all here." He nodded toward his one fan. "I would like to thank the organizers here at CosmiCon for this opportunity to share some of my work with you." He nodded toward an empty corner of the room. "In honour of the occasion I wrote a new story based on what is perhaps my best-known piece, 'The Dread Disciples of Arcturus.' It's not exactly a sequel. I think the correct term is prequel. I call this one, 'The Beast from Arcturus.'"

The fan twined his thick fingers together as if in prayer and nodded his head in encouragement.

Slate cleared his throat and read:

"Sun worshipers joke about the hole in the ozone layer. They turn their naked faces to the sky and predict deeper darker tans and a blissful era in which beaches stretch all the way from the southern tip of California up to Nome, Alaska. A few, perhaps one in a hundred, mention skin cancer. But then they smile and say something about dying young and leaving a beautiful corpse.

"If they only knew.

"There are fates worse than death and a beautiful corpse is not in the cards they have been dealt."

"With each passing year the ozone layer diminishes and the hole expands. Through it passes a strange luminous ray from demon-haunted Arcturus. An illumination I say, but no such illumination has ever been seen before on our lonely planet. It exists beyond the known spectrum, beyond the ultraviolet in what can only be called the metaviolet. No sunblock measured in units of SPF can protect you from it."

Slate was pleased with how he had managed a topical reference to the ozone layer, but the word *cancer* had dropped from his lips like a deformed lead frog and he considered editing it out in a future draft. But this didn't bother his fan, who continued to nod encouragement, the bangs over his eyes flopping in silent applause. Maybe one fan was better than none after all. All it took was a little attention, each reader of the story telling another, and Slate would be back in the limelight again.

❖

"Grrrrawwwww!"

Not ten minutes into his reading, Slate was interrupted by a snore loud enough to rattle the fluorescent bulbs in their sockets. So loud in fact that Slate did not at first believe it to be of human origin. A fire alarm, he thought, and panicked, wondering if he could retrace his steps back to the safety of the upper world. But a second snore returned him to reality. This time he saw the fan's broad face turned heavenward, his lidded eyes betraying not even a glint of pupil. He heard the glottal intake of breath, like an engine revving in a Buffalo winter, and the gurgled exhalation that set the man's lips to fluttering like an obscene flag.

"Damn," Slate said, departing from the text of his story.

There was only one thing to do.

Read louder.

"Then with the scream of a thousand pterodactyls torn wing from limb, a crevice opened beneath the undersea city of Atlantis." Slate pounded down on each syllable like Captain Kirk issuing a command from the bridge of the U.S.S. Enterprise.

Nothing.

He repeated the line a second time, this time as if Captain Kirk had just witnessed a decloaking Romulan Bird-of-Prey. He was answered by a snore equally sonorous to the sound effect evoked by his story.

There was, Slate decided, no sense in his continuing. He took a deep breath, slipped his papers back into his valise, and tiptoed around the table. He began the long walk down the centre aisle, shoes clicking faintly on the tiles.

"What are you doing?"

Slate froze. He had only looked away for an instant but in that time the fan had completely changed position. He now leaned forward, elbows braced on knees, flabby chin cradled in his hands. The intensity of his gaze was enough to give Slate the shivers.

"Nothing." Slate spied the pewter pitcher on the table. "Just getting a drink of water." The pitcher was dented, its rim crusted green. But there was water inside. Lumpy water that plopped clump by yellowish clump into the glass.

The fan was watching.

Slate tipped the glass back, lips sealed against the rim. No way in Hell was he going to drink that concoction. Even so his lips burned as if etched with acid and, when he inadvertently licked the residue clinging to them, his tongue tingled then went numb.

He did not know if he was intelligible, but he no longer cared. *"Then with the scream of a thousand pterodactyls torn wing from limb, a crevice opened beneath the undersea city of Atlantis. For a moment, that splendid city spanned the maw and it seemed she would yet survive, but then the crevice opened a hair's breadth wider and that ancient city of alchemical splendor tipped forward and disappeared into the abyss. She rode a current of pure lava down to the molten core of our ravenous planet. Yes, Atlantis sank once again and the crystal towers became a crystal tomb for the mer-kings, queens, and princes. But the mer-sorcerors had done their work well and the ozone layer spawned from their ersatz cannons withstood the metaviolet rays of Arcturus for many a millennium to come, only to finally fail when exposed to the deadly aerosols of modern science."*

Slate sneaked a glance up at his fan.

He was smiling again as if nothing had happened.

For the first time, Slate wondered if he might be dealing with a psychopath.

❖

"Grrrrrrrawwwwwwwww!" This time the snore slammed into Slate like a crash-landing spaceship, ground shaking, alarms blaring, and passengers screaming their last arias. Slate flung up an arm. His chair squealed back across the tiles.

Remarkably, the fan had not even changed position. He still faced forward, hands curled about his cheeks as if engrossed in the story.

But his eyes were closed.

And there was that God-awful sound.

Slate was less eager this time to leave the room, having weathered the fan's disapproval once already. He sat frozen at the desk, afraid to stand up, but seeing no point in continuing with his reading.

In spite of a face distorted by sleep into a mask of congenital idiocy, the fan looked familiar. What had he said when Slate first arrived? Something about having waited a decade for this opportunity. Slate had probably seen him before at a convention. The messages on his buttons, the sheer weight of all those circular metal disks, attested to his being a regular at science fiction and horror gatherings.

CTHULU LIVES, read one button. That was certainly true. H. P. Lovecraft was orders of magnitude more popular now than he had ever been in his own lifetime.

HORROR FANS EAT THEIR YOUNG, read another. That was just as decidedly false. If anything, horror fans ate their elders. For every H. P. Lovecraft, for every Stephen King or Ramsey Campbell, there were hundreds of good, even great, writers consigned to the ash-heap of remainders. Slate thought of Joy Miller who had broken into Weird Tales with him, their first published stories separated by only five pages. Joy could extract more laughter and tears from a tale of zombie ducks than anyone else he knew. And then there was Clint Ball. Hadn't his short novel "Animatrix Uber Alles" almost been optioned by Roger Corman? Or what about Blake Goodly? He had practically invented the vampire hermaphrodite genre. You never heard from any of them anymore.

What broke Slate's reverie was a stench of obscene dimensions. The fan's mouth sagged open, a suppurating wound framed with yellowed slabs of bone. In spite of nasal passages sealed by congestion and toilet paper, Slate still had to pinch his nose shut and even that was not enough. My God! The fan's unfettered breath was worse than the maggot-ridden chicken carcasses in the KFC dumpster Slate used to pass on his way to the post office. The breath of a thousand opened tombs is how Slate would have described it in a story.

"Grrrrrrrrzzzzzzzzzzzawwwwwwwwww!"

Slate had to get out of there.

He grabbed his story and valise, and hurried down the aisle, face buried in the crook of his arm.

"What are you doing?" The fan raised his head, eyebrows contorted into a frown. "You haven't finished yet." He dropped one hand to a sagging pocket of his cargo pants. There was something heavy and angular inside. A gun?

"I need to go to the bathroom. My nose." Slate's hand shook as he gestured with the rolled pages of his story. "I need to blow my nose."

"Why didn't you say so?' An ingratiating smile spread across the fan's face. "It would be an honour to lend you my handkerchief." He shifted his hand from pants to vest, freed the Velcro tab on a pocket, and pulled out a multi-colored kerchief with a conjurer's aplomb.

Slate accepted the handkerchief between thumb and forefinger and gave it a surreptitious shake. To his surprise nothing slimy or crusty fell free.

"It's freshly laundered."

Slate turned away for privacy and enveloped his nose. He blew. And blew. It seemed the entire contents of his head had liquefied and now passed through his nostrils. He gave a final wipe and turned around, the handkerchief a sodden mass.

"You can keep it. I've got dozens."

"Thank you." Slate folded the handkerchief as a preliminary to stuffing it into his inner jacket pocket. It was only then that he noticed the pattern. Rocket ships. Silver rocket ships zooming past yellow moons and stars on a blue background. A tidal wave of nostalgia overpowered him, bringing tears to his eyes. "I had the same handkerchief as a kid."

"I know. Why do you think I chose it?"

Slate shivered—he could no longer tell if from fear or sickness—and wondered if he had ever revealed anything so innocuous but intimate in an interview.

"Now, how about the rest of the story?"

Slate retreated behind the safety of the table and shuffled through the pages. He began again at random, choosing a page near the bottom of the pile. He had but one mission now and that was to finish and to then immediately leave the room.

❖

"I lost all hope in that instant. I now knew that no matter how fast I ran I could never escape the loathsome beast with the three-lobed eye and the purple mandibles. Were I to catch a plane and fly to the farthest corners of our planet, or better yet purloin a silver saucer and pilot it across the desolate cosmos to Arcturus, even then I would be apprehended.

"I had made one simple and terrible mistake. I had believed that I could save myself from the monster that circled my tiny windswept cabin, that peered through the windows from the depths of that bleak winter darkness, its face a rictus of pure evil. All I had to do was to keep the door bolted and the windows barred. All I had to do was to smash tin cans and nail them across the rat holes in the walls. All I had to do was to plaster over any crack by which that demonic creature might acquire access to my haven."

"Grrrrawwwwrghh!"

A foul stentorian blast rocked Slate. But this time he didn't lose his place, repeat himself, or even raise his voice. He continued as if nothing had happened.

"I had done all I could to keep the creature outside my home."

"Grrrrawwww-aaaah-aaahrghh!"

"But it had never been outside."

"Grrrrawwww-aaaah-aaaah-hrrrrghh!"

"It had been inside with me the whole time!"

"Grrrrawwww-hrraaaah-hrraaaah-hrrrrrrghh!"

Almost too late, Slate realized that he had reached the penultimate paragraph of his story. His ordeal was almost over, the words "The End" clearly in sight, and he sprinted through the final two paragraphs.

"What I had seen in the window was my own reflection. And the horrors I perceived in that hideous reflection were as nothing compared to those of the creature that cast it. For the metaviolet rays of far Arcturus had worked their demon spell upon my own body. Upon my own deformed face. The monster in the window was none other than me!

"Now there is nothing for me but to abandon my wife and son, to leave behind all that I have ever known and

loved. I must seek out and join the ravenous hordes of sun-worshippers, but not those that bask upon the coastal sands. No, I speak of those that only come out when sweet familiar Sol has sunk below the horizon, the ones who raise their naked faces to the darkened sky and worship the luminous rays of that dread star Arcturus. Already I hear their devilish call and I answer with one of my own."

"Grrrrawwww-aaaah-hrrr-hrrr-hrrrghh!" The fan gave one last snore then catapulted to attention, applauding even before he was fully upright. "Bravo. Bravo. A new high-water mark in your already overflowing oeuvre."

"Thank you." Slate blushed. Then weakness overcame him. His head balanced on his shoulders like a fuzzy balloon, his bones quivered like gelatin, and it was all he could do to keep from crashing face-first to the table. "I really appreciate your support. But I must be going before the next reading starts." He rose unsteadily to his feet.

"I don't think so." The fan dropped his hand again to the oddly contoured pocket of his pants.

"What?" Slate sat down heavily in his chair.

"It's not time for you to go."

"I finished the story. What more do you want?"

"It's only ten-thirty-five." The fan raised his left arm, as if Slate could decipher the shimmering display on his digital watch. "You're supposed to read until eleven."

"That's not possible."

"Check your program if you don't believe me."

It took Slate only seconds to find the slim booklet in his valise. He had circled his reading twice in blue pen, marked it with five stars, and heavily underlined the starting time of ten o'clock on this god-forsaken morning.

Slate scanned down the list of names. The next reading after his was scheduled at eleven, and each of the subsequent readings were scheduled at half-hour intervals. The CosmiCon organizers, perhaps because of Slate's perceived stature in the field, had left him an uninterrupted period of one full hour. "You're right." Slate could not hide the despair in his voice.

"Quite an honour, really."

"I'm sorry but I have nothing else to read." Slate rose again to leave.

"Are you sure about that?"

"Of course I'm sure."

"Then I guess it's up to me." The fan slipped a hand into his sagging pants pocket, fumbled inside, grasped something, and jerked his hand upward. The object snagged on the fabric.

Slate flinched. This is it, he thought. I've offended him and now he's going to shoot me.

Another jerk. The fan's pocket twisted halfway around his leg. Sweat dripped from his forehead. He heaved himself upright and began to work on the pocket with both hands. "Hold on. I've almost got it."

Slate stammered out an apology, incomprehensible even to himself.

The fan wrenched his hand free of his pocket, pulling out not a gun but the garish painting of a decayed skull. The image was familiar but it took Slate a moment to place it.

"I brought this along thinking you might sign it."

The Pan Book of Horror Stories. It was the cover to a volume that had featured one of Slate's own tales.

"But maybe you could read from it?" The fan focused a smile upon Slate, but just as quickly inverted it. "On second thought, maybe not. 'They Crawl, They Fly, They Feed' is a bit too similar to 'The Beast from Arcturus.' Why, if you hadn't written both stories, you might be accused of plagiarism."

"Really, I..." Slate marshaled a defense for his literary integrity.

"What do they call it now when you steal someone else's idea. Not a parody. An homage. Well this was an homage to yourself." The fan laughed at his joke then crooked a finger in Slate's direction. "Come over and help me. There are plenty of other possibilities in here." The fan bent over the neighboring chair, his sagging waistband exposing a butt crack deep and long as the Valles Marineris, and undid the flap on his daypack.

❖

In the end it was simple curiosity, and perhaps a smattering of ego, that compelled Slate to join the fan in his bibliographic excavation. Bibliographic, for the daypack was crammed to its straining seams with books, magazines, pamphlets, and papers. Slate's complete works and then some. The fan unearthed mint copies of *Moonrise Comes the Haunter* and *A Hellhound at the Door*, Slate's two most recent novels although both were now a decade out of print. Then came several Ace-doubles including the botched printing of *Return of the Severed Hand*, the cover art reversed so that it illustrating the killer's plebian right hand rather than his demonic left. Each memento from Slate's past was briefly appraised then set aside with a dismissive shake of the head that suggested something more alluring was buried deeper, in a stratum representing an earlier point in Slate's career.

Slate's heart panged at each rejection. His books were the children he had never had, the victims of untimely deaths at the hands of publishers and a diminished audience, and now it was as if each tiny corpse was found deficient by the only re-animator in town. So many corpses, in so many shapes and forms, piled one atop the other. Slate was reminded of how during the plague in London, because of the demand for consecrated ground, priests interred multiple bodies within the same grave, a historical tidbit Slate had used in his zombie story, "Six Feet Deep and Rising." Now that was a story Slate wouldn't mind reading aloud. But the fan also cast that issue of Weird Tales aside when he reached it, digging deeper into strata that held no books or magazines, but mimeographed fanzines.

Both chairs beside the daypack now towered with Slate's lifework, more than it seemed possible for the deflated pack to contain, and still the fan dug deeper. Now only loose papers remained, early drafts of stories, some of which had never been published. Then the supply of these too appeared exhausted. The fan's fingernails scrabbled against the canvas. He beat about inside, rattling the buttons pinned to the fabric, and turned the pack upside down. A single sheet of blue-lined paper fluttered to the chair.

The fan smoothed the page and breathed a sigh of relief. He shook the page before Slate's eyes. "This is it! This is the one!"

It was a grade-school composition, Slate's own work as evidenced by the name in the upper left-hand corner.

"This is the story that brought you to my attention. Here's where it all began. As soon as I read this, I knew you were destined for greatness."

Slate was sure this piece of juvenilia had never been made public. Once again sepulchral fingers wrapped themselves around his heart. Was the fan a forgotten classmate from PS 43 in Buffalo, New York, one who had fixated on Slate and trailed him across the years, pawing through, collecting, and collating his trash?

"A great beginning. A little crude perhaps but you were still young and had yet to learn the rudiments, let alone the intricacies, of spelling and grammar. Nevertheless, I consider this in many ways the peak of your career." The fan thrust the page into Slate's trembling hands. "Go on. Read it."

❖

The title of Slate's grade-school story was "The Jost." This had been circled in red ink and the teacher, familiar with Slate's difficulty in distinguishing between *j* and *g*, had written, also in red ink: "Ghost?" Slate still experienced a certain discomfort with these two letters and avoided the choice whenever possible, describing "cemeteries of emaciated pines and willows" rather than "graveyards of gaunt junipers." But rather than restricting him, Slate believed this had pushed him to become a better writer.

The story covered not quite half the page. It was written in pencil and made no concession to consistency in its use of print and cursive lettering. Grayish smudges and eroded paper pointed to Slate's early penchant for editing and his limited facility with the eraser. Slate began to read aloud slowly, haltingly, correcting spelling errors as he went along. *"Once upon a time there was a dog that did not know that it was dead."*

"Stop right there! I just had the most brilliant idea." The fan clapped his hands. "Although the first sentence is really the highlight of the story, I would like to hear it all the way through. But here's my idea. Why not give your reading in a more comfortable setting? Did you notice the pub upstairs on the main level?"

Slate nodded. "The one with the nautical theme?"

"Precisely. Now how about you and I get ourselves a table up there? You reading, I devouring your every word. The whiskies will be my treat."

Slate was about to protest but then realized this was his big chance. No matter what kind of psycho his fan was, Slate would be safe once he was back among the other convention attendees. "Great idea." He didn't even have to fake his smile.

No sooner said than done. The fan, his bulging daypack hanging from one shoulder and his long black coat slung over the other, led Slate up a circular stairway located only a dozen paces from room 6 but hidden behind an angle best described as non-Euclidian. The delicate botanical metalwork of this Victorian relic shuddered beneath Slate's steps but, to his surprise, did not come crashing down. He made it to the next level without breaking a sweat.

Slate had been under-whelmed by the "Pieces of Eight" tavern when he passed by it earlier in his search for room 6. The pub, with a splintered ship's wheel above its arched entrance, plaster beams painted to emulate wood, and plastic swords nailed to its walls, had seemed a crack-head's version of a Disneyland attraction. But now it positively shone. Honeyed light radiated from the mica windows of hanging lanterns, glanced off the silvery scales of mounted fish, and, refracted through strands of faceted gems, broke into multi-colored lozenges to pattern the walls and customers.

The customers!

Less than an hour before, the pub had been dirty, dingy,

and, above all, empty. Not even a lonely bartender in sight. But now it was packed, chairs jammed seat to seat, the gaily-dressed occupants clanking glasses and laughing madly.

"Grab us two seats. I'll get the whiskies." The fan disappeared into the scrum by the bar.

Slate scanned the room and wondered if there was even one free seat available. All around were pale faces contorted in laughter, grinning toothily, and singing off-key filkish sailor shanties. But in spite of their evident joie-de-vie, Slate found something disquieting about the clientele. He might have puzzled out what was bothering him but was interrupted in his thoughts by someone calling his name. "Paul! Over here." A woman waved her freckled arm just a few tables away. Her puckish smile and the sparkling necklaces woven incongruously through her curly red hair should have been an immediate giveaway as to her identity. But it was not until she winked that Slate recognized her.

"Joy!" Joy Miller. Why Slate had just been thinking about how much he enjoyed her zombie duck stories. And wasn't that Henry LaFollette who used to publish the fanzine *Tooth and Claw* sitting there at her table? Henry had once devoted an entire issue to the subliminal werewolf motif in Slate's writings. And the mole-like man with the pince-nez glasses...why that was Jules Nottingham, the former editor of *Dread Adore*. Jules had once, without asking permission, intruded a necrophiliac nun into Slate's last-man-on-earth story "Adam versus the Cockroach King," but subsequent selection of the story for a Year's Best anthology had proven his editorial intuitions correct.

This was a stroke of luck. Slate waved back.

"Met some friends already?" The fan materialized at Slate's elbow and pressed a tumbler of whisky into his palm. He slid a grayish tongue across his yellow teeth. "I've got a little secret to tell you. Their presence isn't entirely coincidental." He turned from Slate and addressed the room, voice booming. "Friends!"

Every head turned. Joy, Henry, and Jules sat up straighter at their small circular table, faces glowing orange in the lantern light.

"I say friends. I could say fans. Or writers. Or editors, reviewers, publishers. But regardless of what you might be called, there is one thing we all are. Family. Each and every one of you is a member of my family." The fan spread his arms wide as if to hug the entire room to his bountiful chest, then laid an arm across Slate's shoulders, pulling him close as if they were bonded by a lifetime of shared experience. It was their first physical contact, and Slate was shocked at the chill that penetrated his jacket and shirt. "My guest needs no introduction. One of my favorites. One of our favorites. The one, the only, our own John Slate."

The long overdue applause washed over Slate like a benediction, like acceptance, and, yes, like love. He turned from one smiling face to the next, saw the glasses raised, the toasts drunk in his honour. Slate now recognized a few of the others facing him as well: Clint Ball, still affecting a turban; L. Murray Watson in his red velvet suit; Pinky Gore, self-titled Queen of Horror.

"Not only is John with us, but he has a story to share."

More applause.

Slate knew these people. Not just a couple of members from his audience, but all of them. Of that he was now sure. He had only to study a face for a few seconds and old memories burbled up, good memories from when they were all the kings and queens of the pulps. From when they were all each other's biggest fan.

But there was something wrong.

It wasn't so much that he knew these people. Rather it was that he had once known them. If pressed, he could not have sworn that any were still among the living. If pressed, he would have to admit to reading L. Murray's obituary in Locus some years back and wondering why no one had invited him to the funeral.

"Not just any story," his number one fan continued, "but a story from John's formative years, the one the set him on the path to become what he is today." He fluttered the wrinkled grade-school composition for emphasis.

Slate knew what happened next. He could write this scene himself, and had done so at least a dozen times, maybe a hundred times over his career. Nothing subtle, no fading into ghostly translucence, but an ending that went straight for the jugular. Perhaps his number one fan, Death himself as Slate now suspected, wielding an oversize scythe with the felicity of a razor would shave the skin from his body then decapitate him. Or perhaps Joy would give him a congratulatory kiss and, her cold lips mashed against his, he would taste what he took to be tears but then discover were putrefying eyes and flesh streaming down her knobby white cheekbones. Or perhaps the audience would rise for a standing ovation, but then shamble forward, skin sagging from bloody out-stretched limbs, to fall upon and disembowel him with their ragged nails and spastic teeth, his gurgled screams echoing through the tavern long after an acolyte's bite severed his flopping tongue.

Still...they were the best audience he had seen in a long time.

The best he was likely to see in an even longer time.

"Hand me that story." Slate cleared his throat and began to read.

Love Signs

Experiment #1: Daddy's Right Hand

First one, and then the second, angled to form a V. For peace? Daddy doesn't flinch. The third, stripped of its bark and worried into place, protrudes pale and brittle: a ring finger without a ring. The fourth, punctured through the scabrous coat, draws a trickle of blood. Four sticks in a row like warped flagpoles. And now, number five, stationed across from the others, wedged into a crack and glued into place with pine gum.

The thumb.

The thumb sets us apart from animals.

The thumb makes the hand.

But this thumb won't close. The five digits are as immobile as nails in a plank.

A grunt. Not pain. More like surprise. Daddy raises his right hand and looks at the crooked sticks. He waves the stump from side to side. I think he smiles. Maybe he recognizes what he misses. He smiles and smashes his new hand into the ground.

The sticks break loose.

Daddy screams. Yanks against his chain.

One stick, jammed deep, so deep it must have hit a nerve. Or what passes for a nerve. Blood burbles around the broken shaft.

Maybe I should help. But his mouth is a crater, his gray lips peeled back, and, even toothless and his head caged, he looks like he could swallow me whole. He is still screaming.

"Sssh," I say. But he won't stop. "You don't want Mom to hear."
He won't stop. "Be quiet, please. Please?" But it's too late. I
hear the screen door slam.

"Alice!"

I run.

Interview with Mom, Part 1.

Interviewer (Alice Reinhold): Please give your name for the
benefit of those watching.

*Mom (She sets her gin-and-tonic on the porch table and
then pushes a strand of hair out of her eyes, patting it into
place as if looking into a mirror.)*: What was this for again?

I: A school project. We're supposed to construct a
personal history.

M: Do we have to do this now?

I: You promised. The project's due tomorrow.

M: Oh all right. Bring me my pack of Camels, will you?
I think I left them in the living room. In my purse.

I (ignoring the request): Your name?

M: Mrs. Sarah Reinhold.

I: And your husband?

M: Sergeant Samuel J. Reinhold, U.S. Army. Retired.

I: How did you meet?

M: Is this necessary?

I: It's my history and you're both part of that history.
You and Daddy.

*M (She reclaims her glass from the table, eyes the level
of drink remaining, then takes a long sip.):* He hit me with his
motorcycle.

I: Really? Did you die?

M: You're being sarcastic, right? It's not as dramatic as it
sounds. I had just had my hair done and was thinking about...
other things, so I didn't notice the light had changed.

I: What kind of "other things"?

M: Nothing really. I had a date with another fellow from
the base. Dinner and a movie. But I didn't know your Dad
when I made the date, so it wasn't like I was cheating on

him.

I: Daddy ran into you?

M: More like brushed against me with his motorcycle as I stepped off the curb. I fell right on my butt. *(laughs)* Not that my butt was anything to laugh about. You may not believe it but your Mom was pretty hot in her day. Daddy must have laid twenty feet of rubber. Tires squealing, asphalt smoking. The whole deal. Then he came back to check on me.

I: A real knight gallant.

M: More like a soldier with a hard-on. *(snickers into her glass)* He was pretty hot too in those days. Especially in his uniform. He apologized like it was the end of the world. He wanted to take me to the infirmary. It took me the longest time to make him understand that I worked at the infirmary, and I knew I was perfectly all right. Still, he insisted on staying with me, just to be sure he said.

I: Did he take you to the movie?

M (crunches through an ice-cube in surprise): Never! We might have bumped into the guy I made my date with. I wasn't looking to cause a fight.

I: Did you love the other guy?

M: No. We just dated a few times.

I: But you did love Daddy.

M: I married him.

I: Was it love at first sight?

M: It was for Daddy. He may have hit me with his motorcycle, but the only thing broken was his heart. That's what he liked to say.

I: What about you?

M: I required a little more convincing.

I: But you did love him, right?

M: Yes.

I: He was your one and only?

M: My one and only.

I: Then why did you cut off his hand?

M (slams her glass down onto the table): Jesus! Not that again. I should have known. Is that what this is all about?

Document #1 (Oct. 6, 1995; transcript of transmission intercepted by the New World Freedom Alliance):

Operation Hammer... justified... avoid congressional approval... establish the suitable infrastructure... embryonic stem cells for gene transfer... covert information... North Korea and China have initiated similar programs... congressmen who formerly opposed the Operation... long-term commitment... mosaics in the first generation... individuals... the first... must be bred... 36 years... our first fully transgenic adult... the desired number of transgenic individuals... medical evaluation and the need... breeding partners... operation... the same location... government-run orphanages... could be appended... established overseas... overseas... several additional... restrictions... surrogate mothers for the transgenic embryos... methods of in vitro... advantageous ages of consent... Hammer of Justice.

Experiment #2: Food Preferences

Rain clouds blow past and, beyond the fence, beyond the fields, a rainbow arches between the forest treetops and Heaven. Daddy crawls in the mud outside the garage, his chain dragging behind him. He paws at the ground, sometimes with his good hand, sometimes with his stump. He swipes at his face with a muddy fist—his good hand—and smacks the cage that surrounds his head. Gobs of mud cling to the metal bars and splatter his nose, cheeks, and lips. He gnashes his gums, twists out a tongue that is surprisingly pink.

I stand just out of harm's way, barefoot, the mud cool and wet between my toes. I wonder what Daddy is doing.

Then I see it.

Worms.

Daddy is trying to eat worms. They have crawled out of their drowned homes and writhe pale and pink in the puddles. Even as I watch, he grabs another worm in a handful of mud and slaps it against the bars of his face-cage. The severed half of a worm sticks to his cheek and I watch it squirm and fall. I don't think Daddy feels it. I know he doesn't see it because he's already searching for another worm.

Worms.

That gives me an idea.

I return to the house and grab whatever I can from the refrigerator. I stuff the pockets of my raincoat with cheese and cold cuts, pickles and bread. An orange, a carrot, some lettuce. A squeeze bottle of mustard. A package of chicken livers that Mom mistakenly bought for the cat.

The feeding hole in Daddy's face-cage is rectangular, a half-inch high by one inch wide. All his food has to be cut to fit. He used to tear his food apart but he's had trouble with this ever since he lost his right hand. He tries everything I bring him but he doesn't like most of it. He chews a few times and lets the mashed pulp fall from his lips. But he swallows the salami and the chicken livers, just like the chopped hotdogs and hamburger that Mom feeds him.

He likes meat.

But there's one other thing I notice—an important thing, I believe. Although Daddy consumes the meat I brought, he never stops looking for worms. I think it's because they move.

Interview with Mom, Part 2.

Mom (Sarah Reinhold; she takes the pack of cigarettes, lights one, and gazes at the exhaled smoke plume. Her words are slurred.): Thank you my dear...how did you know I needed a smoke?

Interviewer (Alice Reinhold): You had that look.

M (puzzled, as if trying to determine if she has been insulted): Well it was sweet of you...you're a good girl.

I: Can we get back to the interview now?

M: Interview?

I: My school project. We're supposed to construct a personal history.

M: Oh yes...I remember...but we won't talk about what

you promised not to talk about.

I: I'd like to ask you about your pets.

M: About Missy Fluffypants? *(She looks around as if expecting to see her cat sunning itself on the porch; the cat's absence makes her frown.)*

I: Would you call yourself a dog-person or a cat-person?

M: A cat-person, definitely.

I: And Daddy?

M: I don't think he cared one way or another.

I: He told me he used to have dogs when he was a boy.

M: That was his family and that was when he was little... he never complained about my cats...he loved them. *(She frowns again, a combination of anger and sorrow.)*

I: When he was a boy, Daddy told me, he had a black lab named Clemens. Once upon a time an old stray ripped Clemens's nose up and ever after that Clemens had it in for cats.

M: I don't think I like this story.

I: Clemens was afraid of adult cats—because of the one that scratched him—and so he used to hunt barn kittens. He'd kill kittens whenever he got the chance. Rip them to pieces. At least that's what Daddy told me.

M: Why would he tell you such a horrible story?

I (shrugs): It was just something from his growing up.

M: Why would you tell me such a story?

I: Because it's the truth.

M: God preserve me...(she knuckles her eyes and, oblivious, almost lights her hair on fire with her cigarette)... from you and your horrible little truths.

I: Horrible?

M: Some truths are best left unsaid.

I: You mean like what happened to Missy Fluffypants? You mean like what Daddy did to her? And what you did to Daddy?

M: Oh dear God. You just won't let it go, will you?

Document #2 (declassified):

DATE: July 10, 2002, 8:48 AM
TO: xxxxxxxxxx
FROM: xxxxxxxxxx
SUBJECT: Cost-benefit analysis of Operation Hammer of Justice
The projected cost per unit has increased due to an expansion in requested enhancements, resulting in a proportionate increase in R & D. Loss now becomes a significant financial concern and the units can no longer be considered expendable. We propose that R & D be expanded to include revivification. xxxxxxxxx suggests an expansion of the NIH budget, with the additional funding benchmarked for targeted research areas. Somatic cell transformation and stem cell research are obvious targets. There have also been interesting developments in symbiotes, such as the use of engineered spirochetes to replace defective neurons. Funding should be such that we can, within ten years, have an operational backup system capable of activation following a thermal decline in core temperature, one which can be retrofitted to the second generation of H-men.

Experiment #3: Sign Language

Daddy sits on the grass, back braced against the garage, legs straight out in front of him. His boots are military issue and bound with duct tape, so enormous they could stomp the world to smithereens. A cloud drifts across the sun and Daddy moans as coolness replaces the warmth on his forehead. Daddy has just the one hand, his left hand, but that is enough. Each day I try to teach him one new word. I bend his fingers, swing his arm, and repeat the word so many times that it begins to sound strange in my mouth. Mom doesn't know I do this. She would call it dangerous. She says that I should always stay out of the reach of Daddy's arms. She says that Daddy's chain is there for a reason.

"What's the difference between you and me?" I ask.

Daddy slaps at his temple but I can't tell if he means his head or the cage around it. "Are our heads different?" I ask.

He whines but I've learned to ignore his noises. I wait. He taps the top of his head.

"Height? Our height is different?"

He nods.

"You are tall." I sign 'tall' by sliding my index finger up my raised palm. "What else is different?"

He grimaces, lips peeled back, and points at his empty gums.

"Teeth," I say. I tap my own teeth. That was one of the first things Mom stole from Daddy after he returned home. She complained about his biting, although he never bit me, and the army sent over a dentist who put Daddy to sleep with a syringe and then yanked out all his teeth and sewed up the holes. Later Mom showed our caseworker a crescent-shaped bruise on her arm. That was how Daddy got the metal cage around his head.

Daddy is already looking at the stump where his right hand used to be. Maybe he's anticipating his next response. But I don't want to talk about that. So I ask him, "Can you name something the same?"

Daddy points to his left eye. His pupils are brown with flecks of gold that sometimes sparkle. Most of the time he gets that sparkle when he chases worms or a beam of sunlight. But sometimes, like now, they sparkle when he looks at me.

"Yes, we both have eyes. What else is the same?"

He taps his crooked nose. Mom had nothing to do with that injury. I remember sitting on Daddy's lap when I was little and tracing the bent ridge of his nose with my fingertip. He pointed at the TV, at the costumed men massed on the field. "Promise me," Daddy said, "that you will never play football when you grow up." He laughed loudly but I didn't laugh, just nodded.

I think maybe Daddy has forgotten that our noses don't look very much alike. "Yes, we both have a nose. What else is the same?"

His mouth twists and contorts as if it were at war with

itself. He is thinking. Then he raises both his arms and hugs himself, hands crossed over his heart.

For a moment I don't believe what I see. So I make the sign back to him: I raise my own hands and clutch myself. I can feel my heart pounding hard and fast in my chest.

He nods.

I run then. I run back into the house. I'm crying but I don't want to believe in my tears and my reason for crying. "Love," he said. "Love."

Interview with Mom, Part 3.

Mom (Sarah Reinhold): Let me tell you how it really happened. It wasn't because of the cat that I had to...remove Daddy's hand. It was because of you. It was because I love you and I will protect you no matter what.

Interviewer (Alice Reinhold): Does Daddy love me too?

M: He loves you but his love is buried so deep that sometimes he forgets it's there...sometimes it comes out but he isn't used to it and it comes out in the wrong way.

I: He used to come into my bedroom and kiss me goodnight.

M: That was before.

I: No, even after. Daddy used to come to my room at night back when you still had him in the house. He came and stood in my doorway. Sometimes he came into my room and sat by my bed. He didn't say anything but he stroked my hair and held my hand.

M: Oh Darling, you really don't remember?

I: I know what you said.

M: But darling if only you had seen his face...he was like the devil...you were asleep and it was if a devil had hold of you. The government said he was safe and that he would never hurt anyone again but they never saw his face either. A mother knows. *(She takes another drink from her glass.)* A mother knows. I did what I had to do and no jury on earth would convict me...I knew it and they knew it and I did it all for you.

I: But that wasn't when you cut off Daddy's hand.

M: It sure as hell was. *(She slops her drink into her lap.)*

I: No, that's when you chained Daddy in the garage. The hand came later. After he killed Missy Fluffypants.

Document #3: from transcript of the speech given by Admiral Ryan C. Taber prior to awarding of a Silver Star to Sergeant Samuel J. Reinhold on Oct 13, 2034

Sergeant Samuel Reinhold was part of a U.S. operation against insurgent activities of the Golden Sickle terror network. While operating near the Russia-Afghanistan border, in dangerous terrain, Reinhold's platoon was split into two sections for what we call a ground assault convoy. Reinhold was the leader of the front group. He was a role model of courage and patriotism and a natural choice for leader.

The lead group with Sergeant Reinhold worked their way through a steep valley without encountering enemy activity. But the trailing group came under fire and because of the mountainous terrain was unable to communicate with and alert the lead group. Under ordinary circumstances the trailing group should have been able to fight their way clear of the ambush, but our evidence indicates the Golden Sickle used illegal biologics.

When the trailing group failed to reconnoiter with the lead group, Sergeant Reinhold's patrol exited their vehicles and at great personal risk climbed back along the mountainside to the site of the ambush. They encountered sustained enemy fire and, while leading his men toward higher ground, Reinhold was shot three times in his torso and twice in the head. His comrades were forced into temporary retreat and Reinhold was left behind and presumed dead.

However, Sergeant Reinhold was a second generation H-man, part of our country's Operation Hammer of Justice Initiative, a fact that had not been publicized for reasons of national security. We estimate, given the extent of his injuries, that revivification required approximately six hours. Revivification of an H-man initiates a kill sequence and, although it was too late to save his comrades in the trailing group, Reinhold could avenge their deaths. This he did. A local Afghan commander, General Mohammed Bas, confirmed the deaths of at least fifteen enemy fighters of the Golden Sickle at the hands of Sergeant Reinhold. In doing so, Sergeant Reinhold proved himself a potent example of the American spirit in action and a clear demonstration of the importance of the H-men to our military effort.

You may fight us, you may shoot us, you may kill us, but we will still come back and destroy you. That is the message from Sergeant Samuel Reinhold. That is the message from Operation Hammer of Justice. And that is the message from the United States of America.

God bless America and the heroism of Sergeant Samuel Reinhold.

Experiment #4: The Power of Love, part 1:

Daddy's chain is fifteen feet long and stretches from a thick bracelet around his right leg to a cement block buried by the garage door. The block is big as a couch and so heavy that even Daddy, who is stronger than anyone I know, cannot budge it no matter how he pounds and scratches with his ragged hand. He wants to be free but he can never be free as long as the chain binds him. The range of Daddy's chain is easy to pick out: a half-circle worn in our lawn and raked across the driveway gravel. Mom says that I should always stay outside the zone. The zone. That's what Mom calls it and she acts as if I would be vaporized if I ever ventured an inch within its boundary.

I enter the zone all the time. Like the times when I feed Daddy or when I teach him sign language. Still, I always know how distant the boundary is. Maybe it's just Mom's paranoia but part of me never stops thinking about how I would escape if Daddy grabbed me.

I don't know if Daddy wanted to eat Missy Fluffypants or if he just didn't like her. But no matter how Mom pleaded with Daddy, no matter how she pulled and punched at him, he wouldn't release that cat. He just sat there while she beat on him. By the time Mom thought of Daddy's old chainsaw, it was already too late for Missy Fluffypants.

That didn't stop Mom. So goodbye, Missy Fluffypants. Goodbye, Daddy's right hand. Missy Fluffypants is buried in the flower garden, her grave marked by a hunk of quartz crystal that winks angry eyes at the sun. I don't know what happened to Daddy's hand. Maybe it's still down there in the dirt with Mom's favourite cat.

Daddy has never tried to grab me. That's why I trust him. That's why I do what I do now. It's a sunny day with only a few lonesome clouds wandering the sky. Daddy is seated at the edge of the zone, halfway between the garage and the maple tree, picking apart a leaf piece by tiny piece, no easy task with just one hand. I take a deep breath and cross the boundary. I feel suddenly cold even though it is the middle of summer and remember the first time I ever tried to swim in the Atlantic Ocean and how I only lasted a few seconds before splashing back to shore. This time I don't turn back. I walk right up to Daddy and stand in front of him. I lift my arms and cross them across my heart.

I hold the pose because Daddy doesn't look up right away. He's still working on that leaf, removing every last bit of green until all that remains is a skeleton like what you might find inside a fairy's hand. Then he looks up. Even through his face-cage I can see that he is smiling. Daddy drops the leaf skeleton and lifts his arms and mimics my pose. The fingers of his good hand tighten into a fist. The stump of his right arm quivers.

That's when I reach out my arms and Daddy reaches out his arms to me. We hold each other. Daddy makes the moaning noises that I don't understand but now I just listen and say the same words over and over again. "I love you. I love you, I love you, I love you."

Interview with Mom, Part 4.

Mom (Sarah Reinhold): You may not understand, but I really loved your Daddy...I love him very much. *(She takes another sip of her drink, yawns. Her head nods toward her chest.)* But you don't know what it is like to go through what I've gone through.

Interviewer (Alice Reinhold): I know you loved Daddy and I know you loved Missy Fluffypants. But sometimes I think you loved Missy Fluffypants more than you love Daddy.

M: Daddy's a hero but...I hate to say it but...he's also...but you've seen him, you know what I mean. Missy Fluffypants was always a cat...just a beautiful cat and nothing else...my beautiful cat...my baby. *(She nods her head, eyes closed, and smiles at the memory.)* I don't know what got into her to go into the zone. She knew better than that...she knew your Daddy...

I: What did she know about Daddy?

M (jerks her head upright): Let me tell you it's a lot easier to live with a cat than it is with a monster...there I said it, a monster...and Missy Fluffypants had no one but me to protect her.

I: But did you really love him? Do you really love Daddy?

M: Of course I loved him...no matter how hard it got, no matter what he became, I loved him. I still love him. I would have walked through fire for him. *(She swirls the remnants of ice cubes in her glass.)* But once you have a baby you can never love again in the same way...it takes a woman to know that...right now you're still a girl...but you'll know what I mean someday. *(She drains her glass and sets it on the table. She then lowers her head to the table as well, resting it on her arms. Her eyes are closed. Her mouth falls open and she sighs deeply.)*

I: Mom?

M: (no response)

I: Mom? I've got something to tell you.

M: (no response)

I (whispers): Do you know how Missy Fluffypants got so close to Daddy? Do you know why she entered the zone? It's one of your horrible little truths...

M: *(no response)*

I: I was the one who put her there.

M: *(no response)*

I: I was angry then. But I'm sorry now. I want you to know that. I didn't hate Missy Fluffypants. I just hated what you did to Daddy.

Document #4:

Jan. 12, 2036

A.P. Report. Senate launches investigation into alleged misappropriations for Operation Hammer of Justice. There continues to be political fall-out from the Reinhold incident and some members of Congress openly question if Operation Hammer of Justice has a future. Senator Lawrence (R-New York), a former proponent, has suggested that the actions of Sergeant Reinhold's immediate superiors subsequent to his reanimation constitute a cover-up.

"Death by friendly fire is never easy to accept, not for the soldier's family, not for his comrades in arms, and not for our country," said Senator Lawrence. "But here the repercussions from the accidental shooting of Sergeant Reinhold resulted in untold pain and misery. These could and should have been avoided. Those most closely involved with Operation Hammer of Justice claim there was no way to predict that the kill sequence in a resurrected H-man could be directed against his own comrades. They claim that a friendly fire situation was never modeled. I say poppycock. If you've been running a government program for forty years, you goddamn better be asking these questions and modeling these models."

Surviving members of Reinhold's platoon have also begun to make their stories public. "There was no Golden Sickle activity in the area," according to anonymous testimony from one platoon member. "None. It was all Sergeant Reinhold. Every death. These were his friends and he killed them all. He tore them apart with his bare hands, with nothing but his hands and his teeth. He was like an animal. A rabid wolf. But I don't blame Reinhold. He didn't know. I blame the government that made him that way."

Members of the Reinhold family could not be reached for comment.

Experiment #5: The Power of Love, part 2:

Mom lies slumped across the porch table. She looks older than I had thought, her blond hair gray at the roots, her wrinkles pronounced even in sleep. I feel sorry for her. "I didn't hate Missy Fluffypants," I whisper. "I just hated what you did to Daddy." I crush Mom's cigarette out and pour fresh gin into her glass so that, when she wakes, she'll find another drink to carry her through to morning. She won't think about me until later and by then Daddy and I will be gone.

"Sweet dreams," I say. I mean it.

Mom keeps the keys to Daddy's chains and head-cage buried in her jewelry box beneath pearls and earrings and a lace garter from her wedding. That's also where she keeps Daddy's old dog tags and his wedding band. One key is as long as my forefinger and has what looks like a tiny fortress protruding from its end. The other key is squat and circular like the ones you use with a bicycle lock. I take the keys, the cash card from Mom's purse, and my knapsack, already provisioned, from its hiding place beneath my bed.

Daddy is asleep inside the cool mouth of the garage. I'm disappointed, knowing the foolishness of expecting confetti and applause but wishing for something more than snores. The ankle bracelet is banged up, its keyhole clotted with dried mud; the mud crumbles to dust when I insert the key and the key turns like in a dream. Daddy mumbles in his sleep and I think he says my name. "Sssh," I say, sliding into the dark and hoisting his head into my lap. I grapple with the lock on his face-cage. I jimmy the key up and down, in and out, twist it so hard that it slips from my fingers. Daddy is awake now and the whites of his eyes shine like pools of snow. Something catches and gives. The mask clatters to the concrete floor.

"Run," I say. "Run and be free." I pull at Daddy's shoulder and he staggers to his feet. He moans. I steer him toward the door. He pauses, raises an arm as if to protect his eyes. The sun is already down, clouds salmon-bellied in the west, stars peeping from the blue depths of the east. "Come on," I say.

Daddy lumbers forth.

"We'll go to Oregon," I say. "There's folks out there like us. They're wild and they're free. They'll help us."

A few more steps. I'm pulling so hard, I'm afraid Daddy's sleeve will rip. Another step. Another. Then he stops. We're at the edge of the zone. I show him my knapsack. I take out the cash card. "I have everything we need," I say. He stands there smiling down at me. His smile, without teeth, is a black wound that splits his face.

I drag him over the line.

His smile widens to the size of a planet and he screams. Electricity crawls up my spine. Why does he always have to scream? Maybe he just realized his chain is gone. "Sssh," I whisper, pressing a finger against my lips. "Please? You don't want Mom to hear."

Miracle of miracles, he goes quiet. He lurches forward, moving of his own volition, and I think this is it, now is the time, now he's ready, and we're finally on our way. I'm wrong. It's just a few steps, just enough to cover the distance to the maple tree. Daddy embraces the tree as if reunited with a long-lost lover. He falls to his knees. Is this what it was really all about? Is this why Daddy wore his fingers to bloody rags on his chain, why he moaned through the long dark nights?

He's digging. He claws at the dirt with his one good hand. He shoves aside the wadded grass and soil with his stump. He can't do much with his maimed limb and so I join him. I scrape out the earth with my own small hands. Daddy smiles his toothless smile.

I find the first bone. At first I think it's a dirty peanut shell because of the colour and the shape and because it is lighter than a pebble. But Daddy knows. He grabs it and shoves it into his mouth, swallowing it down in one gulp. A finger bone, I realize, the flesh long since decomposed. The rest of his missing hand is down there too and we uncover more bones with each handful of dirt. He eats them all, shoveling the calcified nuggets along with heaps of dirt into his mouth. Black spittle runs down his chin.

In the end, he's eating nothing but dirt.

He settles to the ground beside the maple as if content to set roots there himself. As if he's never heard me talk of Oregon and our future. He's too big and heavy for me to move and I lie down inside his comforting shadow, cradled in the crook of his arm. He's still a broken man but the darkness fills in his broken places and makes him whole.

"Everything will be all right." I want this to be true. Daddy doesn't say anything. The smell of harvested hay blows in from the fields. A chorus of crickets raises their song to the night sky. Daddy doesn't say anything but he doesn't have to. His fingers press against my palm, colder than anything human. The sound of his breathing is soft and low, his pulse steady. He's not asleep. His eyes are open, watching me, watching over me just like he used to do. I smile. A half-smile because I am almost asleep myself, drifting to sleep like a boat coming to dock in a familiar harbor. In these last few seconds before sleep takes me, I want to stay awake. I want to hang on to what I have. "Please God," I whisper to the stars, "let this moment last forever."

THE THREE FAMILIARS

I. The Tale of Legs

Love has many forms. Some forms inspire love, others hate. The witch was the first and only child of a well-to-do family of Boston Brahmins. The doctors told her mother that she would never bear children, and suggested her father content himself with political fundraisers and season tickets to the Shubert Theatre. For this reason, the witch's parents, although compelled by tradition to bless their child with a Christian name, always called her Our Little Miracle. She was doted on with a devotion befitting a freak of nature. Her mother breast-fed the witch until the age of three. Her father read her bedtime stories and once stayed up 52 hours cooling her fevered forehead with a washcloth.

The witch's first words were "I love you." These words were a lie because, in truth, the witch hated her parents. She did not know the primal cause of her hatred but it came to her as naturally as breathing. She lost her pearl necklace to the garbage disposal. She used her best dress to make a kite. She dismembered her dolls, melted their heads on the stove, and fried an omelet for her parents on their wedding anniversary. There were a dozen glass eyes in the omelet. When her parents called in a private psychiatrist, the witch employed the profane language normally reserved for presidents of corporations. The psychiatrist said the witch was testing boundaries to determine if her parents' love was unconditional. Her parents assured the psychiatrist that it was.

The witch sought refuge from her parents' love in

the attic. The house was old but looked new, and the attic was one of the few places where the bones of the original structure showed. There were thick beams supporting the slanted roof, the gargantuan shaft of a crumbling chimney, and a single window with diamond-shaped panes and spider webs. The space smelled of cardboard and memories. The witch found a hexagonal sewing box to use as a table and a five-legged stool. She set these treasures before the window and in the bleary sunlight played Belly Up, Licorice Hill, and other solitary games of her own devising.

One day, while pursuing the court martial for a truant doll, she was distracted by a white mote floating in a sunbeam. She reached out. The sunbeam lapped at her hand. She called such sunbeams The Devil's Tongue. She withdrew her fist from the light and, opening it, saw that she had captured the white mote. It was no bigger than a grain of sand but it moved of its own volition, exploring her palm as if delimiting a new kingdom. Closer inspection discovered eight tiny legs. A baby spider!

"I am your god," she whispered to her captive. "What is your prayer?"

Her answer was a bite that burned.

She laughed. Pain breeds power. "You are hungry. What do you eat?" She scanned her hexagonal table. "Licorice?"

Another bite, one that burned like shame.

"Blood. Blood for you, my pet."

It was only on their first meeting that Legs was allowed to drink from the witch's own flesh. After that the witch brought Legs treats from the house and field. Sometimes a blood-smeared butcher paper, sometimes a fresh-caught mouse, sometimes a wren snared with sticky tape and sunflower seeds. The witch sang as she climbed the attic stairs and wound her way past the boxes and dusty furniture. This is the beginning to her song:

> "Legs up, Legs down
> What's on my gown?
> Legs down, Legs up

What's in my cup?
Legs out, Legs in
What's on my chin?
Legs in, Legs out
What's in my shout?"

The song had many verses and the witch never sang it the same way twice, but she always finished with, "Blood, blood, blood!" At this cry, Legs dropped from her hiding place in the rafters. She landed on the witch's hair, tumbled to her shoulder, and scuttled along her arm to discover the gory treat for the day. By month's end, Legs was thick around as the witch's little finger, her abdomen smooth and pale as a mushroom cap.

Fools will tell you good fortune comes to those who wait. The witch knew otherwise. The average lifespan of a female spider is a little over 100 days but, well before this time, the witch had chosen for Legs a mate. When Legs's eggs hatched and the baby spiders crawled free from their silken sac, there was one among them that was larger than the rest. The largest spiderling did not float away like the others but sidled over to the witch. "Legs," the witch whispered, and lifted her new companion to her lips. There were three generations in a year, and Legs grew with each generation. By the time three years had passed, Legs was larger than a dessert plate.

Do not think that the witch's absences went unnoticed by her parents. When she did not answer their calls about homework or dinner, her parents nodded and pointed upward. "The attic," they whispered. "Don't disturb her." The psychiatrist had warned them about breaking the circle of trust. Nevertheless, like all parents before them, they eventually relented to curiosity. While her mother distracted the witch with sugar cookies, her father snuck up to the attic and there, behind a wall of boxes, discovered the witch's den. He sniffed the air. There was an unpleasant scent like that from a small corpse but he found no casualty. A pallid fungus grew within a crack between two beams but he did not think to mention this when, in bed with his wife later that evening, he made his report. "She plays house. She has a stool and a little table made from a sewing box. There are a few cups and saucers on the table. She may have borrowed these from the kitchen."

"What's in the sewing box?"

The witch's father had no answer. Lacking this, he returned to the attic. The witch heard every creak as he ascended the stairway and crossed the floorboards. She also heard his shriek when he, rummaging through the sewing box, pierced his finger on a needle. "Jesus," he cried. He sucked the blood from his finger. From the corner of his eye he saw a movement in the shadows. He had seen a fungus there earlier. Now the fungus dislocated itself from the ceiling and descended as if suspended on twine. "Jesus," he cried again. The fungus made no sound as it impacted the floor. It made no sound as it scuttled toward him. "My God," he cried, racing for the stairs, "We need an exterminator."

"An exterminator," he repeated to his wife, after he had slammed and locked the attic door and crawled into bed. "Yes dear," she said. She patted his hand. "I'll call first thing tomorrow." The witch was listening outside their bedroom door. Her heart fluttered like a snared bird. She had only the night to save the life of Legs but the nights in New England can be long. The next morning, when the coroner was brought in, he was astonished to find the witch's parents swaddled so tightly in their sheets it was a wonder they could draw breath. In fact, he concluded, they could not draw breath at all. The sheets, although lacking a manufacturer's tag, were of the finest weave and it was a pity they had to be cut to free the corpses. To the coroner's credit, he noted that the witch's parents died hand in hand and included this in his official report. To his discredit, he also noticed a pallid pillow in the corner of the bedroom but did not find it of significance.

So it was that the witch came into her inheritance.

II. The Tale of Hands

The witch lived in an old house that looked new. One day she awoke feeling cold and hollow as if her body were transformed into a cave of ice. She drank a cup of licorice tea and nibbled on a sugar cookie, but these did not fill her emptiness. She fed the rats in her basement but drew no satisfaction from their glittering eyes and chittering teeth. She dug in her root garden, but the sun on her shoulders made her shiver and the dirt beneath her fingernails made her cry. That night, she danced naked beneath a gibbous moon and, horror of horrors, stumbled and fell. An owl hooted in derision.

There was only one companion to whom the witch could turn. She climbed the stairs to the attic. She brushed past a drapery of spider silk and flopped into a hammock embroidered with images of tangled birds. Her familiar, Legs, dropped from the rafters and nestled against her cheek. Legs was round as a dinner plate and coated with hair so fine and pale it was almost invisible. The witch scratched Legs's back. "What brings you pleasure?" the witch asked.

Legs purred. "Birds," she said.

"Anything else?"

Legs craned upward. "Mice."

"Besides food." The witch stopped scratching.

Legs bumped against the witch's hand, begging her to resume. The witch moved her hand out of reach. Legs hissed.

"Tell me," the witch said.

"You won't like it." Legs's voice was a reedy whistle.

"Tell me anyway."

Legs climbed ceiling-ward on a silken strand. "Having babies," she whispered.

The witch shrieked. Although a witch may menstruate, she may never give birth. Her power is in her blood and her womb is as hard as rock. Legs, on the other hand, gave birth to thousands. How many times had the witch watched the spiderling horde gnaw free of their egg sac to then catch air on gossamer wind-chutes and blow across the city? Thirty, forty, fifty times? The sight was beautiful almost beyond belief.

The witch brooded for weeks on the unfairness of

life. But she was young and not yet willing to accept the limitations of fate. I will find myself a mate, she decided, and with him create a baby. To find a mate was not a difficult task. The witch brushed her hair until it shone like a favored memory, wound a necklace of pearls around her neck, and slipped into one of her mother's ballroom dresses. Last of all she pricked her heart line with a thorn, collected tears into her bloody palm, and anointed her lips with the salty mixture.

The witch's father had been tall with unruly hair and a sharp-edged nose. The man the witch chose at the Beacon Hill bar was nothing like him. He was more like what her familiar Legs might choose. He was shorter than the witch by a good three inches, gelled his hair, and had a vanishingly small nose. He sipped a pear martini, his third, and explained patent law to two interns. "Give me your hand," the witch said. The lawyer smiled and fell silent. He held out his hand. "Follow me," the witch said. The lawyer followed the witch to her taxi, and from there to her home. He was drunk and stumbled on the stairway to the second floor, striking his chin on a tread. He cursed. He wiped his hand across his chin and checked for blood, then cleaned his hand on his pants. "It's nothing," he said.

The witch led the lawyer to her bedroom. She lit two white candles and undid her hair. Her bed was as white as new snow on ice. She helped the lawyer out of his clothes and kissed the torn flesh on his chin. "You're sweet," she said. She pulled him down onto the bed. "Stay the night."

The lawyer buried his head in her hair. "Your bed is so warm," said the lawyer. His face was flushed, his arms slick with sweat.

"That is the warmth of fur," said the witch. She stroked the snowy sheet. The fur beneath it prickled and rose to greet her touch.

The lawyer tried to raise himself above the witch. His knee slipped and he fell beside her. He touched her breast. "Your bed is so lumpy," said the lawyer.

"There are many furs," said the witch. She outlined the

rippling shapes with her fingers. She nibbled his ear. She slid a hand along his hip and fitted herself onto him.

The lawyer moaned softly. He rolled away from the witch. "Your bed moves," said the lawyer.

"The bed is hungry and can wait no longer," said the witch. The strands of the sheets parted and a wave of rats poured forth. They were gray and black and brown. These were the colors the lawyer hated most and for good reason.

The witch remained in bed for three weeks, submerged within her mattress of rats. The rats cuddled against her when they grew cold, they fed on the lawyer when they grew hungry. The witch binged on animal crackers and watched *Ratatouille* on a portable television set. She sang to the rats in their own tongue. This is the translation to her song:

> *"Your lives, my life*
> *Your bones, my blood*
> *Hair, skin, teeth, tit*
> *Moon slows*
> *My life, your lives*
> *My bones, your blood*
> *Semen, tears, spit*
> *Life grows"*

The gestation period for a rat is three weeks, less than one lunar cycle. The witch's belly stretched. Her pointed breasts grew heavy, her nipples tender. At the end of three weeks, the witch gave birth. Legs swaddled the newborn child in a cocoon as if to banish it from its mother's sight. "Let me see my baby," said the witch. The bed sheets were barren of blood. Legs cowered at the footboard. These were sure signs that something was amiss, but the witch had eyes only for the pink hands that reached out to her from the cocoon. She touched the palm of one tiny hand and watched with wonder as its five tiny fingers closed around her own finger. She tore the webbing aside, her heart pounding with the same enthusiasm she used to expend on Christmas gifts. Her baby girl, born from a stony womb, was stone herself.

Only her hands had life. The witch held the cold hard thing to her breast, but the lips did not search for her nipple. The witch did not speak or weep. She rose from her bed and, trailed by a river of rats, disappeared down to the basement.

Oh mothers, guard your newborns well! A she-beast prowls the city of Boston. That beast is the shadow of the wind and has a touch lighter than milkweed down. She steals eggs from nested robins. She steals kittens suckling at their mother's teat. The eggs are found crushed, the kittens drowned. Worse yet are the ravaged women. One mother discovered a manikin sculpted from mud and feathers in her baby's crib. Another found only a bottle of bloody milk. There is a rumor of rats. There is a rumor of hands in the darkness. The witch is jealous and although she might cradle a stranger's baby on a moonless night, none survive past the morning. "Another," the witch says to her rat familiar, the largest from the basement brood. The rat has small pink hands. These are sutured at the wrist with threads of finest silk.

In this manner the witch made her peace with the world.

III. The Tale of Eyes

Three is a magic number and so the witch had three familiars. The oldest of these was Legs. Legs was as large as a pillow and trundled about the house on a wheeled cart. The next oldest was Hands. Hands had a touch so deft that she could steal the shadow from the wind. The youngest of the three was Eyes. Eyes was generated from a potato. The witch grew the potato in her root garden between rows of carrots and horseradish. She watered the potato with blood and fed it on crematorium ash. She sang as she gardened and this was her song:

> *"Heart of my heart*
> *Light of my eyes*
> *Breath of my breath*

Rise to my sight."

That autumn, after the leaves of the maple had begun to blush but before the first hard frost, a tapping at her kitchen door awakened the witch. The witch fumbled with the latch. A potato perched on the stoop, russet of skin, pale roots dripping mud. "Eyes," the witch cried, as if she knew the names of all strangers. The witch carried Eyes to her kitchen table and carved a smile with a paring knife. She skewered twin nostrils and ears with a toothpick. The power of a witch is in her blood and thin white scars crisscrossed her arms. A few more scars and Eyes could speak.

"Food," Eyes said.

The witch fed Eyes bacon, hot and sizzling from the stove. The breakfast aroma attracted Legs and Hands. Eyes burped. The witch cleaned the grease from Eyes's mouth. "I have need," said the witch, "for gold kissed by a virgin." A memory stirred in Eyes's potato mind, one bestowed by the crematorium ash on which she was raised. "A pretty girl," Eyes said. "She steals a twenty-dollar gold piece and when confronted by her mother, swallows it. You will find it in an urn at the Fairview Cemetery." The witch turned to where Hands hunkered in the corner nibbling on a cockroach. "Fetch," she said. Hands returned two hours later out of breath but with the coin in hand. The witch praised only Eyes. "You are worth more than gold," the witch said.

If you think that Legs and Hands accepted Eyes as an equal then you, like the witch, understand nothing of jealousy. Legs and Hands chopped a toothy grin into Eyes for a Halloween trick then mashed her for a side course at Thanksgiving dinner. Winter came and the two familiars buried Eyes in a snowdrift, impaled her on an icicle, and lashed her to the top of the Christmas tree. The witch resuscitated Eyes each time. She sewed Eyes's wounds with threads of worm gut. "You're the youngest," the witch said. "They'll accept you in time." When necessary, she spooned the pulped flesh into a fresh potato skin. "A little more time," the witch said. The scars on the witch's arms grew more numerous.

At the tail end of winter, the witch called together her three familiars. "I have need," said the witch, "for a needle blooded in anger." An ash-fed memory coalesced in Eye's mind. "A man," she said. "He paws the oyster-shell buttons in a hexagonal sewing box. He pierces his finger and throws the box to the floor in anger. He is distracted and does not reassemble the contents."

"Where is the needle?"

"Upstairs."

The witch sucked in her breath. "In the attic?"

"Yes. Between a crack in the floorboards."

"Who was this man?"

"Your father."

The witch turned to where Legs squatted in the corner crunching on moth husks. "Fetch," she said. You would not think to look at the witch that anything had changed but, in fact, everything had changed. The witch now regarded Eyes with suspicion.

Spring arrived. The two familiars painted Eyes with circles and stripes and rolled her down a slope intending to lose her at the Easter egg hunt. The witch found Eyes beneath a forsythia bush. Beside her squat brown body, peering up from the mud, was a familiar doll-sized glass eye. A little digging and the witch recovered the remaining eyes from the omelet she had served her parents many years before. Staring into those incriminating orbs, the witch knew what she must do.

That afternoon, while dicing horseradish, the witch called to Eyes, "Come help me." Eyes crawled free from where she napped in the produce bin. The witch rapped the cutting board with the cleaver's handle. Eyes climbed up and settled on the board. The witch kissed Eyes on her wrinkled forehead and then chopped her into small pieces. At the far corner of her garden, shadowed by a crooked pine, the witch maintained a boneyard of unmarked graves. The witch buried Eyes there. She also buried the needle dipped in anger and the dozen glass eyes. The witch placed a fist-sized rock on the mounded earth. The rock was a common sort, jagged and gray and with hints of mica, but this was the first burial the witch ever commemorated.

That evening the witch drank a glass of wine and joined Legs and Hands in playing Flocks of a Different Colour. Legs cheated, producing the Stoat of a Silvery Luster when one had already been played. Hands cursed and refused to pay the loser's forfeit. The witch drank another glass of wine. Hands laid down a pair of Blunted Knives but these were from a different card game altogether. Legs swore and called her a fool. The witch drank still another glass of wine. She lost count of how much she drank. Legs tried to bind Hands with a stinging cord. Hands gnawed through this and attacked her with a potato peeler. The witch burst into tears.

The next day there were three rocks sunk into the soft soil of the boneyard. The witch spent that summer, fall, and winter alone. She read romance novels and played the solitary card games of her youth. She watched *Burn, Witch, Burn* on the portable television set. Sometimes she laughed at the funny parts and sometimes she cried.

The seasons are inevitable. Still, it snowed on Easter Sunday, a dreary leprous snow that fit the witch's mood. She followed the traceries of melted flakes on the kitchen window then wandered out into the yard. The crooked pine was gray in the mist. Three grave markers protruded from the frozen crust. Between them, brown as the mud itself, a gnarled shoot poked skyward. The witch fell to her knees and kissed the tiny fragment that drew its life from those that she had taken. A few days later she saw that a second shoot had joined the first. The shoots grew thick and strong, each crowned with a furry bud.

The witch waited impatiently for the buds to open. This occurred on a glorious spring day when the sun shone bright as butter and the breeze smelled like champagne. The petals were a fleshy pink and there were five to a bloom. The witch reached out, feeling an uneasy sense of déjà vu, and felt the petals wrap around her finger. She touched the second bloom and the petals did likewise. Suddenly afraid, the witch tried to pull away. The tiny hands did not release. For a moment the witch hung suspended, then she sat down with a plop.

The witch had yanked a child forth from the boneyard soil. A girl. The girl's legs were long and thin and bent in unusual places. The hairs on her legs were so pale and fine as to be almost invisible, those on her upper torso dark and thick as a new fur coat. The girl's face, to put it kindly, was earthy. Her cheeks were pocked, her hair stringy, and her mouth lipless. She had only two eyes but these were visible from almost any direction.

"Mama," the little girl said.

The witch took the child to her bosom. The girl wrapped her arms and legs around the witch and wriggled like a nest of snakes. "You're beautiful," said the witch. "I will call you My Little Miracle."

The witch was just as good a parent to My Little Miracle as her own parents before her.

ARE YOU PROPERLY DESENSITIZED?

Once upon a curious time, sensitivity was a valued personality trait. Folks would go to museums and art openings and you would hear discussions on the 'quality of the brush stroke' and 'capturing the essence.' You couldn't throw a rock without hitting some beret-wearing poet and, rather than pound the living crap out of you like a normal person, the poet would weep a single tear, watch it splash upon the pavement, then make some pathetic comment about 'slings and arrows.' Christ, there were even sensitivity training classes back in the 70's. Nowadays, sensitivity is recognized as the liability that it really is and, led by the entertainment industry, every effort has been made to the wipe it out. With a simple click of the remote it is possible to see a decapitation with breakfast, catch some S & M with lunch, and enjoy a little reckless genocide with dinner. But that doesn't mean that everyone has got with the program. Ask yourself: are you properly desensitized?

Part I: Scenarios

1. You are the sole witness to a traffic accident in which one driver is clearly at fault, the other driver as blameless as virgin snow falling on Christmas Eve. The driver at fault offers you one hundred dollars to back a distorted version of the events leading up to the accident. What do you do?

A. Give the driver a hug, saying that you understand their pain but that you cannot accept a bribe. You can, however, recommend a licensed psychiatrist who will help the driver work through the trauma of the accident as well as the inevitable traumas suffered in childhood.

B. Refuse the bribe and report the incident in your accurate account of the accident. The policeman handling the accident compliments you on the legibility of your handwriting. You say that the credit should not go to you but to your second-grade teacher, Mrs. Weatherspoon, who used negative reinforcement to great advantage in eliciting good penmanship from her students.

C. Laugh at the hundred-dollar bribe and say that Ben Franklin was never alone, and, although not well publicized, he was one of five identical siblings. You would hate, simply hate, to see him separated from his brothers. The driver at fault is not an idiot and, later on, you buy him a beer with what used to be his money.

D. Go to the trunk of your car and pull out the pouch in which the jack, tire irons, and lug wrench are normally kept. You long ago figured out that a tire iron wasn't very effective and now keep a pistol with silencer in its place. You kill both drivers and take their valuables, knowing that God, if He exists, will sort out who was right and wrong.

2. You have been working late for weeks at the office trying to debug a software program that is already three weeks behind schedule. Your significant other calls at 5 pm to remind you that today is October 31 and you are both supposed to go to a Halloween party. A costume is required. You, of course, have completely forgotten all about this. Why you barely remember to eat lunch, so how on earth can anyone expect you to remember something as frivolous as a costume party. What do you do?

A. Tell the truth, explaining that the party had completely slipped your mind and asking if your significant other has any ideas for a last-minute costume. You promise your significant other an unreciprocated orgasm to atone for your faux pas.

B. Go into the bathroom at work and steal two rolls of toilet paper. A mummy may not be the best of costumes, but it sure beats donning a sheet with two holes cut out for eyes and going as Casper the Friendly Ghost. Too bad that gray clouds are gathering and it looks like rain.

C. Bring a cup of coffee to a co-worker of the opposite sex. No need to discuss the benefits of caffeine; you're both in this together. After the co-worker says thank-you and leans forward to take a sip, use a heavy paperweight to good advantage. Strip the clothes from your co-worker's body, stuff the body under a desk, and go to the party as a cross-dresser with poor fashion sense.

D. Show up at your significant other's apartment dressed in your work clothes and when confronted about your lack of costume explain that everything you need is in the apartment. The first item on your list is duct tape. The second item is a kitchen knife with sharpened blade. Later that evening, after your preparations are finished, you attend the party as your significant other. The costume begins to smell after a few days but by then the party is over.

3. When your mother died, you...

A. Cried like a baby at the funeral, then that night, while the earth was still loose on her grave, exhumed the body. You now keep her in a chest freezer in your bedroom so that she can watch over you while you sleep, just like she used to do when you were a child.

B. Delivered a stirring eulogy at her funeral and made a contribution to her favourite charity. You take an appropriate amount of pride in knowing that her favourite charity was a secluded group of nuns who still practice self-flagellation.

C. Forgot to attend her funeral because you were playing the video game "Alien Predator versus Jack the Ripper" and had reached level seven. Level seven is where Jack has sex with one of the prostitutes. Level eight, you have heard, is where the prostitute gives birth to a hoard of mini-Jacks, thereby greatly increasing his slashing power.

D. Cried like a baby and delivered a stirring eulogy at her funeral, then that night, while the earth was still loose on her grave, exhumed the body. You sold the dress in which your mother was buried to a second-hand clothing store, her hair to a doll maker, and her skeleton to a medical supply company.

4. On a whim you drive to the town where you grew up, but which you haven't visited in over twenty years. After gassing up your car, downing a chocolate donut and coffee at the local Dunkin' Donuts, and driving through the streets to check which houses you still recognize, you get down to business.

A. Using the same camera with which you won a high-school art contest, you take a series of photographs of the places that were important to you in your youth. You write a short essay to accompany the photos and send it to your hometown newspaper, which publishes it under the title "Return of the Native."

B. You drive up to your old high school and, leaving your car in the parking lot, hike back behind the tennis courts carrying a folded shovel from your trunk. It's here that you lost your virginity to a foreign exchange student. Later, after the exchange student returned to Sweden, you buried a metal box here containing your love letters and a pair of pull tabs from soft drink cans that you had worn on your fingers and called wedding rings. But although you thought you knew for sure where you had buried the box, you can't find it. Maybe your memory isn't very good. Maybe someone else found it.

C. You meet with your high-school art teacher and principal and, with their help, establish a benefactor's fund with proceeds from your most recent book of photographs. The fund will grant teenage girls the opportunity to come to the city and study art during the summers. Once away from home, you will explain to the girls that there is no such thing as a free lunch, which in this case means that in exchange for art lessons that the girls will have to pose for art photographs.

The girls will become very familiar with the phrase, "Pout for me, baby."

D. You seek out Mrs. Weatherspoon and at gunpoint force her to sit down and write an essay on the uses of negative reinforcement as a means to instill a proper respect for good penmanship. Each time her writing fails to attain what she used to call "typewriter quality," you chop one of her fingers back to the next knuckle. When she can no longer hold a pen, you suggest that she write with her own blood. When she faints from blood loss, you lay her comatose body on the floor in a vertical line, arms at her side. You remove her head with a saw and set it below her feet. She looks like an exclamation mark.

Part II: Personal favorites

5. What is your favourite number?

    A. 2
    B. 7
    C. 1
    D. -1

6. What is your favourite colour?

    A. Green
    B. Blue
    C. Black or red
    D. Gray

7. What is your favourite breed of dog?

    A. Border Collie
    B. Golden Retriever
    C. Pit Bull
    D. That dog-human thing from the movie "Invasion of the Body Snatchers." Everyone else went "Eughh" when that came on screen, but you said, "Cool" and began a line

of experimentation that continues to this day. Now that you think about it, the head of Mrs. Weatherspoon is just sitting there...

8. What is your favourite movie?

    A. Bambi (edited for content) or Old Yeller (edited for content)
    B. Top Gun or Pretty Woman
    C. Wall Street or Texas Chainsaw Massacre
    D. Your home videos. Everything else is tame in comparison.

Part III: Short answer/essay

9. Add your own last line to complete the following poem by Lord Byron.

> *In secret we met*
> *In silence I grieve*
> *That thy heart could forget,*
> *Thy spirit deceive.*
> *If I should meet thee*
> *After long years,*
> *How should I greet thee?*

10. You and your neighbors have established your own country. Trusting your judgment they have given you the power to create any governing system that you find suitable. Write a short essay describing your ideal government.

Scoring:

    Questions 1 through 8. Give yourself 1 point for A, 2 points for B, 3 points for C, and 4 points for D.
    Question 9. Subtract 2 points if you even considered answering this question.
    Question 10. Give yourself one point for each use of

the following: secret, torture, police, absolute, Ayn Rand, cannibalism, mutant monkey death squad. Subtract one point for each use of the following: consensus, Marx, healthcare, public, art, education, free, sock monkeys. You may not receive more than 4 points or less than -4 points for this question.

Results:

Score of 37 or above: Properly desensitized but mathematically challenged. Consider a career in government. The presidency is not outside your reach. You will die in a compromising situation but still be given a state funeral.

Score of 30-36: Properly desensitized. Your friends call you the Ice Man. You know that they don't really like you, but they do want to be like you and they spend more on your birthday presents than on anybody else's. The word most often used in your funeral eulogy will be "respect." A close second will be "prick."

Score of 20-29: Room for improvement. You've tried but obviously not hard enough. Watching TV twenty-four/seven simply won't cut it. You've got to get out where it's really happening and stir things up. Trip a nun in traffic. Sell your brother's kidney on E-bay without telling him. Start an office pool on when your boss is going to have a heart attack. Otherwise your ex is going to show up at your funeral, still looking for a handout.

Score of 10-19: An uphill climb. You're probably considering buying a hybrid car and riding your bicycle more often to work. Screw that! Buy a stretch Hummer instead and park it on your neighbor's lawn. Run over his dog, or his children, if he complains. Trade in your ambient ocean tapes for a soundtrack of Baghdad at Night and get on with your life. Otherwise you'll be damned with faint praise at your funeral. That's right, the priest will refer to you as "nice."

Score of 2-9: A hopeless case. You are just a bundle of exposed nerves and break down into uncontrollable weeping every time a bug smashes against your windshield. The two sentences most frequently uttered in your presence are "It's not your fault" and "Don't take it personally." But behind your back, your so-called friends call you a pussy and are secretly plotting to kill you. You will be woken from a deep sleep to the hammering of nails into wood. When you try to get up, your head will bang against a low ceiling. "What a small room," will be your first thought. True, only too true. You will be the only one that cries at your funeral.

Story Notes

by Enoch Soames

Then I look'd him in the eyes
And I laugh'd full shrill at the lie he told
And the gnawing fear he would fain disguise.
              from *Nocturne*, by Enoch Soames

Stories should, in my humble opinion, speak for themselves. Schaller expresses the same thoughts in public, parroting the same old, same old about the purity of the written word, the inconsequence of their *auteur*. In private, however, Schaller prostitutes himself before writerly revelations. He devours the authorial notes in single-author collections prior to reading the stories themselves. "They make me feel like I've been invited into the author's own home, like there's a personal connection," Schaller says, a confession that reveals him as the quintessential student rather than master of his art, because it is only in collections such as *Meet Me in the Middle of the Air* that we find such discursive appendices, these being aimed at establishing a sense of bonhomie between the author and his audience. I use the term *student* here loosely, the term implying some semblance of study, of an intelligence attuned to its advancement or, at the very least, its augmentation, rather than a pathetic desire to belong. A truly original talent would recognize that an understanding of his work will never accrue in his own lifetime but only be bestowed from the enlightened perspective of the future.

For a true original, it's not a matter of life or death, but rather of life after death.

How came I to write these notes, rather than Schaller himself? I could point to any number of factors, of which Schaller's preferred excuse would be an overwhelming weight of conflicting obligations. Might I suggest, as an alternative explanation, the friends with whom Schaller regularly consorts? Their names are Gin-and-Tonic, Martini (with olives *and* a twist), Rosé, Pinot Noir, Sauvignon Blanc, and any number of beers emboldened by an alcohol content inconceivable in my era, back when one's literary credentials were established by a preference for absinthe. Ah, how the scent of wormwood flavored the conversations of my day.

Need I further embellish the details? Perhaps. Picture this: a distraught call from the editor of Undertow Publications, Mr. Kelly, who knows full well the *character* of his author, not to mention my situation, as well as my being privy to any number of revelations due to my being a peripheral member of the writer's circle to which Schaller belongs, these confederates meeting monthly at a local watering hole known as the Salt Hill Pub. Not coincidentally, this pub figures in one of the stories in this volume. "Schaller promised me...he promised me," and here Kelly's voice broke in a most disconcerting manner, "Schaller promised me that he would have the Story Notes completed a good month ago but he hasn't done a d**ned thing. Who does he think he is? Faulkner? Fitzgerald? Ernest F**king Hemingway!" Schaller acquiesced to the editor's recommendation that I assume the mantle of biographer, although not to the suggestion that I pseudonymously craft these notes under his name so as to preserve a semblance of coherence to the collection. Schaller's ego would not permit another to traffic in his name. In truth, neither would mine. If I am to make any claim on posterity it shall be through my name alone.

Perhaps Schaller thought that I would craft a typical paean to a writer's talents. After all, had I not sat silent at those monthly meetings, as though drinking in the bounty of his intellect? Had I not listened to the interminable wailings of the makeshift Irish jam session for which he affected an incomprehensible affinity? Had I not made notes, he no doubt assuming these exhumed the *bon mots* that he proffered and repeated *ad nauseum* at each and every meeting? In truth, I need no notebook to mark his blithe statements, for they are tattooed on my brain. Little did Schaller know how my humble jottings were a far more accurate document of his era than anything he could offer.

Where do you get your ideas?

That question, in a nutshell, is what I understand Story Notes such as these to encompass. When asked this question, the writer Harlan Ellison, who has achieved some measure of success in these blighted times, replies with his typical combination of dissimulation and workingman's bravura, all under the umbrella of humor: "Poughkeepsie." Nevertheless, as another writer pointed out, this is not such a silly question after all. Ideas are mysterious things and the permutations by which they become stories often suggest the interference of the miraculous. Writers rendered idea-less have become suicidal. Indeed, Ellison, in spite of his homage to The Queen City of the Hudson, is one of those writers who has mastered the craft of producing authorial notes of prodigious length, these often eclipsing the stories themselves.

Where do writers get their ideas? Why from their own lives of course, from personal experience wrought fine into the form of fiction. Is this not the basis for that hackneyed injunction: *Write what you know?* A pretty lie. Most writers lack both the quality and quantity of life necessary to inform the multitude of stories they conceive as emanating from their souls. Instead, finding their own lives a frugal repast, they turn to the lives of others, regurgitating these as if of their own invention. Schaller is a borrower at best, and a thief as a rule. He rampages through his life, the lives of family and friends, and, most disreputably, the work of other writers, all the in service of what he grandly refers to as *THE STORY*. My presence here is indisputable evidence of the depths to which he will sink. But I have already overstayed my welcome in this preamble. I am condemned to spend eternity among minds more vacant than the vacuum I now understand exists between the stars. I present to you, in these Story Notes, evidence of a thievery that indicts Schaller and this hapless age in which I am cursed to spend eternity.

The Assistant to Dr. Jacob

This story is inspired by a memory, or rather the debilitated resemblance of that memory to reality. Schaller has written previously about the genesis of this tale:

> "I built an airplane when I was four years old. Not a model, but one big enough for me to fly. I built it in the backyard out of chairs, buckets, bamboo poles, and whatever else my parents failed to nail down. I was quite proud when finished, having made something that indeed seemed capable of flying, something that in memory still is an airplane. Years later, I saw a photograph that my parents took. The photograph shows a boy standing beside a pile of junk assembled without apparent rhyme or reason. The conflict between the airplane of memory and the one in the photograph served as the genesis for "The Assistant to Dr. Jacob."
>
> (from *Nemonymous* #3)

All true, so far as I may attest. Schaller is at least consistent with his oft-repeated tale of origins. However, this statement sets the genesis of Dr. Jacob completely within the realm of autobiography. Might I also point out that this conflict between realities is nothing new to literature. Most significantly, it was the province of Philip K. Dick, an author that Schaller devoured and whose paperbacks, purchased over three decades ago, he still preserves in one of his better bookshelves. Indeed, whenever someone mentions the theater, Schaller finds some way of dragging the conversation back to two Dick-inspired plays he saw performed decades ago at The Broom Street Theater in Madison, Wisconsin: *Ubik* and *A Martian Timeslip*.

The Parasite

Schaller, as he pontificated at length one August evening at the Salt Hill Pub, after returning from a visit to his brother in Vancouver—one might have thought he was the only resident of New Hampshire to ever set foot in Canada—had, while there, discovered a book perched within easy reach on the coffee table. This book contained text and photographs about the parasitic crustacean *Cymothoa exigua*. I will write no more about the characteristics of this parasite, as such information is readily available through the internet. I will only add that its distribution is widespread and includes the Americas. I will only suggest that Schaller's story adheres more closely to reality than some might find comfortable.

Turing Test

The idea for the Oscar Wilde's came first, and with it that Horn of Literary Plenty that Wilde bequeathed to posterity. Note how Schaller spends an inordinate amount of time in reconfiguring the works of Wilde within the confines of his story. Note also that these are rendered in miniature. No greater indictment of this self-aggrandizing age of marvels need be submitted as evidence of its true stature. Schaller talked at length one evening of injustice, of how Turing because of his role in the war effort, had been recently pardoned for his so-called sin of homosexuality. He talked, using his hands as much as his voice, how such an acquittal did not expunge the morally bankrupt notion that homosexuality was wrong, but rather indicated that from the state's point of view it was only something to be weighed on the scales of right and wrong. I submit to you that all moral bluster aside, Wilde's name is still recognized and will be recognized many generations hence, that he won the war if not the battle.

Talking at Sixty Watts

The Salt Hill Pub, as noted earlier, is a real place and one with which Schaller is overly familiar. I also note a peculiar tendency of writers from this age, especially those who write within the confines of genre, to feature pubs, bars, and drinking establishments in their stories. I do not provide any interpretation nor make judgment of this phenomenon; I only bring it to public attention. This is not to say that I have no experience of such establishments but, in my day, when I frequented the domino room of the Café Royale, the overall impression was of gilding and velvet and mirrors, rather than of vinyl and flat-screen televisions. In my day smoking was allowed and the tobacco fumes formed a fragrant veil that extended from tiled floor to painted ceiling, and through which, until the veil was rent, we all took on the appearance of dim apparitions, more ghostly than real.

The lamp in the story is real, one that used to sit near Schaller's bed, animated perhaps by Schaller's memory of the tiny bulb-headed helper who assisted Gyro Gearloose in the Disney comics he devoured as a witless child. But the story is inspired more by a sense of loss than of nostalgia. The section on planting trees is true, after a fashion, although these were planted by Schaller's uncle in consideration for his children, a bounty of hardwood that required only time to accrue. The trees were saplings, easily overlooked in the tall grass, and the man minding the farm ran them over when haying the fields. There is a division between the future we anticipate and that which we obtain, and this division cuts deeper than any knife.

The Baby in the Forest

Schaller never discussed this story at the round-table but, if I hazard a guess, and it is only a guess, the multiple realities, independently ascertained, again owe something to the legacy of Philip K. Dick. As further evidence of his infatuation with Dick, Schaller one claustrophobic evening inflicted Tod Machover's opera reinterpretation of the novel *Valis* on guests at his house, a frugal sharing of wine being a preface to this musical mockery. If I might make a recommendation, although most of Dick's work, in spite of being immortalized through the Library of America, is shoddy stuff in need of proofreading, I nevertheless find his short story, "The Preserving Machine," immensely moving.

To Assume the Writer's Crown: Notes on the Craft

Was there ever a story that owed more to its progenitors? Every section here references something that came before that literally influenced Schaller. The difficulty, and Schaller was willing to expound on this at length, was in whittling the piece down so that some narrative arc tentatively connected all the repurposed material into something that could, cross-eyed, be called a story. The blame for such metafictional enterprises, and blame is the appropriate word here, must be laid at the feet of the notorious Jeff VanderMeer who, through publication of his meta-novel *City of Saints and Madmen*, made genre a haven for such literary jacknapery. It's bad enough that Schaller misappropriates Ursula K. LeGuin, but I have it on good evidence that he also, in an earlier version of the story incorporated Joanna Russ's classic text on *How to Suppress Women's Writing*.

8) – 5.8

The purloinment of Poe, down to the repurposing of his words—Oh Schaller, thou art the laziest of thieves—is so obvious that I mention it only in passing. Instead let me note the suicide booths that make a brief appearance in the story. Schaller's Salt Hill confederates were convinced these were inspired by the Stop-and-Drop suicide booths from the cartoon *Futurama*, Schaller's infantile obsession with cartoons being a consistent target for their mockery. Schaller, oblivious as usual to anything that would diminish his self-aggrandizement, embarked on a half-hour monologue, lubricated by three beers, in which he outlined with a Wikipedia level of inconsistency the literary history of suicide booths. His booths, he insisted, were an homage to an 1895 story by Robert Chambers titled "The Repairer of Reputations." The story was science fiction at the time, my time, as it looked forward twenty-five years into the future. I myself have now traveled over 100 years into the future and I don't know if I am pleased or saddened that, although surprisingly popular in fiction, suicide booths have yet to achieve a physical reality.

This story does inspire in me a peculiar sense of identification, for I understand the predicament visited on Poe in the story—wrenched out of the past and cast into a cruelly indifferent future—as my very own. I wonder if my situation incited Schaller's interest and he, to hide this fact, then displaced my own suffering by transmutation onto Poe: thievery squared if you were to apply the mathematician's rule. Cubed if you take into account Beerbohm's previous misuse of my life for his own ends.

Crystal Vision

This story is all about the house, which exists exactly as described. Schaller passed it twice a day while driving back and forth to work at the University of New Hampshire. It was a big house, with cardboard on the windows, nobody visible either inside or outside, but with an ever-changing menagerie of vehicles in the parking area. Give a writer an empty house and he will populate it. Give a writer an empty house and he will create a story even where no story exists. I imagine, based on Schaller's compulsive collecting of old records, that the scene with the '78's was the most difficult for him to write.

Voices Carry

Schaller has always had a love for insects.

The Sparrow Mumbler

The impetus for this story was the 1811 *Dictionary of the Vulgar Tongue*, by Francis Grose which, against all odds, is still in print more than two centuries later. My mother once told me that I was born under a three-penny planet, a term that I find in this dictionary. Are my works to be forever unappreciated, my life and my literary masterpieces dispelled as easily as the tobacco fumes of yesteryear? Sometimes I wish that my mother had been an *ape leader*, defined in this unhallowed dictionary as "An old maid; their punishment after death, for neglecting increase and multiply, will be, it is said, leading apes in hell." I write this not because I wish that sweet woman any punishment in the hereafter, but simply because the corollary to such an abstemious existence is that I would never have been born, and thus not condemned to this Hell, one where I follow that ape Schaller about like a forgotten shadow.

Cabinet Number 42

Sometimes the impetus for writing comes from outside, another writer creating a stricture designed to elicit stories, and those nominated to participate cheerily donning these shackles. In this case Jeff VanderMeer engineered the conceit of a house with many cabinets. Not surprisingly, Schaller's story involves both apes and automata, these speaking to some recurring and I suppose grand theme in his writing, something more than the alliteration of the letter *A*, but a theme to which I am not privy, and happily so.

The Bright Air that Breathes No Pain

The finest grace of the many fine graces found in *The Dark Descent*, a 1987 horror omnibus edited by David Hartwell, is that it contains three stories by Robert Aickman. According to Schaller, of course. In this respect Schaller is but one among the many yipping hyenas tearing gobbets of flesh from the moldering carcass of horror and suggesting that somehow, as transmuted by Aickman, this rank repast has acquired a rarified air. Which is all to say that any writer of horror who possesses literary aspirations, no matter how misplaced, attempts to produce an Aickmanesque story and just as assuredly fails. Is it only through our failures at emulation that we come into ourselves as writers, that such failures ultimately define our style?

If so, Schaller is a master of style.

Schaller strives for ambiguity in this story, an Aickmanesque ambiguity. Let me tell you, based on personal experience with the supernatural, there is no ambiguity about it. I bargained with the Devil himself—do not laugh—and the Devil I encountered was a flashy but plebian dresser, given to twirling his mustache, more like a sneering villain in a melodrama than Milton's rebel angel. The Devil transmitted me a century into the future, to June 3rd, 1997, where I sought evidence of the transformations that my literary genius, unrecognized by my peers, would have wrought given the enviable weight of a century. *Ahead of his time*, was I thought the honor uniquely to be mine. Instead I found myself only noted as a character within a story by the man I called my friend, Max Beerbohm, my hurts transmuted into fiction and held up as entertainment, and a light entertainment at that, unambiguously so.

Hemoglobin

"When I was in Praaaaague…" Has any worthwhile reminiscence ever started with such a preamble? "When I was in Prague," Schaller says, "I sought out their Asian art museum. This was little visited because it was no longer housed in the city but in the town of Zbraslav, and to find Zbraslav required the decipherment of a bus timetable. My wife and I wandered through the museum's dimly lit galleries, our echoing footsteps re-echoed by a lone security guard. The best was reserved for last: a temporary exhibit of Japanese prints with a ghost and horror theme. We were surprised to find these rooms overrun with kids from a grade-school field trip. But the kids were more interested in each other than in any learning experience. They ignored the samurai warriors, the gargantuan frogs, and the flying monkey demons. Most surprising of all, they ignored the truly horrific images: the decapitations, the murders, the bound and flayed bodies. The moral of the story is, I think, that a kid will ignore anything marketed as educational, no matter how salacious."

This story was an exorcism, or so Schaller referred to it in his typical grandiose manner, arising from the particular fascination that Yoshitoshi's *The Lonely House on Adachi Moor* exerted over him.

Asleep at the Mortuary

This is the earliest story reprinted in this volume. In spite of its brevity, Schaller still manages to reference another author's work, as if a text like the moon could be illuminated with reflected light.

Going Back for What Got Left Behind

Nemonymous.

    Ne-mon-y-mous.

    How is it that this word, for which no concrete definition or etymology exists, can inspire a hazy reverie bordering on nostalgia with Schaller? "The only grammatically correct use of the word," he says, "is along the lines of, 'he has been published in *Nemonymous*.'" Which is merely a preamble to Schaller relating how his stories have twice appeared within the pages of this "megazanthus" edited by Des Lewis, these being "The Assistant to Dr. Jacob" in issue 2 and "Going Back for What Got Left Behind" in issue 8. The stories for *Nemonymous* were routinely selected by Lewis without any knowledge of the author and, in the earlier issues were published without author bylines, these only being revealed in the subsequent issue. Surprisingly, by erasing an author's identity *Nemonymous* inspired greater interest in a story's provenance, a concept I find heartening although I have never benefited from it.

Number One Fan

Schaller has called this story a valentine to the many conventions he has attended, a duplicitous description that evades specifics and also negates the bravery of writers subjected to such monumental horrors of fandom as described here. Or rather the lack of fandom, something only rectified in this story by death, as if death could somehow compensate for decades of neglect, for heads nodding toward breasts at the sound of your voice, for snores that shake the rafters, for children squirming in their seats, for hands raised to inquire when will their torment ever end. If this is the fate of a popular writer, then imagine that visited on me.

My ostensible friend Max Beerbohm once wrote that I was best described by the *mot-juste* 'dim', and this during the period of my corporeal existence. Thrust forward into the future, I spent a single tortured afternoon in 1997 searching for my deserved literary acclaim before I was recalled to 1887. There awaited that miserable bungler Max and the Devil not far behind, mediator of the inevitable ending during which he would claim my life and soul. "Try," was the prayer I threw back at Max as the Devil pushed me roughly out the door, "TRY to make them know that I did exist!"

What was the Hell that lurked on the other side of the doorway? Was it some dull inferno of pitchforks and sulfurous rivers? Was it a glacial hole where demons sucked the brains from still-living skulls? It was a thousand, a million times worse. There was a library. There was a NO SMOKING sign. There was the sickening buzz of fluorescent lights. There was the familiarity of everything I feared. The Devil had once again thrust me into the future, a century hence, there to leave me to an eternity of neglect. There I was and here I am, scribbling away on these Story Notes, now the only remnants of my talent that have any chance of being immortalized in this new century.

Schaller has never even graced me with a *mot-juste.*

Love Signs

There was once a supermarket where the cashiers outnumbered the patrons. Such patrons as you might find were elderly or, if young, were preternaturally aged by the lighting, the hue of young and old alike being of that greenish-gray best described as sepulchral. Schaller and his friends referred to this supermarket as the Zombiemart. One night, hysterical for anything to disrupt the ennui of the age, they drove to the Zombiemart and limped and shuffled along the aisles, heads lolling, jaws agape, emulating the dead returned to life. I have to remind myself, whenever I hear such stories, that all those involved were alive and merely, wittingly or unwittingly, emulating the dead. Likewise, the walking dead on the popular television program of the same name are all actors in disguise. Yes, these are the living. Nevertheless, this age is filled with the walking dead, although most go unrecognized. I refer not only to myself.

The Three Familiars

There are any number of stories, novels, and movies titled, "The Familiar." Writers are notoriously competitive, most forgetting that the accord granted them in their own lifetimes is inversely proportional to the judgment of the future. How else to explain that Schaller writes a story with not one, not two, but three familiars? Are we to be subjected to an 'arms race' of familiars? I do not claim any of my musings here for fact, I merely suggest that the loam of this time period nourishes the proliferation of the familiar (in all senses of the word) as substitution for originality.

Are You Properly Desensitized?

Bart and his sister Lisa watch a movie in one episode of the long-running animated series, *The Simpsons*. Something gory appears on screen and Lisa covers her eyes. Bart says, "If you don't watch the violence, you'll never get desensitized to it." This is a modern inversion of Nietzche's warning, "When you gaze long into the abyss, the abyss also gazes into you."

Story Notes

Some claim that Schaller writes horror stories, that his treatment of characters borders on and sometimes transgresses the sadistic. But a story is just that: a story. I submit to you that it is a far greater torture to be condemned to Hell, to know that you are in Hell for all eternity, and that this Hell is a future you have visited and find in it so little remembrance of your past that you persist as more fiction than reality. I submit to you that mine is the true horror story because it is more than a story. It is my life.

Yet I have not given up.

I have not given up even though my masterworks are all but forgotten, even though Mr. Kelly promotes lesser writers than myself, forgetting that the judgment of history does not come from the past but from the future, and cares nothing for numbers or financial remuneration, only for a genius incomprehensible to lesser minds. It is here in these Story Notes that I stake my claim on the future, casting my words out on the currents of time. My masterpieces from a century ago exist only as fragments. My name is not even heralded on the cover of this volume. But through my words and your eyes, your tongue, dear reader, I shall live again. Fear not to quote me. Fear not say my name and, in saying it, to praise it, knowing that you are engaged in a selfless enterprise, and one more worthy than any you deserve.

Earlier in these notes I reported that the question most often asked of writers is where they get their ideas. I've given an indication above as to where some ideas present in Schaller's stories originated. I will add to this one caveat. The question as typically phrased is not where do you get your idea, but ideas. This plural, although ill considered in its application, is all-important in my opinion. No single idea will support a story. Indeed, I foresee a future golden age in which the idea-count exceeds the word-count or even the character-count for a story, and I believe only then will my works find their true audience.

Even Schaller's creations, although Spartan in comparison to my own, are generated from a spider web of intersecting ideas and the puerile emotions associated with them. Take for example, "8) – 5.8," the most recent story by Schaller appearing in this volume. The petits harken back to such literary predecessors as Mary Norton's *Borrowers*, a *Land of the Giants* novelization by Murray Leinster, and the care-manual for the anthropomorphized brine shrimp called Sea-Monkeys. The projected desires and fears that animate the petits owe much to Schaller's own creations as a child, assembled from Lego's, modeling clay, and such odds and ends as toothpaste caps, key chains, and acorns. There are also memories of trying to carve a quill pen from a crow's feather, of an ivory ship owned by his grandmother in Alaska, and of an entreaty from a panhandler in Littleton, New Hampshire. The park shelter is found in Madison, Wisconsin, and is to where Schaller retreated from a sudden downpour more than thirty years ago. The word *crepuscular* demanded entrance into the story simply because Schaller walked past a houseboat in Paris named *Crepuscule* while working on the final draft. The complexities in the genesis and gestation of a story mirror the complexities of life itself.

"Lean near to life. Lean very near—nearer." These were the words I wrote in my preface to my magnum opus, *Negations*. I leave it to you to judge if Schaller has leaned near enough.

Enoch Soames is the author of three books, the first a remarkable volume titled *Negations*, the second a poetry collection titled *Fungoids*, the third a self-published tome made available to a select audience. Soames's likeness has been immortalized in pastel by William Rothenstein and in prose by Max Beerbohm.

ACKNOWLEDGEMENTS

A few notes on the dedication. The collection is dedicated to my mother because she so effectively imitated Gollum's voice when reading *The Hobbit* to my brother and me as kids that I skipped over the 'Riddles in the Dark' chapter when I later read it for myself. The collection is dedicated to my father because he gave me a copy of Arthur Machen's *Tales of Horror and the Supernatural* saying, "These stories are pretty weird, you'll probably like them." The collection is dedicated to Paulette because she was there for my first published story and because her unwavering support has been worth more than words. I thank the editors who have published my stories over the years. Deborah Layne, Adam Golaski, Yarrow Paisley, Nancy Purnell, Sean Wallace, Stanley Ashenbach, Stephen Ramey and Jamie Lackey, and Bruce Boston and Marge Simon all played critical roles in bringing stories in this collection to light. I am particularly gratified that Des Lewis, Ellen Datlow, Ann and Jeff VanderMeer, Peter Crowther and Nick Gevers, and Mike Kelly each published several of my stories. I also thank Scot Peacock, Neil Williamson, Jeff Ford, Matt Cheney, Rick Bowes, and Luis Rodriguez. All these names are deserving of more than the brief mention here, having contributed in ways too numerous to quantify, enriching not just my writing but my life. Finally, I thank Mike Kelly once again. Not only did he shepherd this collection of stray cats, mongrel dogs, and wayward weasels through streets both broad and narrow, but he also secured Enoch Soames to write the Story Notes at the last minute. I have not yet had time to read these Story Notes but, if they satisfy Mike's expectations, I am sure they more than meet my own.

ABOUT THE AUTHOR

Eric Schaller's fiction has appeared in *The Year's Best Fantasy and Horror, Fantasy: Best of the Year, SciFiction, Postscripts, Lady Churchill's Rosebud Wristlet, Polyphony, New Genre, Shadows & Tall Trees*, and others. He teaches at Dartmouth College in New Hampshire, where he lives in a peach-colored house with his wife Paulette and a cairn terrier named Z. Schaller's stories are influenced in part by his studies in the biological sciences, in their inspiration as well as the unease that originates in a world populated by many organisms—including humans—dependent on but also working at cross-purposes to each other. Schaller's illustrations have appeared widely, and he is an editor, with Matthew Cheney, of the on-line magazine *The Revelator*.

CPSIA information can be obtained
at www.ICGtesting.com
Printed in the USA
LVOW12s1807040516

486686LV00006B/497/P